By The Same Author

The Paris Plot

An Izzy Stone Thriller

Praise for *The Paris Plot*

"This exhilarating underground pursuit is only part of the story, however, and Aragon keeps up an impressive pace throughout the novel…A fast-paced international adventure…" ***KIRKUS REVIEWS***

Five Stars*******AMAZON**

"…[P]itches forward at a speed that very nearly makes the paper pages heat up and burn." **Douglas Glenn Clark**, author, *The Lake That Stole Children.*

"A spine tingling political suspense thriller." **Kevin Montgomery**, author, *The Family Next Door.*

"(Aragon) has taken his experience and woven it into an amazing thriller that will remain with readers for some time to come." **Gerald Lane Summers**, author of the *Mobley Meadows* series and other adventure novels.

CHÂTELET

Secret Service Agent Izzy Stone must stop a cyber terrorist intent on nuclear mass murder

JOSEPH ARAGON

Oakhurst Print, LLC

This is a work of fiction. All of the characters, organizations and events portrayed in this novel are either products of the author's imagination or are used fictitiously.

Although CHÂTELET is a work of fiction, the threat of a mass casualty cyberattack on the Homeland is real, and growing.

CHÂTELET
www.chatelet.us

Cover by L.Mai Designs

ISBN No. 978-0-9981612-1-1

For Ellen

Marc, Conrad, and Andelys

CONTENTS

1

Murder at Châtelet

PARIS

Paris metro commuters don't usually get murdered in plain view of hundreds. But nothing lasts forever, and in the next five minutes someone was going to die violently in the massive underground labyrinth of tunnels known as Châtelet, the world's largest underground subway exchange.

The unfortunate target likely did not foresee that this morning he had less time left on earth than it takes to smoke a cigarette or have an espresso. Nor, for that matter, did U.S. Secret Service agent Isabella "Izzy" Stone, who happened coincidentally to be a few paces behind a man who'd soon be dead.

It was another busy, uneventful morning in the exchange. There was nothing to suggest that death was stalking the metro.

Yet years as lead agent protecting the president of the United States from evildoers had hardwired Izzy with the ability to rapidly scan a crowd and spot the small human tics and clues that signaled danger and set alarm bells clanging deep inside the amygdala of her brain.

As she coursed the massive tunnels to the One line for her appointment at the American Embassy annex located on the Right Bank, she took mental screenshots of those around her.

To her left, the bony young man, threading through the human throng in tight pants, puffy dark jacket with a fake fur collar, dangling metal crucifix and darting eyes, was a pickpocket, scourge of the Paris metro.

Trailing him was a fortyish, athletic man, unshaved, faded jeans, loose-fitting brown leather jacket and sturdy running shoes, likely one of the many undercover police deployed to the vast transit system.

The woman a step or two behind him with a fisheye stare, small black shoulder purse, and large denim jacket that drooped from her wiry build was likely his back-up. A SIG Sauer SP2022, badge and cuffs would be tucked under her jacket in the small of her back. It was an all too familiar scene in the pickpocket-plagued Paris metro. The young man would soon be in cuffs.

Yet, a note of dissonance flashed through Izzy's mind.

Something feels off here.

Farther ahead, a tall older man with a youthful step, a stylish fedora and an expensive looking taupe overcoat moved with purpose through the crowd. His manner was commanding despite his age. His gait, though a bit obscured, suggested he was carrying something.

Keeping pace with him, a slender woman with lustrous blond hair, wearing a dark blue suit, her long strides graceful and distinctive.

Is she his companion?

It was hard to tell in the surging tide of people. Young, runway-handsome professionals in tailored black suits and ties strode around insistent beggars and ebullient American students with trendy backpacks.

Izzy continued past East European immigrants dressed in shabby Soviet-era clothing, busking musicians - some accomplished, others tone-deaf - a stocky man with baggy pants, a grey sweatshirt with the word "Lobos" on the back, his hood swinging loose, an Asian family that looked lost, and a toothless vagrant mumbling incoherently - an odd-shaped rucksack drooping from one hand.

The restless human current was winding its way through the many concrete tributaries leading to and from metro platforms. In other words, a typical day in the Châtelet metro where seven hundred fifty thousand commuters transited each day.

Paris is a global passion. Rich or poor, prince or peasant, everyone wants to be here - and Châtelet sees them all. It's a big world with lots of moving parts.

As she walked, Izzy mentally counted off each second, each step she took. It was an odd, almost unconscious act rooted in her childhood fascination with measurement and time that had stayed with her.

Her life would hang on how reliable that quirk was in but a few days.

There was a slight flurry, an inchoate disturbance in the air. Alarms were suddenly going off in Izzy's head in the way a small bird might sense a predator before it can be seen.

There was no objective reason for her agitation, yet that damned clanging in her brain was in overdrive and the trained agent in her asserted itself.

Then…

"*Arretez!...Police!* STOP!"

The undercover cop was chasing the young man in tight pants who was running fast, shoving people left and right. The fisheye was close behind, shouting

"Police!" as the three disappeared around a turn in the tunnel.

Izzy broke into a sprint.

Something's not right about this chase!

She didn't have to wait long to find out.

"Aaahyeee! Aaahyeee!"

Ahead, a woman was screaming in high-pitched primal terror. Izzy raced ahead as the panicked cries multiplied and commuters dashed wildly in every direction. Rounding the turn in the tunnel, she saw a crowd gathered in a tight circle, eyes wild, hands pressed to mouths in horror as they looked downward.

Forcing her way, Izzy broke through the human knot and saw the body of the tall, elegantly attired man who'd been no more than thirty feet ahead of her.

Damn!

A pool of bright red blood was oozing across the grey concrete floor. She knelt beside him. He was face down, motionless, a small red opening at the base of his skull. *Bullet entry, small caliber.*

There had been no audible gunshot. *The shooter used a silencer.* She touched the man's carotid artery with two fingers, taking great care not to make contact with anything else. *He's gone.* She waved people back. This would soon be a major crime scene and needed to remain undisturbed.

"Police! Police! Reculez-vous!"

Izzy stood and saw two men running in her direction, police badges held high, yelling "Police! Police! Out of the way!" Only a few steps behind them, a six-man squad of soldiers, ubiquitous in the metro system in the wake of bloody terrorist attacks, approached at a fast jog – eyes and automatic weapons sweeping left and right.

As the police arrived and the soldiers set a perimeter, Izzy stepped back and rescanned the crowd.

There was no sign of the pickpocket or the undercover police who'd been chasing him. Nor could Izzy see the attractive blonde who'd appeared to be the older man's companion. If the victim had been carrying something it was now gone.

Somewhere in the crowd a killer just put a bullet into the head of this man and slipped away. I missed something. But what?

She'd stay to tell police what she'd seen. Fortunately, security cameras in the heavily surveilled metro system would have captured the shooting. Izzy checked her watch.

Late for my appointment at the Embassy annex. I'd better file a report on what I just saw. I'm a witness to a murder. I don't want the embassy getting caught flat-footed if the police want to interview me.

She pulled out her cell phone and dialed a number.

2

Hôtel de Seine

Izzy Stone, five-feet nine, dazzling red hair cascading down the back of her form-fitting floor-length Japanese patterned white silk robe, looked out the window of her tasteful fourth floor room at Hôtel de Seine. It was a small Left Bank hotel located on Quai Anatole France not far from France's Ministry of Foreign Affairs. Her shapely body, framed by the window, still radiated the ramrod posture and athleticism West Point had instilled in her years before.

The quiet morning was a welcome change from the previous day's chaotic events at Châtelet. The floor-to-ceiling French windows offered a splendid view of the Seine, and just beyond on the Right Bank, the great Louvre and the vast Tuileries gardens with their rich palette of perennials and annuals.

The Tuileries are really beautiful this year.

She pulled open the tall windows and felt the rush of crisp autumn air. On the street below, auburn, apple-green and burnt-orange leaves swirled in small eddies around the chestnut and maple trees lining the quais and sidewalks. Above, immense white cumulus clouds drifted eastward with ease, a majestic caravan coursing a delicate blue sky. Izzy closed her eyes and filled her lungs with the cool fresh air. She exhaled slowly and returned her gaze to the billowing clouds against the blue of a Monet painting.

She was back in Paris, the city Izzy had come to love as a child when they'd lived there. Her dad, tall and strong, would carry the five-year-old on his broad shoulders as they descended the worn stone steps of the Right Bank's Quai du Louvre to the riverbank. Mom, sleek and lovely, smiling up at her. The three of them promenading the ancient quai, waving back at boisterous tourists atop the upper decks of the *Bateaux-Mouches* plying the river.

She shuddered and felt a chill.

We didn't know he'd be taken from us so soon.

Izzy took another deep breath and slowly released the painful thought, something she'd had to teach herself to do when the dark memories returned.

She closed the windows and picked up the morning copy of *Le Parisien* that had been delivered to her door along with *Le Monde, Liberation* and *Le Figaro*. Izzy was fluent in French, Spanish, Hebrew, Arabic and Russian. Languages came to her as naturally as breathing - an aptitude inherited from her dad, a renowned UCLA linguistics professor. On the front page was a photo of the man who'd been shot at Châtelet. Few details were included. Police were asking the public for help.

She took a sip of the café crème that had been delivered in a steaming silver pot along with fluffy golden croissants, butter and preserves. *Delicious.*

She tried not to dwell on the previous day's Châtelet murder. Not because she was indifferent to the violence. On the contrary. A violent death always troubled her and Châtelet was no exception. She'd seen violence of the worst kind over the years, had been on the receiving end of it more than once, and had employed deadly force protecting the president. One never really got used to it. But her training and experience had taught her that obsessing could cloud clear thinking and lead to disaster.

Never had that knowledge been more important than during her life-death struggle in Paris the previous year as she fought to save the president from rogue French special forces intent on killing him. Had she not been able to remain laser focused on the task of survival, and had they not crossed paths with Victor, the aging cataphile of the catacombs, the president might now be dead instead of sitting safely in the Oval Office.

Her thoughts returned to Châtelet.

The police had taken a brief statement from her and others who'd been near the shooting. Afterward she'd spent the rest of the day at the temporary office of the American Embassy with Lisa Palmer, the political attaché to the embassy. The embassy's main compound on rue Gabriel, steps away from the Champs Élysées, was still being rebuilt following its fiery destruction by rioting mobs the previous year – backlash after an anti-terror U.S. missile strike went horribly wrong, killing twenty-five French school children. That tragedy had been the match that lit the fire of national outrage against President Childs. It almost cost them their lives.

She turned from the window and stepped back into the room. It was decorated in warm earth-tone fabrics and light pastel walls. A mauve satin Napoleonic era *chaise longue* rested by the tall windows. A small study adjoined the room and a door opened to a bedroom.

Izzy had taken an immediate liking to Hôtel de Seine. *Well, what was not to like?* The building was a classic six floor Haussmannian with high ceilings, noble third, *"deuxieme etage"* floor, cut stone facades, wrought iron balconies and zinc roof. The staff was discreet and respectful of the powerful dignitaries and wealthy patrons who stayed there while visiting the foreign ministry or the nearby Assemblée nationale, France's lower house of parliament.

Izzy was neither a powerful dignitary nor a wealthy baroness. Yet her host, the government of France, had decided this was where she should be. It was France's way of showing gratitude for her actions in Paris the previous year, saving U.S. President Leyland Childs from certain death.

In doing so, Izzy had spared the French Republic the eternal shame of having the leader of the free world killed on its soil.

Her mind now clear and calm, she took a last sip of her crème, put the large china cup on the room service trolley, and mulled the strange events of the previous day.

Ironically, it had begun with her decision to ditch the limo and security escort at Charles de Gaulle International Airport. Last minute route changes were part of her security DNA. It was the best way to make a trip uneventful and keep potential threats off balance. *The fewer people know where you are, the better.*

Izzy knew from experience that riding the Paris rail system often included odd passenger behavior. *"C'est normal,"* Parisians said. But instead of having a commute with mildly eccentric riders, she'd found herself in the middle of a murder.

Who was the victim? Was it a robbery gone wrong? And the blonde woman walking alongside. She'd disappeared. Who was she? And why didn't the undercover police who were chasing the pickpocket return when people started screaming? Questions. No answers.

Izzy told police what she'd seen, but offered little about herself, volunteering only that she was an American on a brief visit to France. She provided her name and a phone number that led to a calling service in Topeka. She'd seen no need to identify herself any further, especially given the sensitive nature of her visit to Paris.

Ok, it was an ugly crime, but it's not my job to track down subway killers. Local authorities will take care of it.

The house phone in the bedroom was ringing. She went in and picked it up.

3

Jean-François

"*Allo?*" said Izzy.

"Madame Stone?"

"*Oui.*"

"*Bonjour.* It is Jean-François de Valmont of the Foreign Ministry."

"*Bonjour, monsieur,*" Izzy said.

Though she'd never met de Valmont, the ministry's Under Secretary, she certainly recognized the name as a senior official there. She hadn't been told he would be her contact in Paris. The French government was playing matters very close to the vest. "*You will receive a call from someone at the Foreign Ministry,*" was all they'd said.

"Welcome to France, Miss Stone. I would very much like to meet you. Are you available to drop by the Ministry?" His English carried a pleasant French inflection.

"Yes, I am," she said. "What about three this afternoon?"

"What about thirty minutes from now?"

"Aaah, of course, *monsieur.* I'll have to make a quick call to change some appointments, but after that I can easily walk to the Ministry from here."

"That won't be necessary, Miss Stone. A car is waiting for you at the entrance this very moment."

"Very kind. I'll be down in twenty then." *This is a man in a hurry!*

She walked to the living room, picked up her smart phone and placed a call to Lisa Palmer at the American Embassy annex.

"Palmer."

"Lisa, it's Izzy Stone. Got a sec?"

"Sure. What's up?"

"Just got a call from de Valmont at the Foreign Ministry. Wants me there like yesterday. I need a one minute bio."

"No problem, hold on a moment…Got it. Jean-François Stewart de Valmont, Under Secretary for International Affairs. He is considered second in importance only to the Foreign Minister himself. There are two other Undersecs but he's first among equals, widely expected to succeed the Minister when he moves on."

"And?" said Izzy.

"Well, you'll be impressed. De Valmont's driven and brilliant. He's only thirty-three, but he's had a dazzling rise. Jaw-dropping actually, given modest beginnings and a tragic childhood."

"Hmmm. Interesting. I'll need more on that later. Just text or email me. What's his social profile?"

"Five stars. De Valmont's no wallflower. Active nightlife. Single. Good looking. Adopted. No living natural parents or siblings. Is very close to a woman, a childhood friend, but nothing romantic. Enjoys female company, and is on every A list in Paris."

"Got it. Thanks, Lisa. Listen, can you help rework my schedule for the day?"

"No worries, Izzy. Good luck."

Izzy put down the phone, got dressed, then did a quick check of her outfit in the large bathroom mirror. The smart brown tweed suit and salmon colored silk blouse that she'd brought in her carry-on were matched by a pair of dark brown leather flats. The ensemble complimented her full red hair. She quickly dabbed the hollow of her neck with her favorite Annick Goutal fragrance, grabbed her bag and walked out the door. There would be no gun today. That would arrive later via special courier.

As to why she was in Paris, all she had been told was that the Ministry of Foreign Affairs, as well as the head of the DGSI, France's domestic intelligence service, had asked the U.S. government to make her available on a sensitive matter of grave importance to both countries. But rather than share the details with U.S. intelligence, the French were staying mum, at least for now. There had been too many careless and embarrassing leaks from their American friends recently, and the DGSI was taking no chances at this point in their investigation. The request was unusual given that Izzy's principal function was Special Secret Service agent in charge of the Presidential Protection Division, rather than intelligence operative. Yet the request had come directly from the Élysée palace to the White House.

The Renault four-door armored saloon pulled up to the entrance as Izzy walked out of the hotel. The driver stepped out, did a quick scan of the area, and opened the door. Izzy slipped into the back seat.

4

The Ministry

Soon they arrived at the security gates of the Ministry, and were cleared to enter the courtyard driveway. As the car pulled up to the flag-draped entrance, a tall, slender man with the athletic trim of a runner skipped effortlessly down the stairs wearing a tailored blue suit, his forearms held at a right angle.

"*Bonjour*, and welcome, Miss Stone," he said amiably, extending his right hand as she stepped out of the car. "Jean-François de Valmont."

"*Bonjour*, hi," said Izzy shaking his hand. "Pleasure, and you can call me Izzy."

He smiled. "Then you must call me Jean-François."

She took in his easy manner and striking looks. They brought to mind a young Yves Montand or Sean Connery – two of her favorite vintage film actors. When Jean-François smiled, his broad mouth, full lips and expressive brown eyes widened just enough to convey a startling mixture of intelligence, ruthlessness and flirtatiousness.

"Please, this way," he said, making his way back up the staircase toward the entrance.

5

Victor

Izzy and Jean-François were standing beside a large oak desk in an ornate office of the Ministry. It was furnished in early twentieth century French period. An immense crystal chandelier hung in the middle of the oblong-shaped room. Arched floor-to-ceiling windows set in elaborate black metal frames looked out onto a large green lawn. The light filtering through the glazed windows cast a soft, golden luminescence on the polished oak parquet floors.

"Izzy," said Jean-François, "yesterday morning a man was murdered in the underground tunnels at Châtelet. He was only a few steps ahead of you."

Izzy was surprised by how quickly Jean-François had learned of her presence at Châtelet and her exact location in the busy maze. She wasn't quite sure how she felt about it.

"Yes, I was," she said. "A cold-blooded killing. Pretty disturbing."

"I agree."

"How did you know I was there?" said Izzy.

"Three months ago we quietly added an encrypted facial recognition system to the video feed at Châtelet."

"And?" said Izzy.

"Izzy, you are well known and a much respected *personnage* at the Élysée Palace and the Foreign Ministry.

Your face immediately triggered the biometrics program for high profile individuals."

"I liked it more when I wasn't a *personnage*, as you say," said Izzy.

Jean-François smiled. "I understand. But your actions last year, saving your president's life, impressed my country greatly. And in France, once we take a liking to someone, it is forever."

Izzy managed a brief smile.

"By the way," he added, "your disappearing act at the airport impressed our security detail who were there to escort you to your hotel."

"I like surprising rather than being surprised," said Izzy.

"But you were surprised by the killing."

"True. A weird coincidence," Izzy said. "It left me with a lot of questions. Seemed more than just random violence. I'm sure detectives from the Préfecture are hard at work today, looking for the shooter." She looked at Jean-François and sighed. "But that's not why I'm in Paris, Jean-François. I was asked to come here on a matter of national security – and that puzzles me. Why you? Why the Ministry? Why me? Isn't this more a matter for your domestic and international intelligence services?"

"In fact," said Jean-François, "there *is* an intelligence operation underway at the highest levels. Our DGSI, the *Direction générale de la sécurité interiéure* is involved, as is the DGSE, our external threats intelligence service. For reasons I didn't expect, I've been pulled into this affair also."

"What's my connection to it?"

"Izzy, you remember Victor, the man who lived in the catacombs among the ones we call cataphiles?"

"Yes, I owe Victor a lot," said Izzy. "Helped me get President Childs to safety. We were on the run. Got lost in the catacombs. We would never have made it without him. One of a kind."

"You're right," said Jean-François. "Victor's a legend to the people who live in the underground tunnels of Paris. A highly respected architect who turned his back on fame and took up a renegade's life in the catacombs as a cataphile."

Jean-François reached and opened a drawer in his desk, pulled out a manila envelope and handed it to Izzy. Her name was written on the front of the envelope in awkward handprinted letters. She recognized Victor's writing style.

She noticed the envelope had been opened.

"You've already looked inside?"

"Yes, I apologize. We thought there might be something we needed to act on immediately."

She flicked open the envelope and peeked at the top of the letter.

"I don't understand," said Izzy. "This letter is dated last week. I heard Victor died months ago."

"Victor's not dead. He's in hiding. He concocted a story that he'd died in an accident. We haven't been able to locate him. His cataphile friends helped with the deception. As you'll see in his letter, he's very much alive and he's terrified."

"How did you get this?"

"Victor sent it to me personally," said Jean-François.

"You know Victor?"

"I've known Victor for many years."

Izzy said nothing but found it strange that Jean-François would know Victor, a reclusive cataphile who rarely left the catacombs.

"What Victor says in the letter is alarming," said Jean-François. "There's a passage, a string of symbols, some sort of message we couldn't decipher. We thought you might know what it means."

Izzy opened the envelope wider and pulled out several sheets of paper. She scanned the pages and gave them back to Jean-François.

"Hmmm, not good," she said. "I can see why your government is worried. The passage that you refer to is in cataphile code. It's a message telling me how to meet him."

Izzy took the letter back and looked at it again. "So, Victor overheard a conversation about planned terrorist attacks on France and the U.S.?"

"Right," said Jean-François, "but no details. Apparently, he doesn't want to reveal too much. In the wrong hands that information would be his death warrant."

"Why me?" said Izzy. "He could have provided that information to you or the DGSI."

"You'll have to ask Victor. Our guess is that it's because Victor will only trust you with what he knows."

"Right," said Izzy.

"When do you want to visit the catacombs?" said Jean-François.

"Tomorrow night, but I need someone with me."

"I'll arrange that immediately through our security services," said Jean-François.

"Thanks, but I already have a person in mind. I just need to make a call to Washington."

"Someone we know?"

"Yes, his name is Will Bergen, my second in command. He was with me last year in Paris with the president."

"Do you want the Élysée to make the call?"

"No," said Izzy, "I can handle it myself."

"Good."

"One more thing," said Izzy.

"Yes?"

"I don't want anyone tailing or tracking us. Otherwise I'm on a plane back to Washington."

"You have my word, Izzy."

6

Hôtel de Seine

It's been a long day.

It was after five in the afternoon. Izzy kicked off her flats as she entered her hotel room. The fragrance of roses filled the air. She walked to the study and saw a crystal vase filled with long-stemmed red roses resting on a small table. A card had been placed next to the vase. She picked it up and smiled.

Miss you. Leyland

The card was unnecessary. She knew the moment she saw the roses that they were from Leyland Childs, the man she'd twice saved from death, first in Amman, Jordan and later in Paris, the man who was in love with her – the man who was the current occupant of the Oval Office. He sent her roses each time she was away from him.

Izzy closed her eyes and pictured him. So tall, six-four, with broad shoulders that seemed preordained for the heavy burden of governing the world's most powerful nation. His brown hair, thick and carefully groomed, was showing the first streaks of grey, testimony to the crushing hours and responsibilities of a president only in his mid-forties. A faded scar above his right eyebrow was all that remained of a near fatal enemy round during his deployment to Afghanistan as a Special Forces Ranger. When he fixed his expressive blue eyes on you, the effect was intoxicating.

Izzy leaned into the bouquet and absorbed the rich scent.

Thanks, Ley. So sweet.

It had been an improbable, unthinkable, match. Izzy was a secret service agent whose sole and sacred duty as head of the detail was to protect the president from all harm. When she was appointed Special Agent in Charge of the Presidential Detail, she had approached her assignment with a professional *sang-froid* and badass awareness that personal feelings had no place in her job, a line never to be crossed. Leyland Childs was the president, leader of the free world, married to a remarkable woman, Meg, whom he adored. Izzy was his safekeeper, prepared to give up her life to protect him. That was the beginning and end of it.

But an assassination attempt on the president in Amman, and a subsequent bloody shootout in Paris last year, had changed all that. Their hellish ambush in Amman had spared the president, but had taken the life of the First Lady who was at his side that day.

Months later, still dealing with his grief, he faced a new crisis due to the errant U.S. missile strike that killed that group of French children in Islamabad. The president had been compelled to travel to Paris to make amends, and had once again come under attack. Only Izzy's raw courage and resourcefulness had been able to keep Leyland Childs alive in the relentless onslaught that followed. Amman and Paris had been a searing crucible forging a bond between them that no one could have foreseen. It was not need, but rather the dark journey of battle and blood that had created an unbreakable tie.

Izzy placed the card down and took in the raspberry and lemon fragrance of the flowers. She stepped to the silver cart, poured herself a scotch and water from the well-stocked bar, and slipped into the leather wing chair. There was a lot to absorb. Jean-François was a paradox. If his childhood had been hard, one would certainly never have guessed it. There was internal strength, a polished well-bred finesse and brilliance that telegraphed supreme confidence and engendered trust. Izzy had encountered many extraordinary people in the course of her career. If first appearances counted, Jean-François de Valmont was equal to the best of them.

She checked her watch. Six P.M.

It's noon in Washington.

She took the cell phone from her purse and dialed.

7

Will in D.C.

Washington, D.C.

"Bonjooor, Izzy!" Will Bergen said, drawing out the word *bonjour* with playful sarcasm. "Are you calling me to brag about those high-class French meals you're enjoying, or are you already homesick for your bro'?"

"You'll soon find out," said Izzy. "I need you on a plane in the next ninety minutes. You're already cleared for the flight on Air France out of Dulles. You'll have to hustle if you're going to make it."

"Oh, great! Thanks, boss. I just sat down to lunch at The Old Bailey with a very special friend and a pricey bottle of California merlot. Can't this wait 'til tomorrow?"

"Better step on it. Now you've only got eighty-nine minutes."

Izzy ended the call and looked at her watch. *It's a little after nine in the morning in Santa Monica. Mom will be up. Good time to call.*

Ever since her mom had been diagnosed with cancer, Izzy called several times a week. It was always stressful. Her mom had never recovered psychologically or emotionally from her father's death. After the funeral it had been a downward spiral for decades. The once vibrant family home on San Vicente Boulevard had fallen into mournful silence, and her mom had progressively withdrawn from the world. The more recent cancer diagnosis and treatment had accelerated her decline.

Prepare yourself, Izzy. She needs to hear from you.

***

Will Bergen, Deputy Special Agent in Charge, arrived at Charles de Gaulle in a pounding rain. It was one A.M. Izzy's car and driver, provided by the Foreign Ministry, pulled up to the baggage claim area of Terminal Two.

Izzy opened the car door and stepped out. "Wait here," she said to the driver.

She soon spotted Will rolling a suitcase behind him, a garment bag draped over one shoulder.

"Will, good to see you."

"Oh, oh, that sounds like trouble," he said. "Who's after you now, Iz?"

"No one yet, thought I'd save that for you."

"Thanks boss, really nice of you. Makes me nostalgic for those rounds we were dodging last year."

They walked to the waiting car and got in as the driver stowed Will's luggage in the trunk. On the way back to Paris via the A1 they made small talk, avoiding mission details. They transitioned to Paris's périphérique ring road and eventually made their way to Cours la Reine, Pont de la Concorde, and across the bridge to the hotel on Quai Anatole France.

As they walked into the Hôtel de Seine, Will turned to Izzy.

"Ah, well," he said, admiring the elegant lobby. "Pretty cool digs. Sure beats sloshing around the catacombs."

"Glad you like it, Will, but don't get too comfy. We're not spending much time here. Let's get you checked in. I'll get you up to speed."

8

Canal St. Martin

It was still raining when the battered dark grey van, headlamps off, pulled up at Quai de Jemmapes along Canal Saint Martin in the sometimes edgy, bohemian 10th arrondissement of Paris. It was three A.M. Illumination from the aging street lamps was always poor. But tonight, the light was even weaker as several of the street lamps had recently been vandalized.

Two heavy-set men in dark clothes and caps emerged from the vehicle and walked to the rear of the van. They opened the doors and reached in. With some effort, they pulled a long black bag from the van and carried it to the canal. There was a zipping sound and then the sound of a splash. The men made their way back to the van, closed the rear doors, and drove away.

9

Wong Bai

Paris – next day

Wong Bai, now in his eighties, shoulders stooped, torso bent forward to the point of tipping, made his way with short unsteady steps along scruffy rue de Ménilmontant in Belleville, a working-class neighborhood in Paris's 20th arrondissement.

Belleville had a large Chinese population. Bystanders would have noted little about the octogenarian on the busy street other than his shoddy dress, weathered leather sandals, walking stick and labored steps. Just an old man from the old country. A thick package wrapped in butcher paper with dark brown stains was tucked under the old man's rail thin left arm; likely a left-over meal or scavenger's haul.

Belleville was officially at lunch. Rue de Ménilmontant throbbed with city public service employees, tourists, expats, immigrants, office workers and countless others rushing to get a table at the restaurants, bistros, brasseries, tabacs, Asian food traiteurs, trattorias, salad bars, deli take-outs and sidewalk crêpe makers that unfailingly sprang to life when the lunch hour arrived. Like an enduring pointillist painting, each venue, however grand or modest, contributed to the rich canvas of Paris *à l'heure du déjeuner.*

Wong turned off the *rue* into a dim passage so narrow that it could only accommodate one person at a time.

Reaching an open door along the passageway, he quickly stepped in. Chen Chi was sitting on a small stool in the dingy closet-sized room. An empty food container with the name of one of Paris's most pricey delis sat upon a tall bench in front of him. Young, mid-size and wiry in build, Chen Chi was a man of explosive violence. His deep-set eyes, dark, and in constant motion, suggested someone half-expecting an attack — or planning one.

Large bolts of colored fabric leaned against the walls. Thick rugs hung off metal rods.

"Did you get it?" Chen said in rapid-fire Cantonese, a dialect unusual for the Chinese community of Belleville, where Mandarin was the common language.

Wong said nothing and handed Chen the parcel. He didn't care for Chen. An arrogant upstart who had no respect for his elders. *Our traditions are gone. The young today are as uncivilized as the white ghost Caucasians. He probably plays video games and eats hamburgers like the rest of those savages.*

Chen cast a glance of irritation towards the old man, placed the package on a small round table, and pulled one end of the twine until it loosened. He slowly folded back the wrapped sheets of butcher paper until at last they fell open. He reflexively turned his nose away from the pungent smell emanating from the severed hands.

10

Yuri and the Hacker

Los Angeles – San Fernando Valley

"Watch this," said Eric, a twenty-two-year-old bearded anorexic in faded jeans, tie-dye shirt and bare feet. Fingers flying across the keyboard of the laptop, he typed with the feverish energy of a virtuoso racing through a Bach fugue. A half-eaten slice of pizza and an energy drink sat next to the laptop. The code sped across the screen in long lines until the young man hit the "Enter" key with the dramatic flair of an artist bringing his performance to a thundering finale.

Soon the words "U.S. DEPARTMENT OF STATE " filled the screen.

"Now," he said theatrically, turning to the heavy-set man sitting next to him, "What would you like me to look for?"

The man grunted and moved his hands upward in a half-hearted gesture as if to say he wasn't sure. He looked tired, perhaps in his mid-thirties. He was a man who slept too little and drank too much. His full, round face, dark eyes, broad eyebrows and light brown skin tone gave him the appearance of a latin american.

"Show me some things," the man said in a heavy accent. He'd introduced himself as Yuri.

Yuri, my ass! thought Eric. He doubted Yuri was the man's real name. Maybe it was, maybe it wasn't. Didn't matter. Eric was accustomed to secretive clients with phony names. Besides, his own name wasn't Eric.

For his part, the stodgy looking man already knew "Eric" was not the young hacker's real name. The contacts who'd led him to Eric had told him that, and more.

Eric was not particularly concerned about the motives or cyber requests of this or any client, no matter how morally questionable or illegal others might find them. A ragged trail of legal run-ins with the feds and a twelve-month stint in a federal prison for hacking banks and bedeviling defense contractors with denial of service attacks had relieved him of any ethical qualms about patriotism and the law. Recognizing his talent, the FBI had offered him a deal if he'd join them. "Fuck you!" had been his reply, as he was frog-marched to his sentencing. The reality was that the gargantuan internet was a vast, lawless digital frontier and he was just another gunslinger for hire to the highest bidder—and that did not include some cheesy government salary.

The young man's fingers resumed their mad race across the keyboard and once again struck the "Enter" key with gusto. He looked at Yuri.

"This is a list of the State Department's Top Secret memos on the Chinese Embassy in Washington. The last one is only two days old. Want me to open the files?"

"You make it look easy, but it is hard, no?" Yuri said, his voice thick with inflection.

"Nah," said Eric. "The government says that all the time but they're just smok'n shit. These days a sixth grader could do it. Just a question of using VPN cutouts, a TOR multi-hop chain, neural routing, add some good hacking. Find a point of entry, like a watering hole, a drive-by or a staged attack - even spear phishing. Dude, I've exploited zero-day vulnerabilities, added some good code and 'whomp,' it's the bomb. Most of the tools are almost off the shelf these days. La, la, dude, I can hack from LA and make it look like I'm in a yurt in Mongolia. Want me to open the files?"

"No," said Yuri. He'd stopped trying to follow the man's cyberspeak. He got up with apparent effort, placed a wad of hundred-dollar bills on the table and slowly shuffled his way to the door of the small room.

"I will have work for you soon."

He opened the door, picked up the suitcase he'd brought with him, and walked out.

11

MacArthur Park

Two hours later, Yuri, suitcase in hand, stepped off the crowded, graffiti-marred MTA bus at Wilshire and South Carondolet Street in the Alvarado district, a gang and drug-plagued mid-city area of Los Angeles.

Yuri could instead have easily Ubered to his storage facility in Thousand Oaks. There he maintained a sizeable cache of currency, weapons, documents and his customized $100,000 plus Tesla, always charged and ready. But that would have endangered his carefully curated legend. He checked his cheap plastic watch. Five-thirty P.M.

He walked at a brisk pace down the sidewalk bordering Wilshire Boulevard, a broad, palm-lined, six-lane avenue bisecting sprawling MacArthur Park. To the south of Wilshire Boulevard was the park's sizeable lagoon dotted with paddle-boats and rowers.

North of the boulevard, the once green lawns of MacArthur Park had long ago turned brown and powdery under the racing feet of whooping, adrenaline-charged locals playing soccer with impressive skill. There were picnicking families, homeless transients and emaciated drug addicts. Diminutive Central American food vendors pushed two-wheel balloon-adorned handcarts stocked with hot *antojitos, pupusa, tamales*, soft drinks, pink cotton candy and fresh-cut pineapple.

Yuri crossed Alvarado, turned up a grimy alley and found his way to the rear of a squalid apartment building. He climbed the cracked wood staircase with its flaking sunbaked paint. He reached the top of the stairs, pulled open a dented white metal door, its lock missing, and stepped into a dim, third-floor hallway that reeked of kimchi and pupusa.

Taking care not to trip on loose strands of ragged, paper-thin carpeting, he made his way to a door with a white metal gate, inserted a key, opened it, inserted a second key into a wood frame door, opened and walked in.

He'd paid cash for a month's rental. He'd use it for a total of two hours.

The apartment was in no better condition than the hallway. A vinyl-covered sofa, the stuffing coming out, was the sole piece of furniture in the room. Off to the side was a gloomy kitchenette with a discolored sink, a faucet with a broken handle and a grease-caked two-burner gas stove. There was no fridge.

At the back of the narrow dark kitchenette was a door leading to a small, dank toilet. The only thing that did not reek of mold, bad cooking or stale air was the neat midsized suitcase he'd brought with him. Yuri opened it and removed a small shaving kit, a passport, and the boarding passes from his recent flight from Paris.

In the kitchen, he turned the gas knob of one of the burners, heard it click several times, then struck a match. The burner took hold. He took the passport and boarding passes, lit them one by one and held them over the sink until there was nothing but ash. He turned off the burner, gathered up the ashes, took them to the toilet and flushed.

He removed his jacket, shirt, pants and the thick foam material wrapped around his midsection. He bunched up the clothing and foam and stuffed them into a large trash bag he'd brought. It would soon be in an alley dumpster.

He then removed a final article from his head, carefully placed it in a sterile plastic zip bag, and dropped it in the suitcase. Satisfied, he took a small mirror from his shaving kit and hung it on a nail sticking out from the wall. He lathered his face with a small can of shaving cream, shaved quickly, reached back into the suitcase, withdrew a shrink-wrapped set of clothes and put on the new outfit. He closed the suitcase, picked it up, grabbed the garbage bag, and walked out.

12

"I Have Client"

Los Angeles

"I have client," said Yuri. "He is interested in your services."

Yuri was sitting in the enclosed priest's box of a confessional booth in a small Catholic church located on Dozier Street in East LA. It was eight A.M. on a quiet Wednesday morning. The church, badly in need of repair, was, as usual, empty of both worshipers and clerics.

On the other side of the dark cloth partition was Eric, the young hacker.

"No problem," said Eric.

"Under your seat there is large envelope. Open, please." Yuri heard the envelope being opened.

"Wow! That's some serious money," said Eric.

"Money is for you. Please read note," said Yuri.

A moment later, "Okay, got it," said the hacker.

"Think of this like one of your internet games," said Yuri. "Take money. Put note and envelope back under seat. If you do not like game, tell me now."

After a minute Eric said, "Yeah, no problem. But it will cost more. Some of this I can do, but for the rest I'll have to use some contacts overseas. I mean, is this for real?"

"It is just game. My friend likes play games. Do you want?"

"Yeah, sure," said Eric.

"Good, you go now," said Yuri, as he pulled the silencer away from the partition.

***

Yuri was soon back in a shabby West Hollywood apartment on Sweetzer Avenue where he'd lived for several years. He opened the large metal box concealed under his closet floor and selected two passports, Venezuelan bolivars, Moroccan dirhams, euros, a 3D printed plastic gun and airline boarding passes. He packed a business suit and tie, formal black shoes, shirts and casual wear. He added a makeup kit and a sterile zip lock bag containing his special article.

He walked out of the apartment, set several door locks, then ambled down to Melrose Boulevard where he hailed a passing cab. He took the cab to Normandie Avenue and West Century Boulevard, paid in cash, then boarded a crowded MTA bus to LAX.

13

"Foolish Old Goat!"

Paris

"Foolish old goat! The fingerprints did not match! The hands you brought were from another woman!"

Chen Chi's powerful hands were wrapped around Wong's skinny neck, pressing it against the stone wall of the small shop. The old man was struggling to breathe, his mincing sandaled feet dangling just above the floor. Wong was trembling, terrified of the younger man. He'd seen the violence Chen was capable of.

But I didn't know. How could I? No one told me anything. Chen Chi just told me to go to that address in the 20th arrondissement and collect a package.

The old man did have to admit to himself that when he was given the package, he knew whatever was inside could not be good. The men who'd given it to him were not the kind who gave nice gifts. He would have said all this to Chen, but that was impossible so long as the iron grip around his throat held fast.

Chen took a step back and released his hold. The old man dropped to the floor, gasping. He began to speak, but Chen interrupted, "Shut up old man!"

Chen began pacing the small room, his knuckles pressed to his forehead. *Someone double-crossed me and now I'm in deep trouble with Ajax.*

Ajax Balaskas was a rich Greek businessman who dominated a slice of the Paris underworld, a glowering menace of a beast with a badly scarred face that looked like it had been groomed with a rusty rake. A flashy partier, his immense wealth came from shipping companies and shadowy business connections in Russia.

Ajax sometimes called on Chen Chi for special favors. He'd given Chen a photo, and the address of a woman named Galina Federova. Ajax's Russian friends wanted proof that Federova had been eliminated, and that meant a pair of severed hands. There was no explanation asked for or given. It was a gruesome request, but Chen knew better than to say no to Ajax, a man with a taste for brutality, and connections to powerful people one did not cross.

Chen had tasked the grisly job to an Armenian *sans papiers* named Adur and his two henchmen. Unlike most undocumented arrivals to Paris who'd chosen hard-scrabble honest work, Adur, an ex-felon, had found it more to his liking to work the dark side. There was a feral quality about him, a predator looking for easy prey. His French was limited, but he knew words like "take," "hurt," "bury" and "how much?"

It wasn't the first time Chen had used Adur for messy work. The man was testy but always did the job. Now, something had gone wrong and Adur had sent Chen the severed hands of the wrong woman. *Why?* This was no mistake. It was an intentional switch. Someone had intervened, changed the plan.

Whoever it was must have offered a lot of money, or must have sufficiently threatened Adur such that he was willing to risk Chen's well-known wrath. And bloody wrath there would be.

14

Victor

Paris

Izzy and Will pushed the heavy metal sewer cover to the side and peered into the dark opening. They were on rue de la Comète, a narrow one-way street in the 7th arrondissement of Paris, one of the city's most exclusive neighborhoods. At three A.M., even the club-hopping set and late night drunks were off the streets.

"Looks OK," said Izzy, as she shined her maglight into the opening and onto the steel ladder that led down.

"Gives me the creeps just thinking about how close we came to buying the farm down there last year," Will said, as he looked into the darkness below.

"No kidding," said Izzy. She dropped to her knees, placed a foot on the third rung of the ladder and descended. Will quickly followed, wresting the heavy cover back into position as he climbed down.

They reached the bottom of the ladder and found themselves in a concrete-lined tunnel. Izzy led the way for several minutes until they arrived at an oblong metal door along one side of the tunnel. She pulled it open and stepped into a humid, earthen passage. They closed the door behind them. She panned her light across the walls and floor. It was all too familiar.

I remember this passage. It really was do or die. Running for our lives. The flashback sent an icy ripple skittering down her back. *The president was badly wounded and they were almost down our throats. Thank god we crossed paths with Victor.*

She turned to Will. "Ready?"

"Aaah, nope. But what the heck, let's go, boss. In for a penny, in for a pound."

She gave Will a shoulder pat. "Good man." As usual, Will was into gallows humor, but she knew she could trust him with her life. He was as gutsy as they came. She'd held little back as to why they were trying to make contact with Victor. She was once again putting Will's life in harm's way. He was entitled to know a lot, if not everything. She turned, directed her light forward, and moved into the gloom.

***

"Check this out," said Izzy.

Izzy and Will were looking at a narrow tunnel wall. The wall was a riot of letters, numbers, arrows and garish symbols. They'd gotten there through a circuitous route of menacing passages, some of which diverged into multiple, pitch-black paths. Taking the wrong one could easily lead to a dead end or a labyrinthine maze from which they would never emerge.

"Okay, you're the expert," said Will. "What does all this mean?"

"It means we're close to Victor."

"Victor, or maybe someone who wants us dead," said Will.

"Listen up, Will. We're not here to have a beer and a burger. I can't be sure what we'll find. Maybe trouble, maybe fireworks. Have your weapon ready, but keep it out of sight. I recognized Victor's handwriting on the note he sent. If what he was hinting at is true, a lot of innocent folks are going to be dead unless we stop it."

"OK, no burger. How about just a beer?"

Izzy smiled in the light of their flashlights. "Beer later, and you're buying."

An hour later they found themselves in a huge high-ceilinged earthen chamber. They scanned the walls with their lights.

"This must be it," said Izzy.

"There's nothing here but mud and clay," said Will.

Izzy took a step forward. She directed her light onto her face then panned to Will so that they could be seen.

"Victor! It's Izzy!" she said into the void. "I'm with Will Bergen, you remember him."

"Don't like this," Will whispered.

Izzy touched Will's arm, signaling silence. She turned off her light. Will did the same. They were now in total black silence. For several minutes only the sound of their breathing registered in the quiet chamber. Izzy brushed her back lightly, checking the position of her Sig Sauer.

The silence was broken by a strong, surprisingly cheerful voice.

"Izzy, Will, welcome back."

Suddenly, Victor was standing in front of them under an overhead light he'd just illuminated. The light was bright enough to reveal the three of them, and the ceiling of the chamber that was decorated with a fresco of roses.

"Good to see you again, Victor," Izzy said, squinting in the sudden light. She gave him a hug. *Victor looks stressed and exhausted.*

Victor turned to Will. "Glad you're here, Will."

"Thanks," said Will, "feels like home."

Victor gave a small laugh and motioned with his hand.

"Come with me," he said, as he turned and walked deeper into the chamber.

15

Izzy at DGSI

Paris

Late afternoon. Izzy was sitting across from Jean-François in a large, suspended polymer-enclosed, soundproof room in the basement of the DGSI headquarters in the 20th arrondissement of Paris. There were several people around the table. Although Izzy was fluent in French, today would be in English. She knew DGSI personnel were highly trained professionals with full command of English.

Present were two senior intelligence agents from the domestic security DGSI, an agent from the DGSE, France's external security agency, and a top deputy from the Élysée. The door at the end of the room opened. A man, early fifties, large build, a shock of thick brown hair, green eyes, and sharp jaw line entered, and sat down at the other end of the table. He nodded to one of the DGSE agents, but did not introduce himself.

Izzy took a glancing look. *Looks like one of ours. CIA? FBI?*

"Izzy," said Jean-François, "what did Victor say?"

"Victor believes large-scale terrorist attacks are planned against France and the United States."

"What kind of attacks?" said Jean-François.

"Unclear," said Izzy, "but they involve weapons of mass destruction. He says he heard they will shock the world, kill thousands, maybe millions."

"Does Victor know who's behind it?" said one of the DGSI agents.

"Not sure, but could be North Korea," said Izzy.

"Any proof?" said the agent.

"Nothing conclusive," said Izzy, "but through his large cataphile network, Victor's heard it's a plan to sow panic and death in the U.S. and France."

"Okay," said the agent. "Let's say that it's Pyongyang. Motive?"

"Three words," said the brooding man at the end of the table.

Izzy looked at him. "And those would be?" she said.

"Sanctions, nukes and murder," he said. "The escalation of crippling sanctions led by the U.S., and now France, is devastating what little was left of the fragile North Korean economy. The U.S. has always been at the top of their target list. France's decision to take the lead on European sanctions has made it number two.

Second, the collapse of the denuclearization talks and the ramping up of military rhetoric by President Childs have added to the powder keg.

Third, the attempt on Dear Leader's life has increased his rage and paranoia. He's convinced the West was behind it. It's a damned miracle he survived the bombing. Maybe he wants payback."

"You're right about the paranoia," said Jean-François. "The renewed large-scale U.S. and South Korean maneuvers may have Pyongyang fearing that a pre-emptive strike is imminent. The collapse of nuclear negotiations with the DPRK was a disaster for everyone."

"Negotiations were always a pipe dream," said the brooding man at the end of the table. "Anyone who thought North Korea would abandon its nuclear program had his head up his ass. DPRK wants to be able to pop a nuke anytime, anywhere."

Yeah, he's one of ours, thought Izzy.

She looked at him. "And you are?" she said.

"Powers, - Langley," he replied, referring to CIA headquarters in Langley, Virginia.

He'd spat out the words in a tone that said, "*Careful, I'm not the warm cuddly type.*"

"Okay," said Jean-François, turning to Izzy. "Did Victor have anything more?"

"Yes." She paused and scanned the table. She knew her next words would take the threat to a whole new level.

"Victor said he heard the terrorist 'Lalo' may be involved."

Izzy took in the alarmed expressions. "*Putain!*" said one.

"I had the same reaction," said Izzy. "Lalo's high on our threat list in the U.S. too, as Powers over there can tell you. Lalo's of concern to those of us in the Secret Service Presidential Detail. But we have limited intel on him, or her, or it, whoever or whatever Lalo is."

"I don't know," said one of the DGSI agents, as he pushed his chair back from the table, an expression of irritation on his face. "Let's take a deep breath. You say Victor heard the name Lalo mentioned. Victor's 'Lalo' may just be some Paris barista who's a friend of a cataphile."

"What's your point?" said Izzy.

"My point is, maybe Lalo, maybe not, maybe a possible mass attack, maybe not, maybe North Korea...maybe, maybe, all from Victor, an old cataphile who lives underground. Sounds *trés mince,* very thin. *Bien sûr*, we at DGSI and DGSE have picked up some dark web chatter that is concerning, even alarming, but other than the letter from Victor and your conversation with him, there's nothing solid. We can't go upstairs and tell them World War Three is about to start without more."

"I get the skepticism," said Izzy, "but Victor is not some clueless, aging cataphile with delusions. I would, in fact did, trust him with my life last year." She looked at the DGSI agent. "If Victor heard the terrorist 'Lalo' mentioned in connection with the attacks, you can take that to the bank. Remember, the world of the cataphiles is very different. These are individuals who live off the grid. Some are disaffected in the extreme, are well educated, are active on the dark web, and feel no particular loyalty to a flag, or duty to report what they hear. They have their own ways of getting and passing on information."

"Hmmm," said Jean-François. "It would be a big risk for Pyongyang. North Korea hates the West, but an attack the size Victor's referring to would surely invite massive military retaliation. Hacking banks and movie studios is one thing. They've been doing that successfully and profitably for years. But a mass casualty attack would be a game changer, as you Americans say. I don't believe they'd run the risk of having their intentions exposed."

"They wouldn't have to," said the man from Langley. "If they're using cryptocurrency to lease remote servers, and are working through multiple VPNs, TOR, human cut-outs and dark web encryption, they'll have a lot of anonymity and deniability. That's all they need to create uncertainty – and you can't frigg'n bomb uncertainty. They might feel it's worth the gamble. I'll say this, if they're doing it, it won't be through a North Korean operation. They're wicked, but they're not stupid. You'll have to look somewhere else for the actors."

"I agree with Monsieur Powers," said a DGSI agent. "It could be done with lone wolf proxies, as he says."

Jean-François turned to Izzy. "We need more from Victor and we need it fast. If this is a genuine threat, it could be catastrophic."

16

Video of Murder

Jean-François and Izzy were in the Ministry's safe room.

"We have the video from Châtelet," said Jean-François.

"Good," said Izzy. "Let's see."

Jean-François picked up a remote and toggled. The video began playing on a large wall-mounted LED monitor. It showed people exiting the metro car, then moving through the tunnel.

In the fast-paced throng, Izzy recognized the slender blonde, the elegant older man, the young professionals, the students with their backpacks, the man with baggy pants and sweatshirt, the skinny pickpocket and the tailing undercover officers. It was a human wave rushing towards a murder.

The video ended abruptly as the crowd reached the bend in the tunnel and turned.

"Okay, pretty much what I saw," said Izzy. "Let's move on to the video of the actual shooting?"

"There is no video," said Jean-François.

"What!" Izzy had not expected this.

"There's no video, Izzy. The shooter apparently knew that at that bend in the tunnel video cameras would not capture anything. It's a blind spot."

"Not good," said Izzy. "Two detectives were chasing the young man in tight pants," said Izzy. "Did you interview them?"

"Those individuals, the man and the woman you refer to, are not French detectives and do not belong to any law enforcement body we know of," said Jean-François. "Right now, we have no idea who they are. The same applies to the young man they were chasing. The three could be Eastern Europeans, but could just as easily be from some other part of the world. We have good images, so we think we'll be able to identify them with the help of Interpol and other services, but it will take time."

"So, it was a diversion," said Izzy. *I knew something was not right about that chase.*

"Very possible, Izzy. Looks like a well-planned execution."

"Right," said Izzy. "The shooter had to know in advance that the target would take that route at that exact time."

"Exactly," said Jean-François. "It suggests the victim, a man we've identified as Jens Alders, had someone with him or near him who was in on the killing."

Should I tell him that Victor told me he met Jens Alders? Maybe not yet.

"And no one saw the hit go down?" said Izzy.

"No. People were so distracted by the running and yelling that they did not notice the shooter. The police interviewed a number of people who were walking next to Alders. They were unaware an assassin was putting a bullet in his head. We're working to identify all the individuals who were there, but as you know, there were many in the tunnel."

"And the blond woman?" said Izzy.

"You'll find this interesting. When our detectives were reviewing the video footage, one of the investigators recognized her as a person of interest to the DGSI and the DGSE. There's a strong suspicion she's connected to Russia's SVR intelligence service. Her name is Galina Federova, Russian. It may be a false identity. We won't know what she was doing at Châtelet until we have a chance to question her."

"She could be the shooter," Izzy said. "So, why would the Russians want Alders dead?"

"Another puzzle," said Jean-François. "There's a major operation under way to bring her in. Then we may get some answers, but Federova is smart and slippery. Several weeks ago she disappeared from her apartment. She's on the move but the Châtelet video tells us she's still in Paris. We just don't know where."

"Why go through all the drama of a carefully organized killing in a public place like Châtelet? Why not some dark street?" said Izzy.

"Good question," said Jean-François. "Could be the shooter wanted this to be a spectacle. Perhaps a warning to others. We just don't know enough yet."

"So, what do you know about Jens Alders?" said Izzy. Her question was a probe to see how much Jean-François knew. Thanks to Victor, she had information on Alders that was likely unknown to Jean-François. But she wasn't quite ready to share that information just yet. Victor had asked her not to divulge his sources.

"Jens Alders, Dutch national, sixty-seven years old," said Jean-François. "Operated out of Switzerland. Had an office there, but traveled widely. He's been connected to arms dealing in Africa and the Middle East, money laundering for Russian moguls, and using false flag shipping registries to help North Korea and Iran evade sanctions."

"A busy man," said Izzy. "He was carrying something."

"Yes, we see it in an earlier video. A small briefcase. It's also missing."

"Hmmm. Like you said, Jean-François, too many players, too many angles for a random murder. Any leads on who's behind the shooting?"

"Unsure. But let's consider some of the players. Jens Alders, a man connected to arms trading, Galina Federova, a suspected Russian agent, a carefully planned assassination. It's not a run-of-the-mill killing. There's a lot going on here."

"Right. Jean-François," she said, "we should consider a possible connection to Lalo."

"That is a *big* reach," said Jean-François. "But if Lalo is in Paris, it's not good news."

"What do your folks have on him?" said Izzy.

"We believe he's linked to last year's assassination of a prominent critic of the Russian government in London, and the deadly bombing of the British consulate in Turkey. Also specializes in soft targets."

"Right," said Izzy. "The bombing of Temple Emmanuel in Kansas City during Rosh Hashanah had the markings of his work."

"But he's a phantom," said Jean-François. "Operates deep in the background. No photos or personal details are available on him. A rough, but unreliable composite exists. Frankly, it could be any one of a million people. Like 'Carlos the Jackal,' the terrorist of the seventies, Lalo is a master of disguise and evasion."

"There is one thing distinctive about him," said Izzy. "Like the San Francisco Zodiac killer, he seems to enjoy leaving a calling card. There's always something about his attack that mocks and taunts authorities, a photo of something, a quotation, a piece of fabric, something. But forensically they've all led to dead ends."

Jean-François raised his arms in obvious frustration. "Exactly, but to be honest, Izzy, we're not even sure Lalo exists. Maybe the DGSI is right, and Lalo is just some Paris barista or a barber in Seville. He could be a composite, a complete fiction to keep us off balance. Just 'fake news' as you Americans say."

"Only some Americans say that," said Izzy. "I agree, we're not sure Lalo is a live, breathing human being. But assuming he is, he's working with terror groups."

"And hostile governments as well," said Jean-François.

"Like North Korea?"

"Like North Korea, or Iran, or Syria."

There was a knock on the door.

"Izzy, excuse me for a moment." Jean-François walked to the door and opened it part way.

Izzy could see a man in a dark suit speaking urgently in a low voice. Jean-François nodded twice, closed the door and returned to Izzy, his mouth taut, expression grim.

"The body of a blond woman in blue clothing was just pulled from one of the locks of Canal Saint Martin in the 10th arrondissement. It may be Galina Federova."

"If she was the shooter, Moscow won't be happy to hear its agent ended up in a canal," said Izzy.

"Correct," said Jean-François. "It will take some time to fully identify her. They say the body was a mess."

***

Izzy was back at her hotel. She undressed and took a long, hot shower. She needed it. The murder of Jens Alders and later, the woman found in the canal, had left her unsettled.

Her shower finished, she wrapped herself in the long, white silk, Japanese-patterned robe. She was missing Leyland. He had a way of listening and speaking to the many burdens troubling her that always revived her spirits and eased her mind.

She picked up her encrypted cell and texted: **Miss you.**

A few minutes later her phone chirped.

Leyland.

"Hi," she said.

"Izzy, are you OK?" he said, concern in his voice.

"I am now."

17

Yuri to Paris

Yuri Kouznetsov arrived at Paris's Gare de Lyon in the 12th arrondissement via high-speed train at seven twenty-three P.M. He'd boarded the TGV, *Train de Grande Vitesse,* at Barcelona's Estació Sants station.

Barcelona was only a transit point for Yuri. Using a forged passport, he'd begun his travel in Los Angeles, routing through Caracas and Morocco to Barcelona's El Prat International Airport. The cab from El Prat to the train station was fast.

Evening had fallen on a rainy, darkening Paris. *Good.* Yuri preferred arriving in a city after sunset. It made it easier to avoid detection. He was wearing a tailored black business suit, white cotton shirt, red tie and laced black leather shoes. His skin tone was Latin or Middle-Eastern, his face smooth and clear but for a thin, well-trimmed mustache that suggested self-regard.

Yuri walked out of the train station, a copy of *El País* prominently tucked under his left arm, a brown leather traveling bag and umbrella in his right hand. To other passengers, Yuri would have appeared a quiet, well-dressed man, a bit on the short side, on a business or pleasure visit to the City of Light.

Yuri put the bag down, and popped open the umbrella against the cold, steady rain. He spotted the bus stop for the number fifty-seven bus, pulled out his burner phone, checked the address again, and consulted the bus arrival time posted on the digital screen of the enclosed shelter.

Like most Paris public transit, the fifty-seven arrived right on schedule.

He boarded using the RATP card he'd purchased at the station kiosk. Thirty minutes later, he descended at Porte de Bagnolet in the 20th arrondissement and walked two blocks to a five-story tenement building situated on a dark, narrow one-way street. The eight-foot high dark brown wood doors to the building were massive. He entered the five digits of the *porte-code* into the keypad by the door and heard the click of the release. He pushed and stepped into a shabby cobblestone courtyard. Several pots containing scrawny plants were overflowing with rainwater.

The courtyard was framed on all four sides by apartments in varying states of disrepair. Through the dimly illuminated windows he could see shapes pass back and forth as residents went about their evening. He crossed the courtyard and entered a small foyer. A spindly wooden staircase wound sharply upward. He climbed to the fifth floor, found the door he was looking for and rapped lightly. Footsteps approached.

"*Oui,*" said a voice from within.

"It is Monsieur del Valle," said Yuri.

A door peephole flickered. A lock was turned. The door opened. A tall, blond woman stood before him wearing a red velvet jumpsuit that set off her creamy complexion. Without a word of greeting, he stepped in and did a slow walk through the entire apartment. Apparently satisfied, he turned to her, a question in his eyes. She walked to a small table, picked up a piece of paper and handed it to him.

"This is how to find the old man named Victor. Be careful. The catacombs are a labyrinth. You can get lost."

He took the paper, looked at it, and stuffed it into his coat. "When I'm done, I will need to stay here a few days," he said.

"No more than a few days," she said. "Now go, you don't have much time, *toropit'sya!*" she said.

"*Ya, soglasen,*" he said, as he walked out.

18

Victor

"Victor! It's Izzy."

Izzy and Will Bergen were back at the immense chamber where they had met Victor before. Izzy knew she had to get more detailed information from Victor. She needed to know if the rumored attack was real or bogus.

"Victor! It's Izzy." There was no answer. "It's Izzy and Will."

The two waited in silence for several minutes. Nothing.

Finally, Izzy and Will turned on their lights and moved carefully into the chamber. It seemed undisturbed. Yet Izzy felt unsettled. This was not like Victor. Something was not right. He'd gone back into hiding. *He's afraid.*

The two moved through the vaulted chamber but found no sign of the old cataphile. After half an hour they turned and left.

19

Jardin Luxembourg

"He didn't show."

Izzy sat across from Jean-François at a round grey-metal garden table. They had agreed to meet at a tree-shaded café at Jardin Luxembourg in the 6th arrondissement. Given the sensitive nature of her brief, she wanted to draw as little attention to herself as possible. It seemed every visit to the Ministry brought curious looks and hushed conversation.

"Will and I called out to him," said Izzy. "He didn't answer. We checked the chamber. There was nothing out of the ordinary."

"Maybe he was somewhere else," said Jean-François.

"Possible, but not likely. Victor was very specific about the day and time."

"Any ideas?" said Jean-François.

"If he was afraid, that might explain the no-show," said Izzy. "We should give it a couple of days before trying again. If he's hiding, he won't be in a hurry to return."

"*Très bien,*" said Jean-François. "But if there is a real threat of a coming attack, we need to find him soon."

"Tell me about it," said Izzy.

Jean-François's cell phone was chirping. He reached into his coat pocket, looked at the name on the screen and hit CALL. He pressed the phone to his ear.

"*Oui?*"

As he listened, his expression darkened.

"*Bon, à bientôt,*" he said. He signed off and placed the phone in his coat pocket. He looked at Izzy.

"That was our forensics people at the *Institut Médico-Légal.* They completed their examination of the woman we pulled from the canal."

Izzy leaned forward in her chair. "Yes?"

"Bad news, and now more questions," he said. "The woman we recovered from the canal is not Galina Federova. The hands of the victim were severed and the face badly disfigured. But after studying some of her distinctive facial features and comparing them against the digital images of Federova when she was with Alders at Châtelet, they have ruled out a match."

"How sure are they?" said Izzy.

"One hundred percent."

Izzy leaned back in her chair. "So, Federova is probably still alive. You're right, Jean-François, more questions. Who was the woman in the canal?"

"No idea yet. With luck she'll be reported missing by a relative or co-worker. We can't release a composite. Whoever murdered her wants us to believe it is the Châtelet woman. We're going to leave it that way for now. They took DNA samples and are trying to come up with a match."

20

Adur

Chen Chi was hunting for Adur. He'd hired Adur to get rid of the Russian, Galina Federova, and deliver her severed hands. But Adur had double-crossed him. *Why?*

He arrived at the building where Adur lived. The courtyard door was open. It was trash day and an elderly woman was straining hard as she rolled a large container out to the street.

As he passed her, she gave him an unwelcome look and uttered a testy *"Bonjour, m'sieur."*

"Bonjour," he replied, choosing not to add the respectful *"madame."* Chen despised old people. In his mind the world would be better off if they were simply cancelled at sixty.

He climbed the stairway to the second floor and knocked on the door of Adur's apartment. There was no reply. He knocked a second time. No one answered.

He descended the stairs and approached the aged woman who was rolling a second trash barrel out to the street with considerable exertion.

"Excusez-moi, madame," he said genially, this time with greater civility. *"S'il vous plaît,* I'm looking for the man who lives in apartment five."

"Why ask me, *monsieur?* This not a hotel."

"I thought you might know where he is," said Chen.

"*Monsieur,* I have enough to do. I do not poke my nose in other people's business."

Chen Chi, of course, knew that every building *concierge* in Paris knew more about the personal lives of the residents than their relatives did. He reached into his pocket and took out a twenty-euro bill.

She saw the money. "Are you a relative?"

"Yes, he's my cousin, and I have an important message for him."

"I did not know Adur had a cousin," she said.

Chen smiled. *Yes, she knows exactly who Adur is.* He pressed the money into her hand and was surprised how quickly it disappeared into her apron.

"He never mentioned a cousin, and you don't look anything like him," she said. "But no matter, I can't be expected to know everything." She leaned against the trash barrel. "He left in a hurry. He couldn't take the two suitcases on his motorcycle, so he left one with me and asked me to send it to him today."

"Did he give you an address?"

The woman looked at him and said nothing.

Chen took out another twenty.

"Wait here," she said, taking the twenty.

She returned with a piece of paper and handed it to Chen.

"Tell him he owes me ten euros for the mess he left in the trash room."

***

A half hour later, Chen was standing in a dank apartment in the 15th arrondissement, looking at a wary Adur.

Chen smiled. It was a friendly, good natured smile.

"Are you taking a trip?" said Chen, pointing to a battered suitcase by the door.

"Only for a day or two," said Adur, clearly nervous.

In a flash Chen produced a Karambit knife and slashed Adur's face. Adur screamed and reeled back, collapsing onto a lumpy sofa, his face bleeding badly.

"You sent me the hands of the wrong woman. Why?"

"I, I made a mistake. Believe me, Chen."

Chen drove the knife into Adur's thigh.

"Aaagh!"

"The truth, I want the truth," said Chen, twisting the knife.

"Aaagh! Aaaagh! I made a mistake, it was a mistake!"

Chen was now on top of Adur, pinning him down against the sofa. He placed the Karambit against Adur's ear and sliced it off.

"Uggh"

"You will tell me," said Chen.

***

In the end, Adur told him that he'd found Galina Federova as she walked down a darkened passageway, and was ready to kill her, and carry out his assignment.

But, as he had soon learned, Federova was not a stellar intelligence agent for nothing. Even with his gun against her temple, she'd persuaded him that there was much more money to be made by working for her associates in Ukraine.

"Why do business with people who don't pay enough and give you no protection," she'd said. "Our organization can use your talents. In two years, you will have more money than you ever dreamed. You will be driving a Mercedes and drinking in the best clubs."

She offered him ten thousand euros as a show of good faith. More would come his way in Kyiv. Adur considered the offer and thought of the paltry nine hundred Chen had paid.

A quick trip to the bank with Federova, a gun in her side, and the ease with which she withdrew the ten thousand from her safe deposit box, convinced him she was for real. He was sick of Chen, sick of Paris, sick of having to hustle for business and dodge authorities.

Federova purchased a blue suit at a clothing store.

"Here, take this. Find another woman. Make sure she's blond. Get rid of her, then leave Paris. By the time they discover the truth, you will be drinking vodka with my friends in Kyiv."

***

Chen Chi closed the door and left. Adur's body, bloody and motionless, was slumped against the side of the sofa. The tightly packed wad of euros he'd found in Adur's suitcase would ease some of the anger.

It was only when he attempted to use them at a three-star restaurant that he learned the euros were counterfeit.

21

Victor

Victor, the cataphile, had failed to show up for their last appointment. Worried, Izzy and Will Bergen entered the catacombs the next day, and made their way to the large chamber. They called out his name, but there was no response. They moved deeper into the darkened chamber, each taking a different section, sweeping their flashlights left and right. Izzy's sense of dread grew with each step.

"Oh Christ!" said Will, from somewhere in the gloom.

Izzy removed the Sig Sauer from her shoulder holster and rushed in his direction. She made out Will. He was standing, frozen in place, his light pointed upward.

There, in a recessed part of the chamber, a figure was suspended from the ceiling. Izzy directed her light up...and gasped.

"Victor! Oh, Jesus, Victor," she said.

Victor was hanging head down from a meat hook, ankles bound, his throat slit. Coagulated blood ringed his serrated neck. A dark stain of dried blood covered the earthen floor.

Will pulled a knife from his boot. Together, they cut the heavy rope and lowered Victor's body to the ground.

22

Père Lachaise

"I want that SOB! I want the butcher who killed Victor," said Izzy.

Her demeanor was agitated as she and Jean-François walked through the quiet cemetery of Père Lachaise in the 20th arrondissement. It was seven A.M. Izzy and Jean-François were still processing the shock of Victor's grisly murder.

"I owe it to Victor," said Izzy.

"As do I," said Jean-François. His voice faltered. "He was like…a father to me."

Jean-François's sudden loss of composure and raw emotion surprised Izzy. For a moment the polished, supremely confident voice had broken. And yet, she was still struggling with Victor's puzzling words in the catacombs when they last spoke.

"Izzy," Victor had said, pulling her aside and away from Will Bergen, "Jean-François is like a son to me, but you must be careful. There is darkness there."

She returned her attention to Jean-François. "You said he was like a father to you?"

"Victor risked his life to save me and my sister, Sara."

"I'm sorry," said Izzy... *Sister, Sara?... What?*

"Even after all these years, I have trouble talking about it. Perhaps one day, I'll tell you more."

Izzy noticed that Jean-François's hands had tightened into a grip. Small beads of perspiration had formed on his forehead.

23

Guilt

Two A.M. Izzy was in bed. Wide awake. She knew that she was slipping into self-recrimination and depression, her mind in turmoil over Victor's gruesome murder.

I screwed up. Now Victor's dead.

Yes, she'd told Victor she was worried about him, could provide security above ground. He'd declined, saying he felt safer in the catacombs. Still, she knew she should have done more. Now Victor was gone and anything more he'd known about the North Korean plot, if there was such a plot, was gone.

How did the killer or killers find him? Were Will and I followed?

Then there was Jean-François's startling revelation that Victor had saved him as a child. It was a remarkable coincidence and explained a lot about Victor's relationship with Jean-François. But left other questions. Jean-François had mentioned a sister named Sara. *But Lisa Palmer from the Embassy told me that Jean-François had no siblings. So who's the sister?*

Jean-François had obviously been deeply affected by Victor's murder. Yet Victor had cautioned her to be careful with Jean-François.

"There is darkness there," he'd said. Those words now made Izzy view Jean-François in a different light. What was Victor trying to say? Was Jean-François a danger to her? To the mission? She would have to be on her guard.

She knew she owed Victor her life. How could she ever repay that debt? There was only one way. Find whoever had killed him and make them pay. She thought back on her visit with him, and what he had wanted her to keep secret.

"Izzy," Victor had said, "the photo in the paper of the man who was killed at Châtelet. I met him."

"What? When! Who was he?"

"His name was Jens Alders."

"How did you meet him?"

"One of his business partners, a man named Babin, from Marseilles, is a cataphile. He'd come and go. Mysterious fellow, very short, eyes like a lemur and thin as a stamp."

"What was Babin's first name?"

"Paul," said Victor. "We talked sometimes, not much. He brought Jens Alders. But I found out that the two were involved in arms trading and other criminal business. I was angry. I told Babin we didn't need French police down our throats."

"What did he say to that?" said Izzy.

"Nothing. He and Jens Alders left."

"Did they ever come back?"

"Only Babin. He had a wild look about him. He was very frightened. Those eyes were darting back and forth, looking like a trapped animal."

"Why?"

"Because Jens Alders was going to expose a plot to launch an attack on France and the U.S. Babin said it would be a gruesome death for the two of them if he did."

"Who was going to launch the attack, Victor?"

"Maybe North Korea, but I'm not sure."

"What kind of attack?"

"Something like a weapon of mass destruction."

"A nuclear weapon?"

"No, there was no mention of a nuclear bomb or a missile. But it was something that would kill millions."

"Victor, think carefully. Try to remember. Did Babin say anything else?"

"He said he thought they were being followed."

"Did he say who was following them?"

"The terrorist, Lalo."

Izzy was silent for a moment. Her mind was racing.

"Victor. Are you sure he said 'Lalo'? It's very important you be sure that he said 'Lalo'."

"Izzy, I know who Lalo is, or at least who he's supposed to be. I've heard enough stories about the attacks he's behind, though I don't believe them all. But, yes, Babin said he believed it was Lalo."

"Where is Babin now?" she said.

"I don't know."

"Why would Jens Alders want to cross the North Koreans? That's a death sentence for sure."

"Hard to say. Babin told me he'd begged Alders not to do it. Humans are strange creatures, Izzy. Jens Alders was a greedy scoundrel. But maybe he didn't want to be involved in an attack that could lead to mass murder."

"Jens Alders was carrying something when he was murdered. Any idea what it might have been?"

"Babin told me Alders had documents containing details of the operation. Alders was trying to arrange a meeting with an important contact. He wanted to pass on the information to people who could help stop the attack."

"Did he say who he was meeting?"

"No."

***

Whoever killed Jens Alders also wanted Victor dead. He knew too much. Find the person who killed Alders and I'll find the person who killed Victor.

***

Izzy took another look at the clock. Four A.M. She wouldn't sleep tonight.

It's seven in the evening in Los Angeles.

She picked up the house phone and placed a call to Santa Monica.

"Hallo?"

Izzy recognized Sylvia's voice. Sylvia, the housekeeper who'd been with the Stone family for thirty years. Izzy's mom rarely answered the phone anymore.

"Sylvia, it's Izzy. Is mom still awake?"

"Isabella! I, I mean *señora! Si, si.* She was hoping you would call. Let me get her."

A moment later. "Izzy? Is that you?"

"Hi, mom."

***

Izzy sighed and put the house phone down. *I should be there. I'm letting everyone down. Shit!*

It had been a long, difficult and worrisome call. Her mom sounded weaker, her conversation unfocused and forgetful. Once again, she'd asked her mom to move to Washington. There was more than enough room in her Georgetown townhouse.

"Sylvia is willing to move to Georgetown, mom. You'd never be alone. I'd be able to see you more."

"Izzy, I can't leave my home. All my memories are here," she'd said.

"But I worry about you."

"I'll be fine," she'd said.

68

***

Her thoughts returned to the metro tunnel. She'd missed an important clue. *But what?* It was now becoming clear that somewhere on the planet deadly plans were unfolding. She would have to broaden her monitoring of unusual events in the U.S. and France that might provide clues to the plot Victor had talked about.

She played and replayed each mental screenshot from that morning looking for a clue.

Could it have been the vagrant, mumbling unintelligibly and carrying the odd-shaped rucksack? Was that a disguise? Or perhaps one of the black-suited young men? The man in baggy pants and sweatshirt? Someone else? Someone who'd escaped her notice? Then there was Galina Federova, the blonde. Was she Jens Alders' protector, his lover, maybe his killer? Where are the documents Alders was carrying?

Her mind in turmoil, Izzy tossed until early dawn's blush teased the window of her bedroom.

24

Jens Alders

"Jens Alders was coming to Paris to meet with someone. Was it you, Jean-François?" said Izzy.

"Why do you ask?" said Jean-François.

"Jean-François," Izzy said again, this time more forcefully, "was Jens Alders coming to see you?"

He said nothing for a moment, then looked at Izzy.

"No, Izzy. I never met Jens Alders. I didn't even know he existed until he was murdered at Châtelet."

25

Dinner

After dispatching Adur, Chen Chi took it upon himself to track down Galina Federova and kill her. Ajax Balaskas and his Russian associates wanted proof she was dead. Ajax had given him an address. There was no time to lose.

He found Federova's apartment in the tough 20th arrondissement, gained entry and gripped his knife. Ajax would get his pair of severed hands and Chen would get his money.

But it was not to be, because Chen had struck too soon. An unfortunate miscalculation. And now, Chen, willing instigator of many a violent encounter, Fourth Dan martial arts expert, fitness junkie and exacting epicure when it came to fine wines, classic cuisine and ripe cheeses in Michelin three-star Paris restaurants, knew he was going to die.

Nor did that fact particularly trouble him. After all, he thought, we all die, sometimes sooner than we'd hoped and sometimes under circumstances we would not have chosen, had we had the chance to choose, of course. One might not warm to the idea of early demise, but that was the simple truth of it.

"Hey, that's life," he'd said, with no small irony, on more than one occasion to his pleading victims.

So, no, it was not the thought of dying that was dancing in Chen's agitated mind, but rather the fine dinner he would now miss. All because of the powerful stranger who'd come out of nowhere without a word of introduction, who hadn't had the decency to at least say to Chen, "My name is such and so and I'm going to kill you," the man who was now slowly tightening the piano wire around Chen's neck while methodically preparing to remove ample parts of Chen's wire-tethered extremities with a saw tooth hunting knife.

Would I have foiled this rude surprise if I'd reached Seventh Dan level?

Chen had to admit that in his haste to take revenge on Adur, and kill Federova himself, he'd forgotten the first rule of murder: plan ahead.

Certainly, he'd be the first to say that if he had it to do over again, he would have surveilled the woman's apartment at a later hour, and for a sufficiently long enough time to assure himself she was alone.

But before that bit of business, he would have taken a fine dinner at one of his favorite restaurants on avenue Matignon or Quai de Conti, or perhaps even chanced dining at one of the city's trendy, new, *everybody'stalkingaboutthenewchef* places in the bohemian 11th arrondissement. After all, he did not consider himself "highbrow" when it came to the neighborhood. He'd been raised in the rough housing projects of the Paris banlieue and prided himself on not being a Paris snob.

Unnngh. Chen tried to ignore the man who had begun to work on him in earnest, and retreated to his martial arts training - focusing his mind completely on the task at hand: dinner.

At the restaurant he would have begun with champagne. This was to be a very special evening. So, a bottle, yes, a full bottle of superb *Champagne Louis*

Roederer, his favorite, would have been in order. On the other hand, he might have sought guidance from the sommelier. *S'il vous plaît*, could the gentleman suggest one or two other premium vintages? Something with richness and a round palate? From a fine *terroir* and correct *élevage?* Something with a memorable fragrance, lively, even impertinent!

Chen reasoned that his familiarity with oenophile patter would communicate the necessary *savoir vivre* to the lofty sommelier. After all, one had to plant the exacting culinary flag at the outset, make it clear that one was no tourist or one-off diner spending above his means never to return.

Aah, yes, now on to the food.

Depending on the chef, there might be an artful *amuse gueule* to tease the palate. If so, he would express measured surprise and delight, perhaps even raise his arms and hands as if to take flight.

Ahh, voilá!

He knew his part in a set piece of theatre for both waiter and guest.

For the *entrée*….*aaahgh!*…*deep breath*….why not begin with a *Soupe d'Artichaut à la Truffe Noire* or a *Pigeon de Racan?* Superb. But it had been some time since he'd had a delicious *Filet de barbue à cru avec caviar et noix.* He could taste it even now. One could not go wrong with any of them. Once the entrée was set before him, he might linger over the first mouthful for a long moment savoring each flavor and accent. A brief half-smile to himself signaling approval would be reassuring to the attentive wait staff.

As to the main dish, the "*plat principal,*" the choice was ever conflicted and sublime. The *Homard Bleu Roti* in its shell was exceptional, no doubt, but then again there was the *Noix de Coquilles Saint-Jacques* with ambrosial white truffle sauce *or, or, or,* even an unassuming *Pâtes aux Lardons* pasta dish! The pasta would have been a humble, even inspired choice! - once again demonstrating the confi….*aaahgaah!*….*focus! focus!*...and sophistication of the guest.

The wine? A bottle of dry *Domaine Ramonet Montrachet Grand Cru* from Burgundy would have paired nicely with any of the dishes. Afterwards there would be a refreshing salad of baby greens, followed by a fragrant assortment of ripe cheeses – and freshly baked bread, of course.

Notwithstanding the exquisite meal consumed thus far, he would not yet have been satiated. Chen knew why. It was because the premier chefs of Paris religiously observed the cardinal rule of high cuisine: *less is more!* One should shower the diner with delectable creations aesthetically presented - but leave them wanting. They understood that however splendid the dish, if the portion was too ample the diner might flag. But give the diner less, and the dish became a dish to die for. Ironic, Chen thought, under the circumstances.

To complete the fine meal a dessert, perhaps a *milles…. …unngh!!…milles….aaaahg!...feuilles* or *chariot de glaces.*

And, *bien sûr*, an espresso.

A cognac to finish? Maybe not, as there would still be work to do. Then the check, *l'addition.* Chen was not in the habit of leaving tips. It was bad form since the tip was always included in the bill and correct French diners considered tipping a *bêtise.* Yet, he was feeling expansive and might have whispered to the waiter, "*Another thirty euros to l'addition, s'il vous plaît, monsieur.*" Generous, but not *déclassé.* After all, manners were important, the glue of any civilized society. Thus fortified and in good spirits, he would have returned to his task and lain in wait until the early morning hours, giving him the convenient element of surprise. Alas, he had not, and now it was too…. aaaggh, 天啊!

As the wire tightened and the knife neared the end of its work, Chen Chi, caught between excruciating pain and delirium, had some vague awareness of having answered questions from the man, but could not remember what they were. So he tried with little success to console himself with the advice of those much wiser than he, that after all, no one's perfect, and from time to time mistakes will be made.

So, there it was. *Tant pis!*

26

Jean-François

Jean-François was standing in front of the large bathroom mirror of his designer-curated three-bedroom, two-hundred square meter eighteenth-century rue de Varenne apartment in the exclusive 7th arrondissement of Paris. By Parisian standards it was a large luxurious flat to be greatly envied. Situated only one block from the Hôtel Matignon, official residence of the Prime Minister of France, its location made it all the more prestigious.

Even well-paid Paris professionals could rarely afford a flat of more than sixty square meters in the high-end seventh. Paris real estate, after all, was among the most expensive in the world. Fortunately for Jean-François, he was wealthy, thanks to his adoptive parents, the Count and Countess Stewart de Valmont.

But it was three in the morning, and Jean-François was not thinking about how lucky he was to be living in such elegance and privilege. No, he was trying to decide whether he should use the Sig Sauer hanging loosely from his trembling left hand. It was a recurring, destructive impulse that would slip away for months then erupt with volcanic fury, dark, terrifying. They came without warning, hellish demons and images leaping from their subconscious crypts to torment him.

All his life he'd attempted to bury them. But they were stronger and would not be contained.

His mind reeled; his sanity teetered. He was back on that icy mountain, the terrifying rumble and roar of millions of tons of malevolent snow hurtling towards them, drowning out all thought, all human sound, all hope. The sudden look of horror on the faces of his mother and father just before they disappeared forever.

And after, from the ensuing graveyard silence of the mountain, the weak cries from others he knew he could not save. Except for Sara, only eight years old. He tried to reason with himself. *I was ten and terrified. Sara was badly injured. How much more could I have done? If I had tried to bring them with us........*

But reason was no match for the demons, and in his mind and heart he knew it never would be.

Jean-François took one last look in the mirror. The Sig Sauer dangling from his hand, he slowly turned and half-walked, half-staggered to the bedroom, picked up his cell with a twitching right hand and hit speed dial.

"Jean-François?" A woman said.

"Sara."

It was all he needed to say.

"I'm coming," she said. "Please, for God's sake, Jean-François, please wait! Please!"

27

Miracle!

Izzy was scrolling through a slew of messages that had accumulated over the last few hours. It was a struggle to keep up with the constant pinging of new arrivals, some urgent, some a damnable nuisance. *Scroll, delete, scroll, delete, scroll, read first two lines, delete, scroll, save, scroll, read.* Thirty messages down she saw one from Lisa Palmer at the American Embassy in Paris.

Hi, Izzy, FYI, news story. Bit old, but thought you might find it interesting.

A *URL* was attached. Izzy clicked. It took her to a newspaper story dated February 2, 1998. The banner headline read:

MIRACLE IN THE ALPS!

TWO CHILDREN FOUND ALIVE AFTER ALL HOPE LOST

Izzy speed-read the story. A massive Alpine avalanche had killed four families during a skiing trip. After days of frantic searching, rescue teams had found no trace of the victims and the search was reluctantly ended. A national day of mourning was declared.

Seven days after the deadly slide, a skier named Victor LePrince spotted a dark shape descending from high up the snowy mountain. A reporter interviewed him about that day.

At first, I thought it was maybe a wolf, you know? But what would a wolf be doing that high up the mountain? Then I used my glasses and saw it was a man. Impossible! Crazy! The snow was very unstable. No good mountaineer would be so reckless as that. There had already been several terrible slides. I could see he was pulling something. But then he fell and didn't move. I was afraid, of course, but even so, I went. When I got there I could not believe my eyes. It was a child, a boy, half frozen, half dead. He was pulling a sled with pieces of tenting. I pulled back the tenting and Seigneur! It was a little girl. She was barely breathing, but she was alive. Can you believe it! They were both alive! I swear I don't know how I did it, but I carried them the rest of the way down that devil mountain, the girl under one arm, the boy strapped to my back. It was a miracle, I tell you. I have never seen anything like it. God must have been with them, with the three of us.

The ten-year-old boy, named Jean-François, and a girl of eight named Sara, had been flown to a Paris hospital to treat their injuries.

Izzy closed the article and put the cell down. She realized she'd been holding her breath, and her free hand was wrapped into a tight fist. She exhaled, took a long, deep breath and slowly released it through her lips.

28

Yuri

Yuri *aka* "Eduardo del Valle" was sitting in the dark corner of an aging tabac in the 13th arrondissement, a half-empty espresso cradled in his right hand, his left tapping the table with an index finger.

He'd killed an intruder named Chen Chi in Galina Federova's apartment. Chen had managed to open Federova's door and rush in, a large knife in his hand. By the time Chen realized Federova was not alone, it was too late. Yuri had delivered two savage karate blows to Chen's jugular with lightning speed. When Chen revived, he found himself bound hand and foot, Yuri preparing to sculpt his body with a serrated carving knife.

"Who sent you?" Yuri asked again and again, as he sculpted, but Chen had been a reluctant witness whose screams and incoherent babbling about fine wines and foods with very long names left Yuri wondering if Chen was crazy. Not until the end did Chen mumble through bloody lips, something about a man named Ajax and people in Russia wanting Federova's severed hands. Then Chen was gone, his body lifeless, a puzzling, wistful expression on his face.

Yuri went through Chen's pockets and found an ID with an address in the 13th arrondissement. It was a small rug shop, no more than a hole in the wall, gloomy with a single dismal overhead light. He tossed the place and rifled through a large number of brightly embossed restaurant menus with strange sounding dishes and astronomical prices. There was nothing that could tell him exactly who'd sent Chen to kill Federova.

Yuri lifted the espresso and took a sip. *Cold.* He put it down. The small porcelain cup was dwarfed by his long hands. Out of proportion to his short stature, they looked like they had been genetically designed for brutal work. His low-built body radiated violence in a way that he realized made people nervously cross to the other side of the street when he approached from behind. He was no believer in the spirit, yet he himself sensed that there was a malevolent aura about him that others recognized and fled.

It hadn't always been so. In the beginning there had been trusting innocence. The trust that only a child can have even in the presence of evil. But that was long ago, before the regular beatings by his uncle, before the brutal gang murder of his teenage sweetheart, and before a Catholic priest had stepped forward to mentor him, teach him the catechism, take him to baseball games at Dodger Stadium, and one afternoon brutally rape him in the sacristy. Each experience had been another death for a boy who'd been abandoned by his parents, thrown to the wolves, discarded like a piece of trash.

He murdered the priest one night after drugging him. Police found the prelate in a confessional booth, his throat stuffed with communion wafers. Detectives had questioned the distraught boy, but had not grasped that the youngster inconsolably weeping in front of them had become a consummate liar and dissembler. The murder was never solved.

29

Wong Bai

Paris

Wong Bai in worn remaindered sneakers, shopworn shirt and pants, had been to Chen's hole-in-the-wall rug shop three times. The shop was dark each time and no one had answered his knock. This would be his last attempt to find Chen Chi. Wong certainly had no burning desire to see Chen. The man was prone to violence and had been in a constant rage over Wong's delivery of the wrong pair of severed hands. It was, thought Wong, juvenile behavior over a simple delivery mistake.

But Chen owed him money for services rendered and had refused to pay the forty-five euros he'd promised for the errand. A monumental loss Wong could never forgive. *So little respect for one's elders!*

The much-anticipated sum would have gone to his savings account at the Paris branch of a Hong Kong bank. When asked by snooping relatives, Wong Bai routinely poor-mouthed the account. "Why do you shame an old man! There's barely enough for a sack of moldy rice."

In fact, the account currently showed a tidy balance of five million seven hundred thousand *renminbi*, the result of a lifetime of self-denial, and shrewd investments in Parisian Chinese food *traiteurs*. It was now enough for a comfortable retirement. Still, the loss of the forty-five euros would be deeply felt.

It was odd and troubling that Chen Chi had not returned, if only to fume and harangue. Before his disappearance, he had talked obsessively about delivering bloody vengeance to those who'd sent him the wrong hands. Chen Chi was terrified of the bone-rattling Ajax and needed to make things right with the brute.

As Wong Bai stood at the door considering his next step, giant Ajax appeared. He did not look happy.

"Where's that son of a dog!" Ajax said. Wong looked at Ajax's darkening scowl and clenched fists that looked all the world like large, gnarled tubers, and attempted to shrink himself to a sad lump on the ground. To his dismay, he found he could not. In consequence, he pled ignorance and commiserated with Ajax, assuming this to be a good stratagem. He reasoned that the actual sum of forty-five euros would not be up to the standards of a serious thug like Ajax.

"I know how you feel," Wong said, his voice breaking. "Chen owes me two hundred euros and won't pay! He's a liar, a cheat and disrespectful."

Best to have him think we've both been victims of a major swindle.

"Quiet, old man," Ajax said, as he delivered a mighty kick to the door of the shop, knocking it off its hinges. Ajax entered the darkened shop. It had been vandalized. Furniture, what there was of it, was strewn across the floor. Rugs had been torn from their hangers. Restaurant menus and paper from a ledger lay scattered. Ajax gave Wong, visibly shaken by the shambles, a menacing look.

"Do you know where he is?"

"N'n'no," said Wong. "If I did, I would not be here."

"Find him and call me at this number, or I will come looking for you."

He gave Wong a card with a phone number. Ajax kicked the few pieces of furniture in the shop for good measure, grabbed one of the nicer rugs, threw it over his shoulder and stormed out.

The elderly man realized he was quaking. He had no desire to hunt down someone as violent as Chen. On the other hand, Ajax was even more terrifying.

There was no time for delay. Wong would abandon his dingy, nine-square meter seventh-floor walk-up with its shared leaking loo in the 20th arrondissement, and stay with his ill-humored nephew in Bondy, northwest of Paris, until he could arrange a one-way flight to Hong Kong. It was time to leave France.

He returned to his room, removed a wall panel behind his Murphy bed, and withdrew several large bundles of euros, and assorted pieces of gold jewelry. He stuffed them into a rucksack, went to the door, took one long wistful look at the hovel, and walked out forever.

30

Paul Babin

Lemur-faced, pencil-thin Paul Babin, whose wide-eyed expression conveyed a constant state of alarm, had not slept in days. The brazen murder of his associate, Jens Alders, in the Châtelet metro had made Babin a marked man. He'd tried to reason with Alders, telling him that crossing Pyongyang would be a death sentence for both of them. A threatening message had arrived in his mailbox. The name at the end made Babin's blood run cold: *Lalo*. Lalo, the terrorist!

He begged Alders not to do anything. But Alders, clearly a man with a death wish, brushed off the threat and said he was going to Paris to meet with a journalist. He'd be accompanied by a stunning woman he'd met at an international cyber conference two years earlier. They worked together on sensitive projects. He said her name was Galina Federova.

Now he, Paul Babin, was being followed. He changed his address, but correctly guessed it would not help any more than screaming at the rain would make it stop. His pursuers had connections, people who knew how to find those who did not want to be found. Babin was now an endangered species. He accepted that sooner or later Lalo, or someone else, would hunt him down and kill him.

That insight had been prescient because Babin was now sitting on his creaky bed in a shabby, sixth floor apartment *sans ascenseur*, looking at the business end of a revolver with a silencer. It was resting in the hands of a stranger with eyes more dead than Tutankhamun.

Babin, however, was not one to just let bullies or killers wipe him off the face of the earth without paying a disposal fee. He knew he was not big enough or strong enough to overpower the stranger. It was the abidingly pathetic story of his life. He'd always been the physical weakling, the runt of the group, scurrying head down to the nearest exit whenever a hungry predator approached. He'd compensated for his impotence by becoming an avid note keeper, a meek Dickensian scribe, who'd chronicled the ugly secrets he'd overheard in the years he'd worked with Jens Alders. Secrets whose disclosure would drive North Korea's leader into another bloody purge.

Those notes were now sitting in a locker at Gare du Nord. Access to the locker was linked to an email containing information about its location and the four digit code needed to open it. The email was programmed to go to a specific investigative reporter with a major Paris newspaper unless the email was delayed by Babin himself. He'd delayed the email several times.

That would not happen today - not with a revolver pointed at him that would soon have one less bullet.

But if his executioner expected him to fall to his knees and beg for mercy, he would be sorely disappointed. There would be no groveling. *No, not today. Not this time! Never again. I am Paul Babin! Sensitive. Unafraid! Fierce!*

He took a deep breath, conjured a feral stare, then in his first - and last, act of prideful defiance, reared himself in all his lemur glory and bellowed, *"Connard!"* as

Tutankhamun placed the silencer to his temple and pulled the trigger.

***

A few days later, Paul Babin's email inbox got an auto-reply. It was from the newspaper where the journalist worked.

This is a system-generated message to inform you that your email could not be delivered to one or more recipients. Details of the email and the error are as follows: The email account does not exist.

Paul Babin could not know that, of course, because his naked body was now lying, cold, unclaimed and unmourned in an odorous morgue of a Paris suburb. The journalist he'd emailed had resigned a month earlier for a more lucrative position in Marseilles. The Paris newspaper that employed him had deleted his email address.

Two months later, the rent on the small locker at Gare du Nord having expired, an ill-humored, late-night cleaning crew opened the locker, found it full of papers, shrugged and unceremoniously threw them into a trash barrel.

31

Place des Vosges

It was mid-afternoon and Izzy was sitting at a small outdoor café at Place des Vosges in the historic Marais district of Paris. A half-empty glass of chilled Sancerre rested on her table.

Place des Vosges' four elegant vaulted arcades and sturdy stone pillars enclosed a large grass-covered square set off by four elegant fountains, expansive leafy trees, and an imposing equestrian marble statue of Louis XIII.

Built as a royal palace by Henry IV in the seventeenth century, the Place still retained the stately magnificence of its earlier days of nobility, court music, and earnest - sometimes fatal - jousting.

Even now it was not uncommon to encounter a small chamber group playing Mozart in one of the arcades, or to hear the solo voice of an accomplished soprano or tenor filling the square with a Puccini aria or a lied by Schubert.

But today, Izzy was not there for the view or the music. She was waiting for the broad-shouldered man with a heavy step making his way across the square towards her. He was wearing laced hiking shoes, denim jeans, a dark brown corduroy shirt and an open windbreaker. He had an Irishman's face, round and prominent with a straight jaw line, thin nose, thick eyebrows and a seeming weariness - perhaps cultivated for effect - that would have been well-suited to a hard life at sea, or decades of tilling unforgiving, stony Irish soil with little to show for it.

It was Bill Powers, the CIA man who'd been at the earlier session at the DGSI headquarters. He'd sent Izzy a message asking for a meet. She suggested Place des Vosges. She arrived early and selected a table *en terrasse* that provided a good view of the stone arcades, the apartments above, and the square. But first, she had asked Will Bergen, now back in D.C., to make inquiries about Powers. Predictably, Langley had been opaque. But Bergen had his own sources and got back to her.

"He's a bulldog and one of the agency's best station chiefs," Will said. "Last posted to Pakistan, then back to Langley for a few months. Was in Islamabad when the U.S. missile strike went bad and killed those French kids last year. Powers took it pretty hard. Blamed himself. Almost cracked up, according to some."

"I remember," said Izzy. "The missile was supposed to take out the terrorist Omar Mohammed, but somebody went rogue with the targeting and the result was a bloody mess."

"Yup, pretty awful. Shocked and horrified all of France," said Will. "Not surprised people rioted and burned down our embassy there."

"The target screw-up wasn't Powers' fault," said Izzy.

"Yeah, I know. But he blamed himself all the same."

"What's his brief here?" Izzy said.

"He may be banged up, but he's one of their best. They want him to keep an eye on our French friends, report back on them...and you."

"Right. Thanks, Will."

Izzy looked out to the square. Powers was almost to her.

32

Bill Powers

"Ah, the American Joan of Arc!" Powers said theatrically, and with more than a little sarcasm, as he approached Izzy. He grabbed an empty wicker chair, dragged it across the stone pavement with a scraping noise, and sat down without so much as a "May I?"

Izzy was unfazed. She summoned a delphic smile and imagined an imminent squall. Powers was large, and radiated a crusty impatience. His body language was agitated, territorial. He took in his surroundings as if inviting those around him to fisticuffs.

Will was right, he's a bulldog.

"Having white," Izzy said. "Care for a glass?"

"Bit French for me," Powers said. "Jack Daniels will do. A double, thanks."

Izzy hailed the waiter and ordered. She turned to Powers.

"What's on your mind?" Izzy said.

"What's in your brief?" Powers ignored her question.

"Well, whatever's in it," Izzy said breezily. "You asked for a meet. I'm here."

The waiter returned with the Jack Daniels in a crystal tumbler, a small metal bucket with ice cubes, tongs, and a carafe of water. Powers ignored the ice and water and wrapped his hand around the tumbler.

"Looking for more information. Your French pals aren't big on sharing," said Powers.

"Actually, they are - with their American *pals.*"

Powers looked at Izzy and took a hefty tug of the Jack Daniels. He was quiet for a moment. He put the tumbler down.

"Ok," he said, swiveling his bearish frame towards her, his ample arms now resting on the small table. He jutted his formidable jaw in her direction. "Now that the introductions are over, let's cut the bullshit. You're off your beat here. The ogres at Langley want to know why."

"What, no lions, tigers and bears?"

"No lions, no tigers, no bears. Just ogres. The kind that eat people alive."

"Chew'n my nails," she said dryly. She picked up her wine glass, took a slow sip of the Sancerre, savored it for a long moment, let her gaze do a slow turn of the square, then put the glass down and leaned in.

"Look, Powers, I'll tell you and your ogres as much as my brief allows. No more, no less."

"Go," said Powers.

"The Élysée asked the White House to make me available for a matter of national security. You were at the DGSI meeting so you know it concerns a possible mass attack."

"Why you? It's our sandbox you're playing in."

"Because the source of the information on the threat is Victor, the one we discussed at the meeting you attended. I worked with Victor last year. He trusted me and I trusted him."

"Let's fast-forward, shall we?" said Powers.

"Fine," said Izzy. "Victor wanted to share what he knew about the planned attack, but would only do it directly with me."

"What's your assessment of the source and the threat?" he said.

"Well, to begin with, Victor's dead, you already know that. Someone didn't want him around."

"And you figure there's a connection between his murder and the information he passed on," said Powers.

"Well," she said, "if there's no connection, then it's one ginormous coincidence. Second, Victor would not have gone through the trouble of asking me to come here on a whim or mere gossip. Not who he was. Third, his letter made it clear he was afraid for his life because of what he knew. He was right about that. Bottom line, I believe the threat is real." She paused. "There's more, but that's all you get."

Powers said nothing. He just skewed his large head to the side and rested a ruddy cheek on folded meaty fists, elbows planted on the small table, the weight of his arms threatening to capsize it. He looked out to the square, pensive, as if weighing his next words, perhaps making a decision. He returned his gaze to Izzy. His eyes, emerald green, had softened in aspect. A conspiratorial smile was forming on one corner of his full Irish mouth, a hulk of a man enjoying a bit of mischief. He leaned in closer to Izzy, his massive head only inches away and looked directly into her eyes. The acid voice assumed a disarming tone, the edginess now gone.

"Stone," he said, in a slow, gravel whisper, a mate about to impart a confidence to a pal in a pub, "that was one hell of a magic trick you pulled off in Paris with the prez last year. Odds were you'd both be coming home in a box. But Jesus, Mary and Joseph, somehow you pulled the proverbial rabbit out of a hat. A genuine show-stopper. Command performance. Damn near walked on water. Brought our president safely home to the red, white and blue. Had a lot of us wondering how in merciful heaven you did it."

He leaned back, picked up the tumbler, held it mid-air for a moment then tilted it in salute. The full Irishman's smile, teeth and all, had arrived.

Izzy picked up her wine glass and saluted back.

"Thanks," she said.

I can work with this man.

33

Little River

Little River Nuclear Plant - Georgia

"Holy crap!"

Brad Hollister, the Control Room Reactor Operator was sitting at the control deck of the Little River Nuclear Plant only thirty miles from Atlanta, Georgia. He was aghast. He was not alone. The rest of the staff on the control deck were seeing what he was seeing. *Impossible!*

"Brad, we're having an alarm avalanche! What the hell's happening?" said one, his voice filled with dread.

Hollister had no damn idea. Safety Instrumented Systems should have kicked in. Yet they hadn't. As a result he was looking at a blood-chilling control board filled with warning alarms. He checked the readings on the large overhead plasma displays. Temperatures in the reactor were climbing to dangerous levels. *Why aren't Safety Instrumented Systems kicking in?*

A digital message on the main panel suddenly popped up: ***Cooling System Failure. Excessive Power Surge….***

Brad quickly switched to the hot standby backup computer and ran a second check of the cooling system. A moment later the screen illuminated:

Cooling System Failure. Excessive Power Surge…Critical…Critical…Critical…

Now the Control Room was filled with loud klaxons and the agitated voices of other technicians as they struggled with controls that were not responding.

Hollister was barely holding off complete panic. *It's not possible! What in damnation is going on?*

He went back to his primary computer.

Again!

Cooling System Failure... Excessive Power Surge... ...Critical...Critical...Critical...

Lord protect us. It's happening too fast. If we don't stop this now we're headed for reactor supercriticality and disaster. No time to lose!

He stood and shouted as he'd never shouted before.

"Activating SCRAM! Repeat, I'm activating SCRAM. Now!"

He sat down, said a quick prayer and entered a password to enable the large SCRAM button on his console. After a moment that seemed like an eternity, the button illuminated blood-red. *Thank God.* Hollister pressed the button hard.

A message immediately appeared on his console: *Safety Control Rods Activation Mechanism Initiated.* Within seconds, neutron absorbing control rods would push into the reactor core, terminate further fission, and power down the reactor.

Or would they? Display panels were still hot, hot with readings that were off the charts.

Hollister looked at the control panel with an intensity and almighty terror he'd never expected to experience. He could no longer hear the chaos and cacophony around him, nor was he aware that he was drenched in sweat, had ripped several buttons off his shirt, and that his heart was pounding like it wanted out. He held his breath.

Images of Chernobyl, the nuclear plant in Ukraine that exploded in 1986, flashed through his mind. Workers with horrific radiation burns and painful deaths, towns forever uninhabitable, countless thousands radiated, damage in the billions, criminal prosecution of surviving plant staff.

The only thing that matters now is these damned gauges. Lord, please bring these numbers down.

34

IAEA Vienna

Vienna

The staff member at the International Atomic Energy Agency, IAEA, in Vienna, Austria, was tapping the top of his dark oak desk. He was mulling an unusual report that had arrived that morning at his office in the Department of Nuclear Safety and Security. It concerned a puzzling "incident," if one could call it that, at the Little River nuclear generating plant in the U.S.

How to classify? On the one hand, Control Room alarms had alerted to imminent supercriticality in the reactor, an existential threat. On the other hand, there was zero evidence that anything remotely approaching supercriticality had ever occurred. Nor had there been the slightest damage to reactor, plant, systems, or people. After understandable panic, the Control Room Reactor Operator successfully SCRAMMED the reactor and the computers correctly reset themselves.

A nuclear Incident Level One Event required overexposure of a member of the public, or minor problems with safety components. But there had been no exposure to anyone. On the other hand, the total computer failure had been anything but minor. The mishap was neither fish nor fowl.

Level Two was more serious. It required more than normal exposure of a worker, or member of the public, and/or elevated radiation levels, and significant contamination within the facility. There had been none. Not even one errant REM!

Yes, it was true that a Level Two Event could include a significant safety failure where there had been no *actual* consequences. That might apply, he supposed.

The incident was striking in that it had resulted from an as yet unexplained failure of both computer systems. The defense-in-depth Safety Instrumented Systems protocols that nuclear power plants around the world observed were designed to avoid the failure of not only the main Control Room computers, but their hot standby systems as well. Yet failure of both was exactly what had happened. Troubling.

Okay, of course, a Level 1 or Level 2 Event was no laughing matter, but fortunately it was relatively benign when measured against higher level Events. That was some comfort.

Since 1957 only Three Mile Island in the U.S., Windscale in the U.K., and Kyshtym in Russia had risen to Level 5 or 6. And only Chernobyl in the Ukraine in 1986 and Fukushima Daiichi in Japan in 2011 had reached Level Seven, the highest level on the scale.

Both those Level 7's had been catastrophic, leaving many dead, and countless thousands grievously radiated by the alpha, beta and gamma radionuclides.

Was the incident at Little River the result of some human error? Technical failure? Protocol errors? Something else? He did not like the uncertainty. Nor was he impressed by the explanation provided by EGI, the giant energy company that owned the facility. Just a "minor technical hiccup," they'd said.

This report was an entirely new creature and it was concerning. He picked up the landline and called the Director of Nuclear Safety and Security.

"Director? Something I think you should see."

35

Lapin Rouge

Bzztmm…Bzztmm…

It was eight in the evening and Izzy's phone was vibrating. She took it from her purse, looked at the screen and pressed CALL.

"Jean-François, *bonsoir*," she said.

"*Bonsoir*, Izzy. Apologies for interrupting your evening."

"What's up?" said Izzy.

"Nothing from the office, I'm glad to say. I'm at the Lapin Rouge in the 6th arrondissement having a cocktail with my sister, Sara. She's heard so much about you. Are you free to join us for a drink?"

"At this point a cocktail is just what I need," said Izzy. "I'd like to meet Sara. Shall we say about thirty, forty minutes?"

"*Très bien*, we'll keep an eye out for you."

Izzy had heard of Le Lapin Rouge, the Red Rabbit, a small fabled club in a narrow passage off of rue de Fleurus just west of the splendid Jardin du Luxembourg. The Lapin Rouge's origins dated to an eighteenth century tavern. Over the centuries it had survived the execution of Louis the Sixteenth and Marie Antoinette, the rise and fall of Napoleon, the First World War, the German occupation, the rise of terrorism and everything in between. Like so much of Paris, it was a living archive of remarkable stories upon stories.

She slipped into a pair of dark jeans, black leather ankle boots, peach colored silk blouse, scarf and black blazer, and grabbed an evening clutch purse. A small derringer was concealed just above her right ankle. She ordered a cab.

36

Sara

At 8:45 Izzy stepped out of the cab and walked into the Lapin Rouge. The place was animated, with young attractive women and men dressed in stylish jeans, sweaters, and casual designer shoes. Time, fortune and misfortune had infused the place with an air of mystique and privilege. The main room was bathed in soft lavender lighting reflecting off rough-hewn stone walls and the deep patina of timbered, centuries-old ceilings. American classic rock music, signature of Parisian hipness, thrummed to the deep rhythm of a kick drum. A turn-of-the-century curved zinc bar illuminated a kaleidoscope of colored bottles and decanters. High leather stools at the bar were all occupied.

However humble its origins, the Lapin Rouge was now a preserve of the daughters and sons of the entitled elite of Paris. They were graduates of the Lycée Henri IV, the Lycée Louis le Grand and other exclusive prep schools that were indispensable stepping stones to the *"Grandes Écoles"* of France where the future's most influential and prestigious officials of government and industry were shaped. Well-traveled, supremely educated, impressively fluent in English and other languages, they enjoyed the bottomless benefits French society had always reserved for its anointed.

Gleaming silver and crystal glassware adorned tables of thick, rough-hewn lumber, dressed in immaculate starched white tablecloths. Wait staff in dark suspender pants, white shirts and white aprons moved, swift and attentive, from table to table, to the guests enjoying tapas, drinks and lively conversation.

"Izzy!" Jean-François called out, as he waved from a table set back in a corner of the club.

Izzy raised a hand in acknowledgement and threaded her way through the crowd to the table. As she approached, Jean-François and the woman she guessed was Sara, smiled buoyantly at her. In the suffused light of the club, Jean-François, no longer in a business suit, looked relaxed and happy. He was wearing dark jeans, a blue velvet blazer and white linen shirt. A long wispy grey scarf rakishly wrapped around his neck conveyed a charming insouciance.

In D.C. he'd be every woman's idea of the perfect French lover.

But it was Sara, the woman Jean-François affectionately referred to as his sister, who was most striking. Tall, slender with tumbling chestnut hair, small waist and full breasts pressed against an emerald silk blouse, Sara radiated uncommon beauty. Her cheekbones, high and pronounced, complimented full lips and a delicate sculpted nose that telegraphed strength and breeding. She was stunning.

"Izzy, hi, *bonsoir!*" said Jean-François, as she approached.

"*Bonsoir,*" she said smiling.

He placed a gentle hand on her right shoulder, gave her a fleeting brush on each cheek, then gestured towards Sara with evident pride. "Izzy, this is my dear sister and best friend, Sara."

"*Bonsoir,* Sara," said Izzy. "Thank you for inviting me."

"Izzy! It's wonderful to meet you," said Sara. She embraced Izzy and planted a kiss on each cheek.

Face to face, Sara was even more dazzling. Her large brown eyes were intelligent and inquiring, and enveloped Izzy in a way that left her momentarily taken aback.

They sat down and quickly agreed it would most certainly be a martini evening!

A waiter appeared.

Jean-François ordered a round of martinis made with Few American Gin, easy on the vermouth, shaken hard, three large olives in each. The drinks soon arrived in chilled drawn-stem crystal glasses. They raised drinks, tipped glasses and took a sip.

"Perfect," said Izzy. "Haven't had a martini this good in a long time."

Soon it was time for a second round.

"My turn," said Sara. She smiled at Izzy and said, "I'm ordering us one of Hemingway's favorite martinis!"

"You mean the Mojito?" said Izzy.

"The 'Montgomery!'" said Sara, triumphantly. "They say Hemingway was at Harry's Bar in Venice. He joked to his friends that Field Marshal Montgomery preferred an advantage of fifteen to one against the enemy. Hemingway liked the idea of fifteen to one, and asked the bartender to make him a martini fifteen parts gin to one of vermouth. He called it the Montgomery."

The martinis arrived.

"Then I say we drink to the Montgomery," said Izzy, as she raised her glass.

"To the Montgomery!" said Jean-François and Sara, both now in high spirits and laughing.

Izzy was feeling camaraderie and elation as the martinis took hold. She smiled grandly and raised her glass again.

"To France, to *l'audace!*" she said, invoking the famous words of *audacity* and *daring,* attributed to the beloved French revolutionary, Georges Danton.

"*Encore, de l'audace!*" joined in Sara and Jean-François.

"*Toujours de l'audace!*" the three finished in unison, a wave of exuberance washing over them.

The evening continued and eventually, the three found themselves sharing certain secrets. Izzy opened up about the death of her dad, murdered in a street robbery in Santa Monica when she was eight. She was with him that day and saw him succumb. He was taking her to buy her first bike. Traumatized by his murder, she was unable to speak for a month. Her mother was inconsolable and did not step outside their Santa Monica home for months.

Sara recounted what she remembered of the long harrowing journey she and Jean-François had made down the icy mountain after the avalanche. Tears fell as she spoke of her family and others who'd died instantly, as well as the mortally injured who'd been left behind. Jean-François fell silent, holding Sara's hand until she regained her composure.

Izzy was surprised at how willing she was to share the personal details of her life with Sara and Jean-François, two people she did not know well, as it ran counter to her natural instinct for vigilance and privacy. She knew she was breaking out of her comfort zone. Yet somehow it felt right.

The conversation returned to happier subjects. When Izzy mentioned her fondness for riding, Sara interjected.

"Izzy, let's go riding, the three of us! Jean-François and I grew up with horses. We love to ride." Sara chuckled. "Of course, we terrified our parents with our demented gallops. But seriously, please come, stay overnight. Our parents' home is only two hours by *TGV* from Gare Montparnasse."

"I'll admit it sounds wonderful," said Izzy, "but as Jean-François knows, things are pretty intense right now."

"Izzy's right," said Jean-François. "Neither of us can get into the details, Sara, but we're dealing with a volatile situation at the moment."

"I understand," said Sara. "But the first chance you get, let's do it."

"You're on," said Izzy.

37

Hôtel de Seine

It was almost two A.M. when Izzy returned to her hotel. It had been a memorable evening. Jean-François had been funny, charming and self-deprecating.

Sara was unusual. Her intelligence and beauty were undeniable. Absent were traits of pretense, calculation or prejudgment. Izzy could not recall encountering a person, still relatively young, so wise, seemingly possessing the aspect of an old soul; reassuring, affectionate, as if to say, *We've met before and we will be such good friends once again.*

38

Brad Hollister

Little River Nuclear Plant - Georgia

"You're saying it was just a one-off computer malfunction. It's not as simple as you make it sound."

It had only been a few days since the SCRAM emergency shutdown. Fortunately, within a few heart-stopping minutes, the SCRAM had been successfully executed and in the following days, the reactor was restarted with no apparent damage to people or equipment.

Brad Hollister, Control Room Reactor Operator at the Little River Nuclear Plant, was ticked. He was sitting across the table from Jay Powell, vice president of Energy Global operations, and a small group of blue-suited executives from Energy Global, Inc., owner of Little River. EGI was a multi-billion-dollar energy conglomerate listed on the NYSE.

"Both systems crashed at the same time," Brad said. "That's not supposed to happen. Way not. Something went seriously wrong. The public should have been alerted."

"Alert the public? And then what?" said Powell. "We would have had complete panic in the city."

"But what if there had been a release?" said Brad. "All those folks would have been in danger, including my wife and my kids!"

"Yes, but there wasn't any release, was there?" said Powell.

"Fine, fine, I get it," said Brad, "but don't you think we should at least share that? We need transparency here."

"No, Brad," said Powell. "We're not going to go crying wolf all across Georgia. It's bad enough we had to hustle to keep local and state authorities from going public. Look at it from their position. Nothing bad happened. They don't want panic, they don't want bad press, they don't want a scandal, and they sure as hell don't want to be on the bad side of Energy Global."

"What if it was an inside job? One of the techs?" said Brad.

"Inside job? You're really getting loopy. All tech staff, including you, were recently vetted. Nothing. Nada."

"Okay, okay, but what if we were hacked? Some of the management personnel are pretty sloppy about security."

"Hacked? Get real," said Powell. "Even if some kook was able to hack the administrative side of the plant, it wouldn't get him in. There's no link between management side and the power plant, they're free-standing, independent platforms. Just doesn't happen. Can't happen. You know that. Besides, the plant's SIS, Safety Instrumented Systems, would immediately take action to keep the plant in a safe mode or SCRAM it if there was an intrusion attempt."

"But…"

"Look, Brad," said Powell, "I have family in Atlanta, parents, relatives. Shit, I grew up there. You think if there was any real danger that I would just ignore it? I'm not that big of an asshole, not when it comes to my own blood."

"But…"

"No buts, Brad. We've advised the appropriate federal agencies that there was a computer malfunction and that we're checking our systems. That's all we're going to do. And by the way, even if there was a crazy-ass hack like you say, we're not required by law to report every frigg'n cyber incident. It's our call. There was no harm, no foul."

"Well," said Hollister, "I want it on the record that I disagree."

"Be our guest. But we're not going to have the stock of EGI take a dive on a non-event just because you want a big public selfie. This was a computer hiccup. No explosion, no damage, no meltdown, no release. Nothing. You overreacted, Brad. Sorry, but management says it's time for someone else in that chair."

"You're firing me?"

"No, Brad, we're not firing you," said Powell. "You're going to resign. It's the best way to avoid an embarrassing public reprimand from EGI. You know how that could complicate your career going forward."

Hollister got up and left the room.

"He's all worked up," said Powell. "Hope for his sake he cools down. Don't want to have to trash him in public."

"Right," said another. "I know it sounds nuts, but is it possible there was a hack?"

"I've asked our IT unit to look into it," said Powell. "But for the time being, don't even go there. Hack's damn near impossible, and the suits in New York won't be happy if you raise the subject." He looked at the others in the room. "For now, forget a hack. It's a dead letter."

***

Brad Hollister drove home, his anger rising. The suits had all but said they didn't give a tinker's damn if hundreds of thousands of lives had been at risk, even if only for a short while. Calling an unexplained life-threatening reactor malfunction a mere "hiccup" was not only ignorant, it was totally reckless - showing a cynical disregard for life. *Did they have any idea how radiation affected the body? Victims would die an agonizing death, coughing blood, vomiting, while their internal organs disintegrated.*

He thought of his wife Sue, and their two children, Larry, fourteen, and Margaret, thirteen. *What if it happens again and the reactor does fail, and there's a radioactive release? Will I, and other Atlantans, be notified in time to evacuate, or at least shelter in place? Doesn't management understand the deadly consequences of a nuclear reactor gone rogue? I've been forced out. I won't be there to raise the alarm. Will the next guy just roll over? I should blow the damn whistle. But if I do, I'll be blackballed in the industry. How will I feed my family?*

He'd been chief nuclear engineer at Little River for six years. He'd never seen anything so spooky. It had scared him to death. Something had gone very wrong, and as he considered the possibilities he kept returning to the idea of a hack. Sure, the Safety Instrumented Systems were incredibly reliable and were designed to block or prevent critical systems from being breached.

He couldn't recall an equivalent situation in any U.S. reactor short of Three Mile Island. But in that incident, the release had resulted from human error.

This situation was disturbingly different. The problem, whatever its origin, had been deep within the system itself, and at this point no one had a damned clue as to why. *Why did they restart the reactor? If it happened once it could happen again. Will next time be the real thing?*

Hollister realized his hands were so tightly wrapped around the steering wheel they were white.

39

Energy Global

New York City

"Looked pretty rattled, but I don't think he'll talk. He's got a family. Doesn't want to get blackballed," Jay Powell told the room. He leaned back in his chair at the long, burled-wood oval conference table on the ninety-first floor of EGI's New York City corporate headquarters. With its commanding views of Manhattan and Central Park, the new skyscraper was a powerful testament to the worldwide reach and financial size of EGI, a behemoth provider to the nuclear and gas industries.

Five members of EGI's Executive Committee were seated around the table, bottled water and notepads in front of each.

"What's the contingency plan if he does?" said Trish Combs, Chairman of EGI's Executive Committee.

"Off the record?" said Powell. "Our HR and public relations departments are ready to push the narrative of a disgruntled employee who couldn't handle the stress of the job. Started exaggerating even the smallest maintenance issues way out of proportion. Possible personal problems outside of his EGI work, maybe marital, maybe money, maybe drug abuse, a girlfriend. We're set if he goes off the reservation."

"Alright, Jay," said Combs, "now what do we know about the incident so far? You told us our IT folks are saying it might have been a hack, but don't understand how it's possible. That's not good enough. We've brought Little River back online, and we want it kept online. But we can only push the narrative of an unstable employee so long before we get serious press inquiries. And we sure as hell don't want some ass wipe in Washington breathing down our necks before we can get a handle on things."

"Our cyber team has been on it since the event," said Powell. "It's something they've never seen before. If it was malware, it's very sophisticated. They can't locate it, can't find a point of entry, can't identify a source or method."

"In other words, they don't know shit! Not good enough, no way. What the hell are we paying these guys for?" said Combs.

"Trish is right," said a second board member. "If our team's not good enough, let's bring someone else in. Maybe it's not a hack, maybe it's just some bizarre software issue. But until we know what it was, we have to tell everyone it was just a hiccup, a small gremlin of no big consequence. If we don't, it will scream major problems. We're in the middle of negotiations for four new plants in India. A bad story will tank the deal and our stock."

"I get it," said Jay. "I'll bring in a firm with more depth. That means we'll be getting folks involved who aren't EGI. If the story leaks, there will be an investigative shitstorm. If I'm bringing in another team, I'll need a greenlight from you…and I'll need it in writing."

40

Izzy and Joy

Paris

Izzy was sitting at Moustache, a brasserie in the 11th arrondissement, with Joy Morin, a twenty-nine-year-old French cybersecurity wizard who, like nearly all educated young French Parisian professionals, spoke English fluently.

They'd arrived just before noon, an unfashionable time for Parisians, who rarely took lunch before one P.M., considering it *déclassé* to arrive early. But early was better today because Izzy would have her choice of tables. She wanted a place where she could pick Joy's brain about cyberhacking without too much eavesdropping. If bad actors were going to use the techniques Bill Powers had mentioned, then she wanted to know more.

Her cell phone was vibrating. She picked it up and looked at the text message. It was from Will Bergen.

FYI Couple of stories for you. LA Times is reporting arrest of a man threatening to poison Echo Park reservoir. Story from Cleveland Courier about married couple arrested for plan to sabotage natural gas pipeline. Also check this link to GNN breaking news. Nuclear Plant Whistleblower. Cheers!

She looked at the stories. The LA Times story on the reservoir concerned a local activist with a history of mental disorders. *Nothing there.* The story about the married couple read like a Keystone Cops caper. *Not serious.*

Only the last one piqued her interest. She checked her watch. Almost noon in Paris. Almost six A.M. on the East Coast where GNN was located.

"Joy, excuse me for a moment, will you?"

"No worries," said Joy. "Take your time."

Izzy stepped out of the brasserie and found a quiet place close by. She opened the desktop on her phone and tapped the GNN link.

GNN Breaking News: Former Nuclear Plant Control Room Operator Alleges Coverup of Serious Nuclear Incident at Little River nuclear facility. Fears it could have been a cyberhack. Plant operator EGI calls charge "absurd." Claims man is disgruntled employee.

Izzy walked back into the brasserie. She handed the phone to Joy Morin. "Can you tell me what you make of this news story?"

Joy read the article and looked at Izzy.

"Honestly, Izzy, I don't know what to make of it. I've never heard of computer systems at a nuclear power plant failing that way. Crazy time. Really strange."

"He says he's concerned about a cyberhack. Is that possible?"

"Hmmm, extremely difficult, I'd even say near impossible because of safety instrumented systems, firewalls and hardware. They're the last line of defense for nuclear power reactors all over the world." She paused, scrunched her face and tapped her lips with an index finger. "BUT ...yeah, it could be done," she said. "Would have to be a group that was very good."

"So, are we talking about government cyber experts?"

"Not necessarily. Could be lone wolves," said Joy.

"A nuclear power plant? Now *that does* sound crazy," said Izzy.

"It was, until 2010 when the Stuxnet worm was born. It was a powerful multi-exploit cyber worm created by the U.S. and Israel to target Iran's nuclear program. Stuxnet was the most complex, brilliant, and dangerous zero day cybermalware that had ever been created. Unfortunately, it escaped into the wild, and Pandora's box opened. Since then, the world of cyberhacking has evolved so rapidly that lone wolf hackers can now bring down critical systems easily. Cyberhacking has been around a long time, but Stuxnet was a game changer."

"Joy, tell me again. You're saying a nuclear power plant could be hacked by lone wolves?"

"It's possible. A lone wolf group named Black Ghost Knifefish with alleged links to Russia is suspected of attacking national power grids.

Another clandestine group has used malware called Triton, developed by a major Russian research institute. Triton is capable of defeating the ICSIS industrial control and safety instrumented systems of nuclear power plants. It was used to cyberattack the Petro Rabigh oil refinery in Saudi Arabia in 2017."

"Truly frightening," said Izzy.

"Not as frightening as what I'm about to tell you."

"Yes?" said Izzy.

"Like I said, there's been an exponential growth in the world of dark cyberhacking. Hackers, sometimes mere teenagers, are bringing down systems of scale."

"Teenagers? Are you serious?"

"Deadly serious, Izzy. Teenagers, and I'm not talking about script kiddie wannabes or pointless nuisance, denial of service attacks. I'm talking about teenagers capable of launching kinetic hacks that can destroy and kill. Cyberterrorism has gotten easier, more invasive, more malevolent, by several orders of magnitude. The theft of Eternal Blue exploits from the National Security Agency in 2017, and their release into the wild has made sophisticated cyberattacks much easier. It's not stretching the truth too much to say the exploits, the tools, are now about as available as a Mickey D's Quarter Pounder."

Izzy sat back in her chair and sighed. "So now, teenage hackers we've never heard of, who may be sitting in some walkup apartment somewhere on the planet, are capable of unleashing a nuclear inferno? Insane."

"I don't know that I'd go quite that far…yet. But it's a brave new world, Izzy. I live in the cybergeist. In my field, I am considered an expert. Even I have a hard time keeping up with new threat models. Only a few years ago we were talking about the danger of single zero day exploits. But now the game is all about packaging multiple zero days in one attack."

Izzy stood up. "Okay," she said, "assuming that Little River could be hacked by lone wolves, whatever their age, what's the potential for harm?"

"In one word? Apocalypse," Joy said. "When the Chernobyl nuclear power plant exploded in Ukraine in 1986, it took several hundred thousand workers…yes, Izzy, that's right, several hundred thousand, to contain and clean up the radiation damage. Deadly radiation from that reactor caused devastating injuries, like thyroid cancer, leukemia, bone marrow cancer, genetic damage, and compromised immune systems. Whole villages and thousands of acres of land around them will be uninhabitable for the next twenty thousand years."

Izzy pursed her lips and folded her arms. *Shit!*

41

Bill Powers

"What's your read on the GNN story?" said Bill Powers, raising his beer for a slug. Izzy had sent Powers and Jean-François the link to the story. It was evening. Powers and Izzy were at a small terrace table outside La Source, a welcoming corner bistro in the artsy Batignolles neighborhood of the 17th arrondissement.

It was a straight-on question, the tone easy, the restive body language absent. Ever since their meet at Place des Vosges, Powers had morphed from prickly porcupine to collegial chum. She liked that.

"Not sure," said Izzy. "Could just be a coincidence that has nothing to do with North Korea."

"But you're not buying that," said Powers.

"Who knows?" said Izzy. "All sorts of unusual events happen every day. Might be nothing. Might be something. So, let's assume for a moment that there's a connection, that we're looking at a cyberattack on the Little River nuclear power station. I spoke with a cyber expert yesterday. She says a successful hack of the plant's systems is almost impossible, but, and it's a big but, she did not rule out the possibility that lone wolves might be able to pull it off."

"Bad stuff," said Powers. "Energy Global says the engineer is just a disgruntled former employee making this stuff up. Say they did a complete vet of the incident and they found nothing more than a minor software hiccup."

"Yeah, saw that," said Izzy. "They're making him out to be a bit of a crackpot, and maybe he is."

"Right, maybe," said Powers. "We need to find out more."

Powers asked for the check.

"I've got it," said Izzy. "I'm just going to stay here a bit longer. You go ahead."

"Right," said Powers. "See you."

After Powers left, Izzy ordered a hot chocolate. It soon arrived, pleasantly hot, a cinnamon stick in it. She took a sip and took a nip of the cinnamon stick. *Delicious.*

Though it was chilly, sitting outside *"en terrasse"* with its broad southwest view of rue des Batignolles, was one of Izzy's favorite pleasures.

La Source was a charming classic bistro with early twentieth-century dark wood paneling, and a handsome circular zinc bar. There was something uniquely Parisian about how the bistros, cafés and restaurants were transformed as daylight waned and evening unfolded. The soft golden lighting created an inviting fresco that made each venue the perfect place to be at that moment.

The scene was one more bittersweet reminder of her childhood days in Paris when her parents would take her for a croissant, a hot chocolate and people watching - simple but memorable moments for a child of five.

And it occurred to her now that her lifelong love of Paris and fascination with people had likely begun there, *en terrasse,* as she sat with her parents, watching them observe and comment on the passing human pageant, its richness, its stories, its mysteries and its tells.

42

Liam

Izzy's room landline was ringing. "*Oui?*" said Izzy.

"*Bonjour, madame*, it is the front desk. There is a Mr. Liam Cabot on the line. He says he is an old friend and would like to say hello. Shall I put him through?"

"Yes, in one minute, please."

"*Bien sûr, madame.*"

Izzy reached for her purse, removed a voice recognition module, and turned it on. It illuminated green. She held it close to the receiver. A few seconds later there was a click.

"Yes," said Izzy.

"Izzy, hallo! Liam Cabot here, and many thanks for taking the call."

Izzy checked the screen of the module…*Cabot, Liam…verified.*

"Liam, hi. Bit of a surprise. You in Paris?"

"As it happens, yes. Was passing through. Beastly trade show. Heard you were in town and thought how fun to have a chat, catch up on the amazing Izzy Stone."

"Sure, sounds good," said Izzy.

"Brilliant!" said Liam. "Maybe Galerie Vivienne on rue des Petits Champs near Palais-Royal, around three-thirty today? There's a small restaurant there, Le Vidocq. The bar's very quiet in the afternoon."

"I know the place," said Izzy. "See you there, but let's make that four."

"Outstanding. We'll see you then," said Liam. "Cheers."

He knows why I'm in Paris.

Izzy knew there was no such thing as a random encounter or "chat" with Liam Cabot, her former lover and master spy from Britain's MI6 intelligence service. Nor did she believe he'd just been passing through Paris. In all likelihood Liam and MI6 had been tracking her ever since she'd landed in France.

Liam was six-foot-three, athletic, and a human chameleon, sometimes appearing as a mid-level diplomat, other times as a salesman or stuffy academic, depending on the need and the setting. She knew she could count on him. The previous year in Paris, he'd helped her spirit the president to safety.

Liam was a warrior, an adventurer, at heart. She'd been drawn to that. As a Secret Service agent, she too had chosen the life of a warrior. They mirrored each other in that way. Their affair had been brief but memorable. She was still fond of Liam, and considered him a confidant and friend. He was so different from Leyland Childs.

"Leyland," the way she addressed the president when they were together and away from official duties, offered her unwavering love that made her feel alive, valued, desired. Leyland was a builder, a visionary, and a leader. America would be a more just, and bountiful nation because of him. Like Leyland, Izzy too, wanted to be a force for good in a world of daunting challenges.

Each in their own unique way, Liam and Leyland spoke to the duality of her own makeup and stirred conflicting emotions. *If I choose one over the other will I one day regret having closed my heart to an essential part of myself?*

Could I live with that? I don't know. Perhaps there's no way I will ever be able to bring myself to make that choice.

43

Galerie Vivienne

Izzy got off the Number One metro line at Palais-Royal at the foot of the immense Louvre museum. She crossed rue de Rivoli and made her way through the flowering rose-filled garden of the Palais-Royal, birthplace of the French Revolution, where on July 12, 1789, Camille Desmoulins had leapt onto a table and delivered a fiery speech that ignited the revolt.

She turned up rue des Petits Champs, proceeded to Galerie Vivienne, and entered the impressive *passage*. Built in 1823, the exquisite neo-classical hall with its soaring glass canopy, mosaic floors, delicate paintings, unique shops and tasteful bistros conveyed an air of bygone elegance.

Izzy found Le Vidocq and walked in. The lunch crowd had departed. Staff were preparing tables for the evening. The dining area led to a small elegant bar with green leather tub chairs and dark wood paneling. She stepped into the bar. It was empty, but for a heavyset bartender with mutton chops, dressed in white shirt and black pants. He was busy drying glassware and arranging bottles of spirits. She said *"bonjour,"* and took one of the two tub chairs next to a small round cherry wood table with a good view of the entrance and side door.

Liam hadn't arrived. Nor had she expected to find him there. He would have wanted to be sure Izzy wasn't being followed.

The bartender approached. Izzy ordered a Badoit and told him she was waiting for a friend. She checked her watch. *It will be about ten minutes,* she said to herself. The Badoit arrived. The bartender poured for her.

"*Merci,*" she said.

"*Je vous en prie, madame,*" he said.

Almost to the minute, Liam appeared at the side door and quickly walked over to Izzy. She stood.

"Izzy. Lovely to see you. You look grand."

"Good to see you, Liam."

Liam planted a peck on both her cheeks. They each took a chair. Liam hailed the bartender.

"Talisker scotch, neat."

While he waited for the drink, Liam assumed the bonhomie of someone having a lively conversation with a good friend.

"Enjoying your stay here?"

"It's Paris," she said. "What's not to enjoy?"

"Bravo," he said. His drink arrived. Liam took a swallow. He smiled approvingly and looked at Izzy. "By the way, my latest business card. Took on a new position." He slid a card across the table to her.

"Thanks, and congratulations," said Izzy, as she took the card and looked. "Nice," she said. She turned the card over – and blanched.

Powers. Be careful.

Izzy re-read the words, her mind in overdrive.

She looked up at Liam, her eyes reflecting barely contained alarm and asking the unspoken question.

Liam blinked once, smiled, his head nodding almost imperceptibly. He resumed his light banter accompanied by more smiles and laughter, then finished his drink.

"Got to run now, Izzy. Have to be back in London this evening. Was great to see you." He stood, gave her a quick peck on each cheek again. "Dinner, sometime soon?"

"I'll think about it," she said.

"Cheers, then."

He left twenty euros for the drinks and off he went. This time through the main entrance.

Izzy stepped into the restaurant bathroom, closed the stall door, took a photo of the card, encrypted the photo, then tore the card into small pieces and flushed.

44

The Note

Liam's card had left Izzy reeling. *"Powers. Be careful."* *Why?* Now Izzy was delving into her photographic and auditory memory. Exactly how much information had she imparted to Powers? Was there anything she'd missed about the way he'd queried her? Was there any hint of betrayal or deception? Liam's wave-off was hard to believe. Everything she'd sensed about Powers told her he was the genuine article.

Yet Liam was an extraordinary operative, not given to reckless off-the-cuff judgments. He knew something, or at least thought he knew something about Powers, that was troubling.

45

L C Automotive

"Miss Stone? Front desk here. There is a package for you. It was hand delivered a few minutes ago. Shall I send it up?"

"Does it say who the sender is?"

"*Oui*, from L.C. Automotive."

"Can you hold on for a moment?" said Izzy.

"*Bien sûr, madame.*"

She selected Liam's private phone number from Contacts and sent a text message.

Package?

A moment later, a reply: ***L.C. Automotive.*** Izzy smiled. Liam's reference to automobiles was his way of reminding her of a running joke between them. He was a bottomless well of minutia when it came to all things automotive and enjoyed teasing Izzy with arcane references to 1920s' clutches, piston sizes, vintage cars and Formula One races.

"Yes," she said to the front desk, "please send it up."

The package soon arrived, a three by five-inch padded envelope. She opened it. There was a thumb drive inside. She turned on her laptop, made sure it was not connected to Wi-Fi or Bluetooth and inserted the drive. A video file popped up. She double-clicked. The video had been shot from a distance. It showed a busy square, automobiles and pedestrians on the move, a corner bistro with patrons sitting at outside tables under an overcast sky. It was hard to determine the location or signage but in the distance she thought she could make out the distinctive profile of Prague's fifteenth century Powder Tower. *Ok, looks like Prague.*

The camera zoomed in. A couple was seated at one of the outside tables. A woman wearing a dark coat with a hooded top, her back to the camera, was sitting across from a man. The shot tightened and the couple came into clearer focus. The lens tightened more and framed the man's face.

Bill Powers.

Hmmm. Powers with his massive build and Irish face in Prague with a woman. So what! He travels. He has female friends.

The couple stood. The woman was tall. Without shaking hands or exchanging a kiss on the cheek, the two simply turned and walked off in different directions. *Odd. Wait! Hold on!* Izzy hit Pause. She'd seen something. She moved the video slider back three seconds and hit PLAY.

There it was again! Something about the woman's long, distinctive stride was familiar. Izzy hit STOP.

I've seen that stride before.

Her mind was racing. *Could I be wrong?*

She pressed PLAY and let the video continue. At the intersection the woman stopped and hailed a cab. As the ride pulled up, she removed her coat and stepped to the street. As she did, her long lustrous blond hair spilled down her back.

Dammit! It's Galina Federova from Châtelet!

Izzy hit stop and sat back, stunned. Angry. *Powers, you've got a lot of explaining to do.*

46

Savoy-sur-Mer

Savoy-sur-Mer, France

"Merde!"

Stéphane Sauveterre, the Control Room Reactor Operator at the Savoy-sur-Mer nuclear power station in western France, one of the world's safest nuclear power generating facilities, was looking at a control panel:

> ***ARRÊT AUTOMATIQUE...***
> ***ARRÊT AUTOMATIQUE...***

The operator could not believe it. The reactor was signaling an automatic shutdown. The reactor was in full charging mode. He knew that an automatic shutdown while the unit was charging could lead to a thermo-hydraulic transient, resulting in a dangerous buildup of pressure in the vault. Enough pressure, and critical components could fail. Disaster would result. He quickly booted backup systems. His pulse accelerated as the displays illuminated:

> ***ARRÊT AUTOMATIQUE....AUTOMATIC STOP.......***
> ***ARRÊT AUTOMATIQUE....AUTOMATIC STOP.......***

"*Non! Putain!*" Klaxons were now sounding throughout the plant as technicians scrambled to their consoles.

He tried going to manual override to return the reactor to a safe fallback state. His answer came back fast:

ÉCHEC D'ANNULATION....FAILED TO SHUTDOWN...........

"*Seigneur!* Lord!" Sauveterre was in full panic. He grabbed the hotline.

47

Damn!

Paris

Izzy's cell phone was buzzing. She looked at the clock on her bedstand. Five-thirty in the morning. She picked up the phone and looked. *Jean-François.*

"Do you *ever* sleep?" she said, her voice tired, but not angry.

"Izzy, apologies for the hour," he said, "but I've just learned that last night there was an incident at our nuclear power plant at Savoy-sur-Mer."

"Yes?" said Izzy.

"The preliminary report indicates a problem similar to the one at Little River."

"Damn!" said Izzy, now wide awake. "What happened?"

"All we know so far is that there were warnings in the system. The Control Room attempted to SCRAM the reactor manually but the system did not respond."

Izzy's heart was racing. "Was there a release?"

"No release, no damage. The system reset itself after seven minutes and a controlled shutdown took place. But as you can imagine, there was complete chaos until they were able to confirm a safe shutdown."

Izzy's phone purred, indicating another call.

"Hold on a moment, Jean-François," she said, and went to the incoming call.

Bill Powers.

"Powers, have to get back to you in a few," she said.

"Make it soon," said Powers. "We need to talk."

She switched back to Jean-François. "Okay," she said, "if it was a cyberattack, it looks like the North Koreans may have just made a move."

"Yes, possible, but we'll need more proof they're behind it if we want to act."

"What's your government's next step?" said Izzy.

"The Élysée Palace is preparing to go to a total security lockdown of all nuclear facilities in France. But the problem is that more than seventy percent of France's electrical production comes from our nuclear plants."

"And you can't shut them all down."

"It would be a catastrophe. It would plunge the entire country into the dark ages," said Jean-François.

"How can I help?" said Izzy.

"I need everyone at the Ministry at seven A.M."

"I'll be there," said Izzy.

"*Bon. À bientôt.*"

Izzy checked the time. There was no way she was going to get back to sleep. She picked up the laptop on her side table, logged in and began searching the internet for any further information on the incident. There wasn't much. She put the laptop down, picked up her phone and speed dialed Bill Powers.

He picked up. "Savoy-sur-Mer. Best guess?" he said.

"I'm not into guessing," Izzy said.

"Forget the guessing then, Stone. What do you know?" his irritation coming through.

"Probably less than you." Izzy's sarcasm was evident.

"Meaning?"

"Meaning, oh, I don't know," said Izzy. "What's your best guess?"

"Look, pal," said Powers. "We have a second nuclear power plant that just went AWOL, and I'm smelling trouble. We don't have time for Wheel of Fortune. Let's get back on the same page."

"I would…but I don't read Russian….pal," said Izzy. She ended the call and walked, still agitated, to the large windows of the front room, taking in the tableau beyond. First light was breaking on the Louvre and the Tuileries. It was a moment of great beauty, yet her mind was in turmoil.

First Little River and now Savoy-sur-Mer.

The contrast between the peacefulness of the morning and the ghoulish spectre of a nuclear plant in ruins was jarring.

48

Musée des Arts et Métiers

We need to talk….now.

Izzy looked at the text message from Bill Powers. It was noon.

She replied: ***Arts et Metiers museum, three P.M.***

They had both been at the seven A.M. Ministry meeting. It was short. There was little new information on Savoy-sur-Mer. Powers had remained silent throughout.

And now, several hours later, Izzy was in a leather chair looking at him. Powers was leaning against the wall of a quiet reading room at the Musée des Arts et Métiers on rue Reamur in the 3rd arrondissement. They were the only two in the room. On a mid-week afternoon, the whole museum was empty but for a few security staff sitting on folding chairs.

She'd arrived before Powers, wanting to check for uninvited company. Prague had put her on her guard. She spent an hour in the museum's galleries, admiring displays of science and rare technology spanning centuries, the aging wood floors breaking the silence with creaking sounds as she walked.

"You asked for a meet," Izzy said to Powers, her tone dry and businesslike.

"You're pissed off. What's on your mind?" said Powers.

"What's in your brief?" said Izzy, with caustic irony, ignoring his question.

"Just a government grunt taking orders, doing his job."

"Like chumming with a known Russian agent in Prague?"

"Meaning?" said Powers.

"Meaning, that the blonde you were with may be involved in the Châtelet murder, and that gives me a bad feeling."

"Sorry, can't help you."

"Yeah, right," said Izzy. She stood. "Have it your way. And by the way…," she leaned in and dropped a newspaper on the table, "brought you a copy of Pravda. Fun reading… if you like fake news and propaganda."

"Thought you didn't read Russian," said Powers.

"I lied," said Izzy, as she hoisted her purse and walked away.

49

Harry's Bar

Bill Powers was not having a good day. The meet at Arts et Métiers with Izzy had not gone well. Afterward, he'd made a beeline for Harry's New York Bar at cinq rue Daunou in Paris, not far from the opulent beaux-arts Garnier Opera House. He took a seat near the back and ordered a Bloody Mary, or "Blewdee Mehree" as the French pronounced it. It was soon gone. He hailed the waiter and ordered another. It arrived promptly and could not have tasted better.

The bar was not busy, but would soon be packed with late afternoon and evening drinkers. He took a swallow and surveyed the storied place, a near-shrine boasting illustrious visitors like Ernest Hemingway and Rita Hayworth. George Gershwin had reportedly composed *An American In Paris* on the piano in the downstairs bar.

He took another swallow and began mulling the problem at hand. Galina Federova, the tall, blond Russian SVR agent he'd been running for several years had gone to ground. She had not shown for their scheduled meet at the safe location in the apartment above a deserted plumbing shop in the 18th arrondissement. The building was near the bustling Marché aux Puces, a vast, sprawling open air market of seventeen hundred vendors, an ideal venue for concealment and evasion.

The following day, per an agreed protocol, he tried again at Les Philosophes in the Marais. He sat outside the bistro at 2:30 P.M. drinking a glass of Sancerre, reading a white cover copy of André Farkas' *Budapest 1956,* a dark red bookmark sticking out of the book. He had set the alarm on his watch to vibrate at 2:55 P.M., five minutes before the rendezvous. He did not want to be looking up from his book too often.

At 2:55 his watch vibrated gently. Five minutes later Federova should have casually walked by, and raised her cell to her head to signal an imminent drop. Her phone would have been turned off to prevent GPS tracking. An hour later Powers would have entered the church of St. Roch in the 1st arrondissement, knelt behind the middle wicker chair of the third center aisle and extracted an encrypted USB thumbnail drive taped to the bottom of the seat. The drive would contain a series of sensitive SVR documents, reason for the non-meet at Marché aux Puces, and instructions for the next rendezvous.

But Federova had not shown at Les Philosophes and there was nothing at St. Roch.

Powers was getting nervous.

He dashed off an encrypted message to his case officer in the Directorate of Operations at Langley. *Dave, sorry to hear about Susan. Hope for her quick recovery. Best, Don.*

The day after the Les Philosophes no-show, he began surveillance of Federova's apartment building. He took a room in a small low-budget hotel just across the street. He told the dyspeptic clerk behind the counter that he was claustrophobic and needed a room with windows facing the street. The clerk was unmoved.

Thirty additional euros got Powers what pleading had not.

After observing Federova's apartment complex for two days without any sign of her, he decided to make entry. He waited until evening, then approached a resident who was going into the building.

"Hi, *bonjour!*" he said with classic American geniality, pointing to the door. "*Moi*, American. *Mon ami* lives here. Can you let me in, *s'il vous plaît?*" which came out sounding like "silver plate." The man, accustomed to tongue-tied Americans, punched the door code and held it open for Powers. It was easier than spending five long minutes deciphering mangled Franglish.

There was no elevator. Powers walked up the creaking wood stairs to the 5th floor. He did three quick taps on door 5G followed by two slow taps. There was no answer. After a long minute, he inserted a wire tool into the key slot and was soon inside. The apartment was empty and in good order. If it had been tossed, a good cleanup had taken place. Federova's clothing and personal belongings were still there. If she had fled, it had been with the clothes on her back. A quick walk through produced nothing. With one exception - a grey stain across the bedroom floor. *Damn!* Powers knew what dried blood looked like. Someone had done a quick wipe. Judging from the large stain a lot of blood had been spilled. *Was it Galina's?* He would have to alert Langley.

***

Powers had been running Galina since his posting to Ukraine several years earlier. He had arrived in Kyiv using the cover of Michael McClister, adjunct professor from Clemson University. He was writing a biography of the celebrated Ukrainian writer, Taras Shevchenko, he told the serpent-eyed agent at passport control. "Michael" took a two-room apartment located in the Goloseevskiy district, a mere five minute walk from Taras Shevchenko park. It squared nicely with his legend.

Powers wondered more than once whether he'd recruited Federova, or she had sought him out to be recruited. A "chance" encounter at a folk festival in Kyiv had led to an invitation to a performance of Ukrainian folk dances. "Cahm, professor, you weel have sahm fun," she had said, in an engaging Russian-inflected English soaked with "ah's" and "ee's." A week later he reciprocated, inviting her to a concert at Lysenko Hall to hear a piano performance of Gershwin's Rhapsody in Blue.

"Vonderful! I love Ameriken moozic," she said.

After the concert Federova suggested dinner at a small restaurant on Prorizna Street. Over chicken Kyiv and a bottle of Koblevor Cabernet Sauvignon, Powers, in his guise as Professor McClister, talked about the biography of Taras Shevchenko he was writing. Federova spoke about her work as an information specialist for a Ukrainian tech firm.

"I travel great deal. And so much foolishness, Michael!" she said with a charming laugh. It was a full, inviting laugh, filled with humor and possibility. "There is always new problem somewhere," she added, her sapphire blue eyes shimmering in the candlelight. When dinner ended they taxied to his flat near Taras Shevchenko park and tore at each other until dawn.

He vetted her through Langley, and was not entirely surprised to learn she was likely connected to Russian SVR intelligence. *Well who wasn't? It was, after all, the Ukraine.*

Over the next several weeks, "Michael McClister" and Federova took day trips to places connected with

Shevchenko's writing and to less traveled historical sites Federova knew.

One evening over a wine infused dinner at a country restaurant she said, "Michael, you must have many friends at the American Embassy in Kyiv, no?"

"Afraid not, just the junior staffer who helped me once with some travel arrangements to Shevchenko's home in Morynski."

"Ah, of course, Shevchenko's birthplace," she said. She leaned closer to Powers and lowered her voice. "You know, Michael, I have dear friend who works at your embassy in Kyiv. Do you think your staffer might like to know maybe a little bit more about him? My friend has very interesting background."

Powers suspected a dangle but went along. "Perhaps," he said. "I'd have to ask him. What is your friend's name?"

Federova's help in exposing a mole in the Kyiv embassy was the beginning of an important recruitment. Over the next three months, Galina provided valuable information on the current staff structure of the SVR. He was surprised by her extraordinary knowledge of its inner workings.

The mandarins at Langley were giddy with delight once they'd satisfied their robust skepticism about her. One of the Agency's counter-intelligence pagans had expressed serious doubts early on. "Her real name is Manya Lebedev. She has deep family connections to the SVR. She's too good to be true. She'll be feeding us red herrings."

Yet Federova had held up over time. Her information had helped disrupt several serious attacks on U.S. interests.

When Bill Powers was subsequently posted to Islamabad, Galina refused to be tasked to another CIA handler. It was nothing new. There was always a deadly risk in being a double agent. Trusting your handler with your identity and your life required an audacious leap of faith. So, Galina remained "Michael's" asset, periodically traveling to Geneva or Prague for a debriefing by Powers.

But something had changed in the last few months. Galina was more guarded during their encounters. That troubled Powers, who read the small cues with increasing alarm. She was worried about something. Something she did not want to, or was afraid to, share. He persuaded her to take a holiday in Greece with him. Each of them concocted a reason for a getaway. She never told him what excuse she'd given her SVR handler. He'd told Langley he was working on a possible recruit and needed to be out-of-pocket for a few days.

They spent four days in a whitewashed hilltop rental on the isle of Sikinos, with stunning west facing views of the Aegean. There was intimacy, but Galina's love-making had seemed distant and joyless. They took long walks down to the seaside village below, savoring local dishes of bobota dipped in saganaki cheese and tyrokafteri, oven baked sardines in lemon, herbed lamb, chilled uozo and assyrtiko wine.

He'd probed for reasons behind her changed behavior.

"Eez nothing with you, Michael. Just all theez arguing with contractors who work on my dacha. Should be finished months ago. They driving me crazy."

Now Federova was in Paris. And so was he. Izzy Stone was asking uncomfortable questions about his Prague meeting with Federova. What else did she know?

50

Galina Federova

Galina Federova was thirty-seven, brilliant, with expensive tastes and an impressive coterie of admirers. A person much to be envied - but for the fact that she was a walking dead woman. The visit by a man named Chen Chi, intent on killing her, had made that clear.

It was a lamentable fate she'd brought upon herself. She'd followed a false star navigating the dangerous waters of espionage and betrayal, confident she could maintain a steady course while making profitable ports of call in Moscow, Washington and Pyongyang. It had gone well for a while.

Her decision years earlier to work with the Americans while still an intelligence agent for the Russian SVR had proved a financial boon. The American wallet seemed bottomless, an acknowledgement of her value to the CIA.

But Galina was an ambitious spy with needs. There was the dacha in the Ukraine to renovate and the Alpine cottage in Switzerland, not to mention the expensive Swiss boarding school for her nine-year-old daughter Katia, center of her life, child of a misadventured tryst with a Bolivian who was no longer in the picture. So, when she was approached with a platinum offer at a cybertech conference in Singapore by an agent of the North Korean Reconnaissance General Bureau, the clandestine intelligence service of North Korea, she could not resist. The impressive sum of money they were prepared to provide in exchange for her technical help on cyber operations, and intelligence on the SVR, though laden with great peril, was too tempting to refuse.

She mused about the fountain of money she would have enjoyed had she also revealed her work for the Americans. But that would have set off too many alarms in Pyongyang. She now could see that in her oversized hubris, she'd underestimated the challenge. She'd assumed she could successfully juggle several explosive relationships. Not without reason. After all, she'd been born to espionage, deception and deft movement. Her father was a senior KGB officer, her mother a celebrated Russian ballerina. From childhood, Galina's talent for dissembling and cunning had revealed a precocious, shape-shifting, liar prodigy.

At the age of twenty-two, following her graduation from the prestigious Moscow Institute of Physics and Technology, her father arranged her appointment to a low-level position with the SVR intelligence service in Moscow. Galina rose fast. Within five years her outstanding technical skills in the cyber field combined with her natural beauty and ability to extract useful information, mostly from moon-eyed male admirers at big international meetings of scientists and cyber experts, made her an invaluable asset of the Russian government.

But those halcyon days of easy profit and prevarication were over. The cyber demands of Pyongyang, her new employer, had grown from network disruption and denial of service attacks to progressively darker assignments. Soon, ransomware, and extortion of financial institutions, multinational companies and public utilities, as well as cyberhacking of government databanks, were producing millions for Pyongyang.

Her work had also involved assignments with Jens Alders, a Dutch citizen whose connections in Europe, Asia, the Middle East, Africa and the United States had facilitated the targeting of the attacks.

When Pyongyang made the decision to disrupt nuclear power plants, Jens Alders had balked, and decided to expose the plan. Galina Federova had her own misgivings, but by then she was in too deep. If North Korea revealed her work for them, Russia or the U.S. would soon put a bullet in her head - the money gone, her daughter orphaned.

She agreed to assist in the assassination of Jens Alders in the Châtelet tunnels. Pyongyang's Dear Leader had a penchant for dramatic murder in public places. Paris would be a perfect setting. She'd had no choice. Jens Alders was about to go public. He had to be stopped and the dossier taken from him.

Although the handler from Pyongyang's RGB had told her that an individual by the name of "Eduardo del Valle" would do the hit, he had not offered more. The murder of Jens Alders happened so fast that she had not seen the shooter. "Eduardo del Valle" showed up at her apartment on a rainy night several days later. He told her he needed to stay at her place for a few days.

She considered saying no, but thought it risky. There was something about his manner, the way he looked at her, the way he moved about the apartment, as if sniffing for prey, that terrified her. He asked if she had the small briefcase Jens Alders had been carrying. She told him it was safely stored. He made no reply. But she felt death was in the room. She gave him directions on how to get to Victor, the cataphile, who also had to be eliminated.

Ironically, she was grateful that she'd agreed to let Eduardo stay with her. He'd been at her apartment when Chen Chi came looking to kill her. Chen Chi had been difficult to break, but after a long, ghoulish "enhanced interrogation" by Eduardo in the small bedroom, Chen mumbled that someone in Russia wanted her dead.

The uncomfortable truth was that both the Americans and the Russians had probably discovered her treachery. It would not have surprised her if the Americans wanted her dead. As between the two, Federova reasoned it was not likely the Americans would move on her. On the other hand, Moscow ordering the murder of a traitor to the Homeland was guaranteed. A long, painful interrogation at Lefortovo prison, followed by a one-way trip to an open furnace would be a predictable end. Her relationship with Michael McClister had lasted years. Would he be open to a deal in exchange for the information she could deliver on Pyongyang?

After all, she now was in possession of the briefcase and the dossier that she'd taken from Jens Alders when he'd been murdered at Châtelet. The documents it contained would set off alarm bells throughout the world.

Michael was looking for her. She'd avoided him because he'd been asking too many uncomfortable questions. She had moved in with a Ukrainian friend but left her belongings at her apartment. She felt things closing in, and was desperate. Michael might be the answer.

I'll send him a message requesting a meetup and hope Moscow doesn't find me first.

Unfortunately for Galina Federova, the Russians were the least of her worries.

51

IAEA

Vienna

It was ten in the morning and the IAEA staffer was reading the report from France's *Autorité de Sûreté Nucléaire*, the agency responsible for overseeing the safety of French nuclear power plants. The previous day a nuclear generating station at Savoy-sur-Mer had experienced a system failure triggering a critical alert in the Control Room.

Despite efforts to conduct a SCRAM shutdown, the system had failed to respond. After seven harrowing minutes, the system had unaccountably restored itself, and a second attempt by the Control Room Reactor Operator to SCRAM the reactor was successful. A rapid inspection of the reactor and the facility had revealed no physical damage or leakage. *ASN* immediately dispatched a team to Savoy-sur-Mer.

The staffer put the report down. His pulse was racing. He reached into a tall pile of reports sitting on his desk and yanked out the file entitled "Little River Nuclear." He punched a number on his landline.

"*Ja.*"

"Director, I need to speak with you urgently."

52

Liam and Izzy

Paris

"Yes?"

"Izzy, it's Liam. I'm in the lobby."

"Come on up. I'm in four-ten." She'd asked Liam for a meet. He'd agreed to fly to Paris from London. She wanted more clarity. MI6 was warning her off from Bill Powers, a long-time CIA operative with a solid reputation at Langley. The video of Powers with Galina Federova in Prague was troubling. What else did MI6 know?

Moments later Liam knocked on the door. Izzy let him in.

"How was the flight? Get you a drink?"

"Bumpy," said Liam, dropping into an armchair. "Thanks, whatever you're having."

"Scotch, then," said Izzy. "Hotel sent up a bottle of Talisker yesterday. Neat?"

"Talisker. Brilliant. Neat, thanks."

She took two crystal tumblers, opened the Talisker and poured. She gave one to Liam and took the other for herself.

"The Prague video of Bill Powers," she said. "Why?"

Liam took a short sip, savored it, and looked at Izzy. "Because you're working with French DGSE and

DGSI on a sensitive matter and Bill Powers is in the conversation. He's an intelligence operative who's been spending a lot of time with Galina Federova, a known SVR operative. So that makes us wonder what's up."

"Well, MI6 has been busy!" said Izzy. "But you said it, Liam, sounds like an American intelligence officer doing his job and running a source. What's the problem?"

"Or maybe she's been running him," said Liam.

"Just taking a flyer, or do you have something?"

"Only circumstantial at this point," said Liam. "After Prague they both pulled a disappearing act for several days. We'd like to know where they were."

"Romantic involvement?" said Izzy.

"Who bloody knows? Maybe they were having Stoli and chumming with the boys from Moscow Center in some safe house. If Russian intelligence turned Powers, you need to seriously rethink his role."

"Okay," said Izzy. "Maybe there's a problem there, maybe not. Maybe they just couldn't keep their hands off each other on a lost weekend. Unless you've got more, I can't shut him out. Above my pay grade. He's in Paris because Langley wants him here."

"Fine," said Liam. "Let's go with that and say Powers *is* running Federova. Let's assume he's not compromised. A nice fellow. He's Mr. Rogers in the neighborhood…but if he is, he needs to watch his back."

"Because?" said Izzy.

"Because MI6 has reason to believe the SVR has targeted Galina Federova for action with extreme prejudice."

Izzy had not expected this development. *Moscow wants her dead? Did they find out she's working for us? Did Powers tip off Moscow?*

"How good's your source?" said Izzy.

"How good's your Russian?" said Liam.

"It's ok. Not what it was at West Point. What've you got?"

Liam pulled a folded document from his coat pocket and passed it to Izzy.

"This is an intercept of a message from an SVR operative in Moscow to two expats in Paris. One of the expats is Ajax Balaskas, the Greek shipping tycoon, spends money like it's water."

"Who's number two?" said Izzy.

"Igor Nochenko, a former Spetsnaz special forces no regrets killer. We believe Balaskas and Nochenko have been tasked to terminate Federova. Take a look."

Izzy unfolded the document and read. She looked up. "I've heard of Ajax Balaskas here in Paris. Lives large, likes expensive toys, and both genders." She handed the document back to Liam. "How did MI6 come by this adorable missive?"

"The SVR operative got sloppy with his email."

"You hacked him? Good work," said Izzy. "Has this been corroborated?"

"We have a second source."

"Did you pass this to French intelligence?"

"Thought we'd let you know first."

"Thanks. What's your assessment of the threat to her life?"

"On a scale of ten, it's a twelve," said Liam. "The only thing missing is a toe tag."

"You think the SVR found out she was working with our side?" said Izzy.

"Not necessarily. There's another possibility."

"I'm listening."

"That she was working with a third-party actor and the SVR found out."

Izzy's mind was turning cartwheels. *Christ, this has more layers than a French pastry!*

"A *third* party?" said Izzy. "China? Israel?"

"You might want to take a stiff pull of that scotch first," said Liam.

"I'll wait, thanks."

"Fine. We obtained information from a Swiss banking source showing Galina Federova had several six-figure deposits made to a bitcoin account she opened in Geneva. Cyber forensics traced those transfers to a Malaysian bank with ties to the DPRK. If Moscow also knows this, it might explain why they want her gone."

Izzy was taken aback. *DPRK? North Korea? Liam's right. If the SVR knows about the Swiss transfers, she's as good as dead.*

"Think I'll have that drink," she said. She lifted the tumbler, took a hefty swallow, and sat down on the chaise longue facing Liam. Both sat quietly for a long moment, absorbing the implications.

"So, when did you begin Russian?" said Liam.

"A woman named Anna Popov, a Jewish émigré from Moscow. Anna was my Russian nanny and tutor when I was growing up. But she was much more than that. Really a wonderful caring woman, kind of a doting grandmother. I was having a hard time with dad's death and she helped me through it. That was my first Russian. After that, there was high school and then the Point for more."

"Hmm, Anna Popov. Backstory?"

"Right, Anna was a distinguished professor of history at Moscow State University. After the Berlin Wall came down, she and her father, Radion Popov, a Russian officer, emigrated first to Israel, then to Los Angeles. It was a tough decision. Anna once told me they would have stayed in Russia after the wall came down but her father, a decorated colonel who'd been to hell and back during the Soviet occupation of

Afghanistan, knew that as a Jew, he'd hit an iron ceiling in the military hierarchy. Besides, everything was in flux and Radion was concerned about a revival of rabid anti-semitism in Russia."

"Why didn't they remain in Israel?"

"Sort of a mystery. All they ever said to me was that they didn't feel welcome. I never asked why."

"So, then to the good old USA?" said Liam.

"Right. It was a hard landing for both. There was no demand for Anna's professional skills in LA, and her father found no market for his military experience. He'd risen to a very senior position in the Ministry of Defense in Moscow, but in Los Angeles he was just another immigrant with a bad accent. Offered his services to the feds, but there were no takers. So Anna became a tutor and a nanny to support the two of them. Quite a humbling experience, given their former positions. Fortunately, she was fluent in English. Radion much less so."

"How long did you know her?"

"She tutored me until I graduated from high school."

"Is Anna still in Los Angeles?"

"Not sure, I haven't spoken with either of them in several years. Just one more ball I've dropped. Makes me feel like crap."

53

Musée Guimet

"I need some advice, Michael."

Galina Federova and Bill Powers *aka* Michael McClister were standing by a marble column in the darkened rotunda of the ornate neo-classical library of the Musée Guimet. He'd been surprised to hear from her. She'd disappeared into a black hole. Now she wanted to talk. Federova had seriously violated tradecraft by contacting him directly, but she had sounded desperate. *Midnight. Rear entrance. Musée Guimet,* he replied. The Guimet was closed for repairs, but Powers knew a way in. They would be alone.

"Yeah?"

"My family is not happy with me."

"And?"

"They want me to go away."

"How do you know?"

"They sent someone to tell me."

"Go away? How long?"

"Permanently."

"Unfortunate."

"Yes. They feel I've been rude and ungrateful."

"Because?"

"They think I've been traveling too much and talking to people who are a bad influence."

"Right. One does have to be careful about talking to strangers."

"I will try to remember that."

"Anything else on your mind?" said Powers.

"Actually, yes. It's a surprise for you. I know how much you like to read good stories. I found an exciting one and thought you might enjoy it."

"Is it another fairy tale? I didn't like the last one about the lady who was fixing her dacha."

"Mmm, no. It's more of a horror story."

"Aaah. I finished a dark story recently. It was about a very clever woman who mysteriously disappeared. People thought she'd gone to live with bears. You may have read it."

"I know the story. But in it, she didn't disappear. She just lost her way and got frightened when she found out the bears wanted to eat her. She decided to find a new home."

"Ah, yes, hungry bears. They've been known to eat spoiled food…. and home would be where?"

"I was hoping you could tell me."

"I might have some ideas. You know, I do like a good read, even if it's a horror story. Perhaps the one you have will be interesting enough. Can you send it to me?"

"I have two copies. I will send one to you as a gift. But after that I want to go on a long vacation, somewhere I can relax and where I can be safe. Can you help me with travel arrangements?"

"I'll see which travel packages are available… after I've read the story."

54

Questions

WHAT'S GOING ON AT NUCLEAR PLANTS?

Control Room Reactor Operators in U.S. and
France describe sheer terror as safety systems fail

The headline in the New York Daily Journal was only one of many front-page stories in news outlets around the world. Somehow two nuclear power plants, separated by a vast ocean, had experienced unexplained failures of computer systems in remarkably similar ways. Why? How?

EGI, the owner of Little River, with new nuclear power plants under contract in India, the UK, China and Africa, immediately launched a multi-million-dollar ad campaign dismissing the seriousness of the incident at its plant. The slick ads promised a full investigation while suggesting that it was likely the result of a minor software glitch.

EGI pointed out that state of the art security protocols, that could not be disclosed, were more than adequate to interdict any attempted intrusion. After all, there had been no release of radiation, damage to the plant, nor to any person.

Influential members of congress in charge of oversight committees dismissed calls for an investigation by environmental groups. The fact that the legislators were the recipients of substantial campaign contributions from the energy industry, and had family members who were profiting greatly from business dealings with China and Russia had no bearing on their decisions, they insisted.

55

FBI Visits Brad

Brad Hollister, former Senior Control Room Reactor Operator at Little River, looked out of his living room window in a quiet Atlanta neighborhood as the four FBI agents walked to their government vehicles and drove away. Across the street a small crowd had maintained a vigil ever since the arrival of the agents. Hollister saw that several had smart phones pointed in his direction, no doubt taking video of the visit.

The interview had lasted four hours. Hollister and his wife, Sue, were exhausted. The agents had been professional and courteous to a fault. Yet it had been a grueling experience. They had asked Hollister to walk through the nightmarish sequence of events at Little River minute by minute. It was clear from the questions the agents had put to him that they were interested in any information that might suggest a rogue technician, the presence of malware or active cyberintrusion. He also sensed they were probing for some nefarious role on his part. He understood they had to consider that angle as well.

He told them what he'd told the New York Daily Journal. He did not think the event at the plant was a one-off "never will happen again" event. "No," he'd said, there was something screwy about the whole thing. Both computer systems had reported imminent reactor failure, yet there had been none. He'd quickly SCRAMMED the reactor with zero complications.

There was no good explanation yet, as far as Hollister was concerned. If it happened once, it could happen again - and that was not good. What was also not good was that he was now blackballed in the industry. EGI had done a real piece of work on him. *Unreliable, panicky, delusional.* That was the narrative, and that was all it had taken to make him an untouchable in the business. Yet he did not regret his actions. Unexplained system failures in a nuclear generating facility were no small thing, as Chernobyl and Three Mile Island had dramatically demonstrated. EGI's dismissive attitude and public efforts to downplay the incident were inexcusable. Until now, most of his expressions of concern had gone unnoticed. That had changed and others were now asking tough questions.

It was ironic, but Hollister was almost relieved by the reports of a similar incident at a French nuclear facility. People were paying attention. Maybe this would lead to answers.

56

Where's Babin?

Since the nuclear event at the Savoy-sur-Mer generating plant, Izzy had shuttled from one high-level meeting of intelligence, defense, and cybersecurity experts to another. Now the political and security apparatus of not only the United States and France, but other European nations were paying serious attention. She'd been asked to recap her conversation with Victor. She decided to reveal his interaction with Jens Alders and Paul Babin. It was total transparency. Still, the jousting between the U.S. and French intelligence agencies, and the possibility of leaks worried her. Everyone would now be on the hunt for Paul Babin. She didn't want him to disappear. But where was he?

57

The Tunnel

"Jean-François, have you ID'd everyone who was in the tunnel?"

Izzy was walking alongside Jean-François, passing the seventeenth-century Fontaine Medicis on a tree-shaded path of the immense Jardin du Luxembourg. She was anxious to know what his intelligence services had learned.

"Almost. We've been able to identify and clear everyone with a few exceptions," said Jean-François. "Nothing remarkable. For the most part the people in that tunnel were what they seemed, Parisians and tourists with no serious criminal records who were on their way to jobs, hotels, hostels or sightseeing."

"What about the phony detectives and the pickpocket?" said Izzy.

"The woman and man who looked like metro detectives are Bulgarian nationals. Our Border Control shows they entered France on a Bulgaria Air flight the day before the murder and left immediately after."

"And the young man they were chasing?"

"Not yet identified, but we have to assume he is also Bulgarian."

"What do you know about them?"

"Low level criminals. Not much else. But they didn't have a complicated role. Someone likely paid them a few euros and told them to just make noise."

"Yeah," said Izzy, "didn't require a lot of talent. What does the Bulgarian government have to say?"

"Unfortunately, not much. Bulgarian authorities have not been willing to provide any information on them or their whereabouts."

"And the few exceptions?"

"There's the homeless man with the rucksack. He was close to the murder victim when the shot was fired. An odd fellow. He's a familiar busking musician. People call him 'Saxophone Man.' We're still investigating him."

"Go on," said Izzy.

"There were two men, mid-thirties in suits, we still haven't identified. There was an Asian couple with two small children. No ID yet, but not likely assassins. And then, a stocky man, early thirties perhaps. Baggy pants, sweatshirt, a sort of swagger."

"Hmmm. What do you know about the baggy pants guy?" said Izzy.

"Name is Eduardo del Valle. We matched his video image from Châtelet to passport control. He entered France on a Venezuelan passport, but there's nothing on him beyond that. Here's the passport photo."

Izzy took the photo and looked.

"Hmmm. There must be some bio material on him somewhere."

"I agree, but right now it's a blank slate. Keep in mind that Venezuela is a chaotic place right now. The country is on the brink of economic and political collapse. The last thing on their list of priorities is a passport background check. We've queried the Venezuelan Passport Office, Interpol, other intelligence services, Facebook, Instagram, Messenger, Twitter, Snapchat, etc. Nothing."

"Nothing? His face doesn't show up anywhere but on a passport? What does that tell you?" said Izzy.

"Everything and nothing. True, it's out of the ordinary, however it wouldn't be the first time we come up with a blank. Facial ID libraries and profiles are growing fast, but we still don't have every human in the system. He may just be from some small town in Venezuela that's hard to pin down. Sometimes the record-keeping isn't great."

"Is it possible the Venezuelan government does not want him identified?"

"You mean an intelligence operative? Who knows," said Jean-François.

"Is he still in France?"

"Maybe. We don't have any evidence he's left."

"I'd like to get a copy of the Châtelet video," said Izzy.

"I'll have one sent to your hotel this afternoon."

"Thanks."

58

Lalo and Galina

Lalo, *aka* Yuri, *aka* Eduardo del Valle, was standing over the bloodied body of Galina Federova - the very woman he had previously protected when Chen Chi came looking to murder her at the behest of Ajax Balaskas and the Russians.

Yes, Lalo had saved Federova from a messy death at the hands of Chen Chi. But things had changed, and Lalo felt loyalty to no one but his paymaster - and his paymaster now wanted her dead. The Reconnaissance General Bureau, Pyongyang's spy agency and Lalo's mercurial employer, wanted the Jens Alders dossier and any copies Federova had squirreled away. Federova had served her purpose and now was expendable. An intelligence officer at North Korea's RBG had occasioned a laugh when he told his staff that she'd become radioactive.

After Lalo had dispatched Chen Chi, Federova fled, terrified by what she had witnessed. A few days later, she returned, perhaps to recover the hidden dossier. Lalo was waiting for her.

At first, Federova refused to show Lalo where she'd hidden the dossier and the copy. But Lalo was a persuasive interrogator, and fifteen minutes later he had them in his blood-soaked hands. The killing had been relatively problem-free. She'd struggled of course, a snarling, clawing opponent. One would expect that of her. Unlike other victims, Federova was no invertebrate, but the outcome was never in doubt. In the end she'd fixed a blood-shot stare through swollen eyes. "Get it done *svin'ya!*" she'd said.

He'd obliged.

Afterward, Lalo walked to the tiny kitchen of Federova's apartment. He blew out the pilot lights of the stove's two grease-stained gas burners. He turned the gas knobs to maximum, pulled a small incendiary device from his backpack, and set a timer. Satisfied, he tucked the dossier and the copy under his arm and walked out of the apartment.

59

Yuri and the Hacker

San Fernando Valley, California

My friend wants to play the second part of the game. Your Bitcoin fee has been sent. A large bonus will follow once it is done. Please confirm - Yuri.

Eric, the twenty-two-year old anorexic hacker re-read the message he'd received through an encrypted TOR-aided, triple-hop virtual private network.

This was getting serious. "Yuri," the strange man with a heavy accent, had given him a second set of instructions. And they were not about just scaring the bejesus out of people. No, they were a lotworse, and Eric was having second thoughts about "the game" as Yuri called it.

Eric wasn't too picky about folks who wanted to steal secrets or play tricks, even scary tricks on others. But what he was being asked to do could result in dead people, maybe a lot of dead people. He fired off a reply.

Don't think I want to play the game anymore.

He soon got an answer. It was a dark web message with a URL link. Eric clicked and a video popped up. A manwas being tortured in a gruesome and methodical way. It ended badly for the victim.

The video was quickly followed by a second video. A person, face obscured, was standing at a doorway, a large saw-toothed knife hanging from one hand. The room beyond was dim, the curtains pulled across windows. The camera slowly panned the room. Beer bottles and pizza boxes littered the floor. Eric's eyes widened.

Shit! My room! He felt the angel of death upon him.

60

Searching

Izzy was back in her room at the hotel. She'd just picked up the Ministry envelope with a thumb drive containing video of the Châtelet murder.

The choice to do the killing at a point where there were no cameras had been clever. Investigators had studied the video carefully but with no success in identifying the shooter. Yet Izzy felt there might still be something they'd missed.

"Jean-François," she'd said, "send me the video from the time the metro stops to the time everyone leaves the tunnel."

"Of course," he'd said.

Izzy booted up her laptop and inserted the thumb drive.

This will take hours, but it's the only way to make sure we didn't miss something.

She clicked on the file. The video showed the metro car coming to a stop at the quai. The doors opened and passengers exited, as those waiting to board stood to the side of the doors. The metro doors closed less than a minute later and the train sped off. As the video shifted from one surveillance camera to the next, Izzy studied the passengers frame by frame, their body language, their faces.

She followed them to the point where the murder had taken place, first disappearing into the blind spot then reappearing, confused as some remained and others fled in horror. One by one, Izzy studied the young men in dark suits, the phony detectives, the phony pickpocket, the students with their backpacks, people who appeared to be tourists, the man with the rucksack, the guy wearing the grey Lobos sweatshirt, Federova, and Jens Alders. It was a slow, time-consuming job.

Now and then she paused a frame, looking for any hint of the shooter. No luck. Calculating the pace and stretch of each step, one by one she culled the metro passengers, eliminating them from her list of possibilities. She found no clue among the suited men, the students, or the Asian couple. She studied the homeless man with the rucksack, the man Jean-François had referred to as "Saxophone Man." He did not appear agile enough. Or was he only pretending frailty as he made his way through the crowd? The rucksack could easily have contained a weapon. But as she counted and measured his steps, she decided he could not have been close enough to the victim at the time of the shooting.

Then there was the man that Jean-François had said was from Venezuela, the man with a Hispanic countenance and a swagger. He was wearing a grey sweatshirt with the word "Lobos" peeking out from under the hood. In the tunnel he had moved to a longer, loping stride as he passed her. Something about his body was gnawing at her, but she couldn't quite put her finger on it.

She opened her browser and did a search for the word, "Lobos." A score of web page hits popped up.

There was a Lobos Tamales restaurant in San Diego, a Lobos political party in Bolivia, a Lobos cartoon character from the forties, a Lobos bar in Maine. She scrolled through them and others without success. She would never have guessed that the name Lobos could be so popular. The websites led nowhere. It was a dead end.

She returned to the video of the stranger and hit PLAY. The easygoing shuffle, shoulders tilted back, arms in a seesaw motion finally clicked in her mind. That walk, that body language reminded her of Hispanic gangbanging homies she'd seen in the crime-plagued Alvarado district of Los Angeles, a city she knew well. She decided to take a flyer.

What's to lose at this point? Get out of the box!

She opened a new window and typed, *Lobos Los Angeles.*

Her eyes widened when a single web page popped up with a URL link to the *Boyle Heights Courier News.* The web page contained a blurb on the paper. *Boyle Heights Courier News* was a bi-weekly neighborhood newspaper located east of Los Angeles with a circulation of 553 copies. She checked the date - six years ago. An adrenaline rush made her pulse quicken.

She clicked on the URL.

Boyle Heights Kiwanis Club opens new hall - Council race heats up - Local Lobos bikers to help with annual neighborhood cleanup.

She wrote down the address and phone number of the paper, closed the window and did a Google search for *Boyle Heights Lobos bikers.* Nothing. She tried different word combinations to no avail. *The bikers must have disbanded.*

Izzy returned to the video and watched the homie make his way through the tunnel. As he climbed a connecting stairway and was about to disappear from camera view, a gust of tunnel wind blew the hood of the sweatshirt to the side.

There!! It was a mere fraction of a second. She hit Pause, backed up the video, and froze the frame just as the hood was momentarily blown to the side fully exposing the back of the sweatshirt.

My God!

Illuminated in the diffused tunnel light the words *"LA Lobos"* appeared across his back.

Heart pounding, Izzy grabbed a pen and a blank sheet of stationery from the bedroom desk, and furiously wrote down the seven letters in consecutive sequences.

LA Lobos...LAlobos...LAL...obos...

LALobas... LALO!

There it was. His calling card, his taunt. No token, no photo, no note this time. Instead, his sweatshirt!

It was right in front of us. Lalo was the Châtelet metro shooter. A cold-blooded killer who'd diabolically planned a public killing and had left a chilling clue to taunt investigators. Jean-François and DGSI/DGSE intelligence were wrong. Lalo wasn't from Venezuela nor was he an invented terrorist. No, Lalo, one of the most feared terrorists in the world, was a damned one hundred percent home-grown Los Angeles homie! And that was very, very bad news for France and the U.S.

Suddenly the false alarms at Little River and Savoy-sur-Mer made sense. They were not jokester cyberhacks meant to bedevil governments.

A cold chill took hold as Izzy considered the terrifying implications. Joy, the cyber expert, had said it. *Apocalypse.*

She picked up her encrypted cell. Should she call Jean-François? She hesitated. Could she trust him? What if in some sordid way he was connected to Lalo? A crazy thought, but it had to be considered. She should have pressed Victor for more when he'd warned her about the "darkness" in Jean-François.

Then there was Bill Powers. He had brushed off her questions about being in Prague with the Russian agent Federova. Izzy wasn't buying it.

She wouldn't tell either one that she'd discovered Lalo. Not until she was sure they could be trusted. She'd have to work this on her own.

61

Izzy calls President

The White House - Oval Office

U.S. President Leyland Childs' desk phone chirped. It was Hannah Wellborn, his secretary.

"Yes, Hannah."

"Mr. President, it's agent Izzy Stone."

Childs rose from his leather chair in the Oval Office and turned to his National Security Advisor who had been discussing the Daily Briefing Book.

"Andy, I need a few minutes." It was one P.M. in Washington.

"Yes, Mr. President," said Valucek. "I'll be outside."

"Thanks."

"Okay, Hannah. Put her through."

Izzy wasn't someone who just called to chat in the middle of a workday. Personal calls between them took place in the evening - sometimes into the early morning hours, and he loved those long talks. No, something was on her mind, something was wrong. With considerable reservation, he'd agreed to tasking her to Paris. The French government had stressed that Izzy was crucial to helping them deal with a national security threat, one that could also affect the U.S. He understood it could be dangerous for Izzy, and that weighed on his mind constantly.

She had kept him updated on the investigation and what she was learning.

"Izzy, you okay?"

"Yes, Mr. President, but…" said Izzy.

She used "Leyland," or "Ley," when she wasn't on duty. But this was business.

"Go," said the president.

"I believe I've had a breakthrough on the Paris assignment. I think I've identified Lalo."

"What!"

"He's an American. It's possible he's shuttling back and forth from Europe to the U.S. I need to find him."

"But there's a problem, right?"

"Yes. For several reasons I can't share my information with either my French or my American counterparts in Paris at this point. They won't be happy when they find out."

"Are you concerned about a possible leak?"

"That, or worse," said Izzy.

"I don't follow."

"The intelligence officer Langley dispatched to Paris is, in my view, a possible security risk. I passed that on to Langley through our Service Director. I thought they should have a heads up."

"Izzy, are you in danger?"

"No. But I'm not taking anything for granted."

"How can I help?"

***

Izzy updated the president without going into a lot of detail. He was a busy man. He did not need to hear chapter and verse. She told him what she needed. He'd make it happen.

After her call with the president, Izzy scrolled through her missed calls and saw one from Liam Cabot.

She pressed CALL.

"Izzy! Greetings. How's Paris?" said Liam.

"Very French, thanks," she said.

"Good to hear. One never knows."

Liam was in character, offering as he sometimes did, odd comments that were impenetrable.

"Back in London?" said Izzy.

"Am, but returning to Paris tomorrow. Was hoping for a quiet dinner on the Left Bank with the dazzling Izzy Stone. *Le Bougnat*, perhaps?"

"Dinner sounds good," she said, "but we'd need to change the venue a bit."

"Brilliant. You're thinking Right Bank?"

"Mmnn, no, more like Santa Monica."

"Ahh….as in Santa Monica, California?"

"As in Santa Monica, California. My Air France flight leaves De Gaulle tomorrow morning at ten."

"Wee bit of a dining detour, wouldn't you say?"

"Sorry, but I have to see someone in LA."

"Hairdresser?"

"You're so perceptive. Want to come?"

"Thanks bags, but I'll have to take a rain check. Let's try again when you return."

"Suit yourself. I'll have a margarita and miss you. I know the best place."

"Have two, and miss me more," Liam said. "Does this margarita shrine have a name?"

"El Coyote, in Hancock Park, my favorite."

"Enjoy, then. *Adios!*"

"Same to you, *señor Cabot*. Bye."

62

Los Angeles

Los Angeles International Airport

It was one in the afternoon. Izzy stepped out of the Bradley International Terminal B and went directly to pick up the Chevy Camaro coupe she'd requested. With a 6.2-Liter, naturally aspirated V8, the LT1's 455 horsepower engine could clean the road.

She was soon speeding north on the churning 405 Freeway. The 405 was a twenty-four hour Mad Max free-for-all with thousands of howling, dodging vehicles and petrified, newly-arrived tourists braving their first Los Angeles drive.

Yet, as batty as an LA freeway might be, Izzy felt very much at home with her hands on the wheel of the roaring beast. She'd grown up on LA freeways and had mastered the unspoken rules of Southern California road survival.

To her west lay yacht-heavy Marina del Rey and quirky Venice Beach with its broad concrete boardwalk, its vast expanse of soft sand, and beyond, the spectacular deep blue Pacific Ocean.

Venice Beach reached north to tony Santa Monica where, as a child, she'd spent happy days sitting on a Disney beach blanket in her pink tulle tutu listening to her mom read dreamy fairy tales, then scurrying to build sand castles with her dad, her peaked princess cap with its wisp of white tulle fluttering in the salty breeze.

Santa Monica was also where Izzy's father had been murdered. It had been a terrifying, searing experience that she knew would never heal. For years after his death, in her child's mind, she'd believed she could will him back to life.

In time, she found the strength to accept the finality of his death. Her mother was not as strong. The murder broke her. She retreated from the world and rarely left the house. That was when Anna Popov, Izzy's beloved Russian *"babushka"* nanny and tutor entered her life. It was Anna who took Izzy back to the warming sand and sea, Anna who told Izzy colorful stories of her homeland, Anna who spun magical tales about the sandpipers, seagulls, cormorants and plovers as the feathered creatures jockeyed on wet sand, then took flight with speed and grace.

In her teenage years Izzy played beach volleyball with friends and classmates, then raced them to cool in the waiting ocean as the sun arced a deep blue sky. Those were lighter days. Yet, there were moments when the beauty of the vast ocean, the sound of breaking waves, the flutter of birds in flight, and the intoxicating smell of the sea filled her body and soul with a profound sadness that took her to darker places.

***

Izzy segued off the 405 and transitioned west to Santa Monica. Ten minutes later she turned onto Wilshire and the magnificent Pacific, glistening in the afternoon sun, came into full view. Waves without number moved across the vast panorama, their peaks sparkling like diamonds for a mere instant, then disappearing and reappearing as dozens of small craft, white sails billowing, tacked across the horizon.

At palm-lined Ocean Avenue, Izzy pulled into the driveway of the red-tile-roofed San Simeon Hotel. The San Simeon was a handsome Mediterranean structure of white stucco walls, arcades, mosaic floors and flowering plants.

She checked in and took the elevator to her room on the eighth floor. Placing her small suitcase on a luggage rack, she walked to the sliding glass doors, pushed them open and stepped onto the balcony. For a long moment she took in the stunning theater of sea and sky. A light wind off the water infused the air with salty essence. Izzy took a deep breath, savored the familiar fragrance, then exhaled slowly.

A sense of well-being washed over her. *Home.*

63

L.A. Freeway

After a quick shower, Izzy donned denim jeans, a mauve blouse, a cream linen jacket and white athletic shoes. She placed a quick call to her mom, promising to drop by before leaving Los Angeles.

She then scrolled to the number she had saved and called it from the hotel room phone.

"Boyle Heights Courier News," said a woman with a Hispanic accent.

"Hi," said Izzy. "I'm a reporter. I was calling to see if I could drop by and spend a few minutes with someone from your paper."

"Sure," said the woman. "No one's here except me. I'm a student volunteer. Can I help you?"

"Maybe. I'm doing a series on neighborhood papers and I wanted to talk with someone, maybe the editor or someone else?"

The woman chuckled. "Yeah, that's Ruben. He does like almost everything. He's back in about an hour if you want to come by."

"That would be great," said Izzy.

"What's your name?" the woman's voice said.

"Jennifer," said Izzy. No need for her real name.

"Are you like, with a big paper or something?"

It was Izzy's turn to laugh. "As if! No, I'm just an independent writer, reporter. I sell my stories to papers. Helps pay the rent, know what I mean?"

"Sure. Okay, I'll tell Ruben you're coming by."

Izzy shouldered a small bag containing cash, credit cards, two IDs, a notepad and pen, her cell, and her Sig Sauer. She asked the front desk to bring her car around. Twenty minutes later she reached the massive downtown interchange with the LA skyline rising before her.

Los Angeles, or better said, greater Los Angeles with its many municipalities, was a riddle. Though the central downtown business district contained impressive high-rise commercial and residential buildings, it paled in comparison to the striking architectural forests of New York, Tokyo and Hong Kong which projected dominion. Yet the vast underlying political, economic and cultural power of the great metropolis of Los Angeles was in a class of its own.

Gertrude Stein had once said of Oakland, "There is no there, there." What might have been true of that Bay area city was not true of Los Angeles. Granted, a new visitor driving past miles of endless strip malls in search of "the city" might get the unsettling feeling of always approaching - never arriving. But in fact, there was plenty of "there" in LA. Just not in one place.

It was one of the exotic features of Los Angeles that the far-flung enclaves, each existing in its own reality, could give one the sensation of traveling from one eye-popping, shape-shifting film set to another. In Izzy's mind, greater Los Angeles in its many incarnations, was a vast backlot of multiple dream factories, each with leading actors on set, playing out well-rehearsed roles ordained and directed by their respective zeitgeist.

Malibu was not just a beach colony but a unique state of mind. It was a self-contained, self-absorbed place, as were Silverlake, Brentwood, Encino, Pasadena, Compton, West Hollywood, Sherman Oaks, and Boyle Heights.

64

Boyle Heights

It was four in the afternoon when Izzy pulled up in front of the small wood frame bungalow on Esperanza Street in Boyle Heights. Located just east of downtown L.A., Boyle Heights had once been a thriving diverse community of Jews, Latinos, Japanese, Portuguese and Croatians, one of the city's oldest neighborhoods. But massive freeways, driven by government bigotry and opportunism had ripped through the heart of the ethnic enclaves, forcing dislocation. Over the years, a burgeoning community of working-class Hispanics emerged.

The bungalow was among a string of similar homes on the narrow street. Close by, Odd Fellows Cemetery with its cracked pavement paths and sad headstones was receiving a funeral cortege.

Izzy clicked the car's remote lock and walked to a four-foot-high wire fence with an aluminum gate enclosing a small lawn with dirt patches. She paused when two pit bull terriers ran to the gate barking loudly.

"Honey, Marcos, down!" said a steady voice from within the bungalow, and the dogs scurried away. A man soon emerged, tall, medium-build, thirtyish, Hispanic with a broad, open smile.

"They're not dangerous, just like to make noise and play," he said, as he approached the gate.

"Come on in. Lupe told me you were coming. You're the writer, right?"

"That's me," said Izzy, extending her hand. "Name's Jennifer. Need ID?"

"Naw, you're cool. You know, it's not like I'm TSA, 'Hey show me your butt,'" he said. "I'm Ruben, sorry about the house, not fancy, but it's my office."

"No worries, Ruben," she said. "Thanks for seeing me."

"Want something to eat?" he said, as they walked up the worn wood steps into the modest home.

"Sure," said Izzy, "but sounds like a lot of work."

"Easy," said Ruben. "Besides, like Cesar Chavez said, 'If you really want to make a friend, go to someone's house and eat with him.'"

"*Simon!*" said Izzy, with an easy laugh. "What's to eat?"

"I just picked up some fresh corn and chicken tamales."

"No way!" said Izzy, segueing with ease into the SoCal patter she knew so well. "Just got into town and was really looking forward to some awesome Mexican."

"*Órale!*" he said.

"*Órale!*" she replied, with her own broad smile.

Izzy took a slatted chair at a small round folding table in a tiny alcove room. Several black and white photos in thin dark plastic frames rested on shelves of a grey metal etagere. One appeared to be Ruben.

He was wearing a cap and gown, a hint of pride in his expression. On a sagging Ikea style bookcase, she noticed a collection of weathered *Harvard Classics*.

Silverware, paper napkins, and plates with blue and red Mexican floral designs soon appeared. Ruben brought two large white ceramic bowls piled high with steaming tamales wrapped in cornhusks. A deep bowl of refried beans accompanied the tamales. He returned a moment later with two chilled bottles of amber Mexican beer, a rim of salt and a slice of lime with each.

"Want a glass for the beer?" he said.

"I'm good, Ruben. Food looks *muy sabrosa.*"

They both dug in with gusto. Ruben was easy to talk to. It was a welcome change not having to measure each word, be on guard for hidden agendas or motives.

"That's a nice photo of you in a cap and gown. High school graduation?"

"No, I dropped out in tenth grade. Got in trouble. But got my shit together and got my GED."

"So, what's with the photo?" said Izzy.

"Cal, Berkeley. Got my MA in English lit. Was a long haul, man."

"Hey, that's really nice, Ruben. Congratulations. So, how'd you get into the newspaper business?"

"I had job offers, but I wanted to write about my community. Just my thing, you know?"

"Right, it's a good story. I want to write about you, the Courier and the LA Lobos bikers."

"The LA Lobos? Wow, that goes back. Why them?"

"Just kind of a human interest story. Saw a reference to them in one of your earlier issues."

"Earlier is right. More like years ago."

"Do you remember them?"

"Sure." Ruben took another tug of his beer. "LA Lobos. Kind of a wild bunch of homies who rode hogs when they weren't low-riding and messing Bloods."

"A biker gang?"

"No way, LA Lobos wasn't really a biker gang. Just a bunch of *vatos*, you know, dudes who'd get together, ride around and hassle motorists. But sometimes they upped for the community like doing the beach cleanup thing. Never figured how they got the money for all that bike."

"LA Lobos. Cool name," said Izzy. "Where's it from?"

"Heard it was from the '60s, a Chicano gang called LA Lobos, you know, 'wolves.' Guess they dug it. Least that's what I was told. But who knows?"

"I'd like to do a story on them. Where can I find them?"

"Gone, man. They just went like, disappeared."

"Oh, that's too bad. They sound interesting. Do you have a photo of the group?"

"Hold on, let me ask Lupe."

He returned five minutes later, a photo in his hand. He gave Izzy the photo. She looked at it for a long moment.

Lalo's not in this photo!

She tried not to show her disappointment. "Thanks, so there are seven guys here," she said. "Do you remember their names?"

"Not all, but this guy here in the front is Chulo, really funny dude. I heard he's doing time at Pelican Bay. And that's Bad Penny. He was killed in a drive-by."

"Sorry, life can be tough," said Izzy.

"Yeah, whatever," said Ruben, his tone philosophical.

"Who's this guy?" said Izzy, pointing to another.

"That's Two-fer, he was best *carnal* of this guy here."

"And what's *his* name?" said Izzy.

"Oh, that's Lalo. Crazy dude."

What!

She placed her finger on the man Ruben was pointing to. "His name is Lalo?"

"Yeah, it's a nickname. They all had nicknames. They never said their real names. Nobody wants to be doin' shit and say, 'Hey, by the way, I'm like, John Wayne,' you know? Anyway, Lalo was like the leader.

Vato's a genius but a real *malvado*, you know, mean as shit."

"Mean, hunh?"

"Yeah. Was always kind of angry, you know? They say after his girlfriend died, he was like an animal. Scared the shit out of people."

"How did she die?"

"It was bad. Gang rape and murder. I heard he paid back big time."

Izzy pointed to the figure again. "Ruben, I'm sorry, but you're *sure* that's Lalo?"

"Yeah, that's him." Ruben seemed irritated about being asked again.

Izzy's mind was reeling. *That's not the man in the Châtelet metro! His face is different, and he looks much thinner.*

"He looks on the skinny side," said Izzy. "Was he always like that?"

"Lalo? Sure. Like the dude never ate."

"Sounds like a guy who was headed for real trouble. Is he doing time, or did he check out like Bad Penny?" said Izzy.

"No, man. But he's like gone with the wind, you know? Heard he took off for Lil' Em. But that was a long time ago." Ruben cocked his head to the left and squinted at Izzy. "Why you asking so much about Lalo? You a narc?"

"No way!" said Izzy, with an explosive laugh, as though he had just paid her a compliment. "Wish I had their pay. I'd be doing piña coladas in Cabos. Naw, just me. I write about bike clubs and he was like leader of the pack, sooo, you know?"

"Whatever. Want another cool one?"

"No, thanks, I don't want to get pulled over. Life's too short to get busted for a DUI. In LA it's a one-way ticket to the poor house."

It was Ruben's turn to laugh. "Man, you? A beautiful Anglo? No way. Cop would let you skate. Me, I might end up dead, you know, resisting arrest, like they always say."

"How about a glass of water?" said Izzy.

"Got it. Right back."

As soon as Ruben disappeared into the kitchen, Izzy took her cell from her purse and took two stills of the photo. Ruben returned with a large glass of water.

"Thanks, Ruben. So, you said, Lil' Em?" said Izzy.

"Yeah, it's what we call Little Moscow, part of West Hollywood. So, you gonna write about my paper?"

"*Simon!*" said Izzy. "Tell me all about it," pulling out the small notepad and pen.

65

Back to Square One

Izzy was back at her hotel. Things weren't adding up. Unless Ruben was mistaken or lying, there was a huge disconnect between the Lalo in the photo and the man in the Paris metro. It didn't make sense. Was Lalo up to another of his infamous deceptions? Had he planted another person at the metro killing in order to confuse and throw off investigators? She thought she'd made a breakthrough, but was now back at square one.

Izzy hoped that the forensics team that she'd asked the president to make available to her might be able to provide additional clues. She'd provided a copy of the video and a passport photo from DeGaulle's Passport Control. She asked for an in-depth analysis of the target. What could they tell her about his age, weight, health, nationality, race, etc.?

Lalo was emerging as more elusive than she had imagined. He was most certainly planning a devastating attack either in the U.S. or France...or both. If she didn't get a break soon, a lot of folks were going to die. One thing was certain at least. "Lil' Em" was quickly becoming ground zero in the hunt. She checked her watch. Six P.M.

Got to see mom.

The family home was only minutes away from her hotel. Izzy called for the car and soon after, pulled up in front of the attractive Mediterranean style home with its broad green lawn and palm trees. Like other homes on San Vicente Boulevard adjacent to the Riviera Country Club, with its expansive golf course, the house was large and prosperous in appearance.

It was also close to the private all-girls school she had attended, a beautiful Spanish Colonial Revival building on Sunset Boulevard. The words *Ambitious, Joyful Learning* suddenly popped into her head, and for a moment she realized how much she missed those happy years of challenge and discovery.

Izzy parked the car, walked to the door, and rang the bell. The door soon opened.

"*Hola, señora!*" said Sylvia, the family's longtime housekeeper. "It is good to see you. Come in, come in."

Izzy stepped in and gave Sylvia a big hug. "It's good to see you, Sylvia. But you don't have to call me *señora*. Remember, I'm just your Izzy. Have you forgotten?"

"No, but you are *so* important now!"

Izzy laughed and hugged the four-foot nine woman again, bending to do so. "I understand, *mi amor*. Yes, I am all grown up, but I still think of myself as Izzy with the braids and braces when I see you. Tell me. How is my mother?"

"Not so good. Most of the day she is in her room. She is having trouble walking, even standing, and she doesn't eat her food. The doctor is very worried."

"Yes, he told me," said Izzy.

They walked to the bedroom door. As Izzy was about to enter, Sylvia gently touched Izzy's arm. It was a caring, protective gesture Izzy recognized from her childhood.

"Izzy," said Sylvia, her voice subdued yet betraying emotion, "she will not look the same as when you came last time."

Izzy took a deep breath, turned the handle, and walked in.

***

The doctor and Sylvia had not overstated her mom's condition. Izzy was shocked by the stark decline in her physical and mental state. Her mom had trouble forming complete sentences and seemed frailer and thinner than Izzy had expected, even given the doctor's disheartening report. Izzy tried to converse with her, but ended up just sitting next to her, holding her hand and revisiting long ago childhood experiences, until her mom nodded off.

It was nine by the time Izzy returned to the hotel. It had been an exhausting twenty-four hours. She took a long shower, ordered room service, and crashed.

66

Little Moscow

West Hollywood - "Little Moscow"

Little Moscow is a small but vibrant, Soviet émigré community in the city of West Hollywood that grew out of the massive migration of immigrants fleeing Russia and its satellite republics after the collapse of the Soviet Union.

No longer trapped in the suffocating Soviet police state, large numbers of the intellectual, scientific, military and bureaucratic upper class fled to America. Many of those who abruptly left their professional lives, worldly possessions and homeland were of Jewish heritage, and did so fearing the escape window might suddenly slam shut once again. The Hungarian Revolution of 1956 and the Prague Spring of 1968 had brutally shown how short-lived freedom could be when it came to Moscow.

West Hollywood was a logical destination. Over decades, a small Russian-speaking community had sunk roots in the neighborhood. Many of those residents, once émigrés themselves, had maintained ties to family members still trapped in the Soviet Union.

To the new arrivals America was a dazzling cornucopia of goods, opportunity, and personal freedom previously unknown to them, even as former members of the Soviet Union's elite. Something as common as a visit to an American supermarket overflowing with fresh produce, eggs, fish, coffee and meat was an eye opening revelation.

They were anxious to establish a footprint in their new country, and it mattered little if that meant leaving behind a hard-earned professional career for less prestigious, even bottom-feeding work. A once respected Moscow physician might be found tutoring Russian for twelve dollars an hour, living with distant relatives in a shabby third floor apartment while seeking a way to re-enter the medical profession. The craggy-faced former Soviet gunner from Latvia, once trained to shoot down NATO aircraft, now waited tables at an IHOP on Santa Monica Boulevard to pay the rent on his closet-sized Hollywood apartment and the insurance on his prized possession, a wheezing, over-mileage Mercedes diesel.

Hollywood and my own Mercedes! Who would have believed such a thing possible in Riga!

The exodus of former Soviet citizens also included criminal elements. Some merely transferred their personal law-breaking talents from one country to another, while others created a profitable U.S. link in a chain of illicit activity reaching back to their native countries. Dining in one of the numerous Russian restaurants, one could expect to be not only among former members of the arts and sciences, but also among peddlers of stolen goods, counterfeit currency, drugs and other contraband.

A visit to Plummer Park just off Santa Monica Boulevard, where chess was the preferred pastime, might find former academics deep into the next chess move, as well as retired members of the Soviet military. The portly Russian ex-pat sporting a remaindered short-sleeve Hawaiian shirt and loose-fitting Kmart pants once commanded thousands of battle-ready Soviet troops.

Although growing gentrification and expensive housing were driving some to the San Fernando Valley, Little Moscow still retained a colorful ex-pat community of Soviet personalities, professions, and secrets.

67

"Lil' Em"

Little Moscow, or "Lil' Em," as it was called, was Lalo's neighborhood and sanctuary, though in that Russian-speaking community, he was known as Yuri.

Born in Saint Petersburg to Pyotr and Nataly Kouznetsov, a professional couple, and members of the *nomenklatura*, Yuri was sent to America at the age of ten to live with a domineering uncle. Terrorized by the man, the young boy prayed each night that one day his parents would magically appear to save him. But years of letters and a child's prayers went unanswered. Yuri never heard from them again. Just another Russian mystery.

The uncle lived in a cramped two-bedroom apartment in a gang-plagued public housing project. He never explained to the youngster why he'd chosen to live in Boyle Heights, a place that was predominantly Spanish-speaking.

Abandoned by his parents and subjected to regular beatings by the habitual drunk, who often brought home sketchy types with criminal ties for vodka-drenched all-nighters, Yuri learned that he was on his own. He felt rootless, neither Russian nor American. Any hope of affection from family or country had been smothered in a child he no longer recognized. Life's only gift to him: rage.

Surrounded by struggling Mexican and Central American immigrants and vicious street gangs, the next several years had been hard, as Yuri struggled to attend school and survive the gang culture of the housing project. At the age of thirteen, the only path forward, short of a trip to the graveyard, was joining a gang. Loners soon became victims.

He got jumped in, endured the initiation in stoic silence, and was allowed to join. The rape/murder of his girlfriend by a rival gang had only hardened his view of the world.

In school he mastered English in a way that impressed his teachers, though he feigned the accent and vocabulary of a poorly educated Russian immigrant when it served his purpose. He learned homie Spanglish on the streets, and the life and sign language of his gangbanger bro's. His uncle's insistence that he speak Russian at home ensured that Yuri became trilingual.

He took on the nickname "Lalo" and prospered in the gangs due in part to his Russian roots, which made him something of a trophy. His zeal for shooting rival gang members while cruising Brooklyn Avenue in a low rider impressed his *carnales*. Beyond that, his rugged intelligence and unique ability to dissemble with police, teachers and all forms of authority was what made him most valued. More than one serious gang arrest had been averted due to his talent for invention and his ability to convincingly lie with such facility that even hardened detectives were taken in.

But time was passing, and by the time he was twenty-three, Yuri - "Lalo," decided gangbanging was a dead end in more ways than one. He'd already been shot. Another half inch and the bullet would have torn through his carotid artery. Life expectancy was short. He knew he'd be crippled, dead or doing hard time at Pelican Bay before the age of thirty.

Besides, he was ambitious and had larger plans. During the years he'd been stealing cars, shaking down vendors and moving amphetamines and other drugs with his gang, he'd also been soloing darker jobs for his uncle's criminal friends.

Yuri was only five-feet-seven, and would never grow taller. Slender, with a smooth face that almost never needed shaving, he was quiet, and forgettable. But Yuri was smart, fast, and quick to anger. When he fought he respected no rule of combat, and tore into his adversary with a ferocity that only bottomless rage could account for. He made a reputation among his uncle's associates as a gifted criminal, a nimble dissembler, and a cold-blooded predator. They told him there were powerful people who would pay handsomely for his skills.

Yuri listened, saw his future, packed his belongings, pocketed the fifty grand he'd salted away from his illicit activities, and moved to Little Moscow in West Hollywood. There, he rented a cheap apartment on Sweetzer Avenue and disappeared into the woodwork.

His ground floor apartment, like his attire, spoke of neglect. Located in a poorly maintained seventy-five-unit wood and white stucco apartment complex built in the 1950s, the dim one-bedroom place had a stained carpet, faded wallpaper and bad plumbing. The complex was mid-block on Sweetzer Avenue, its entrance obscured by immense ferns, banana plants, and towering sycamores that concealed the decay within.

No one had ever been invited into his apartment, and never would be. He always paid his rent two months in advance. The apartment manager was a short, ill-tempered Ukrainian who walked with a limp, right hand nervously buried in his pocket, who would not have resisted the temptation of an unlocked window or door. But Yuri made sure his place was heavily secured.

Meddling with his apartment would not have been good for the Ukrainian's health.

Over the years, Yuri's network of criminal connections in the underworld flourished. By the age of twenty-seven, his reputation for stealth and creative violence had made him a go-to person for the most demanding tasks. The biggest benefit for his employers: Yuri left no tracks.

"He's good. A real talent, and no footprints," they said.

"Lil' Em" was a place where he easily disappeared into the community. He was to the world, a nondescript Russian émigré making his way with limited income and second-hand attire.

An inquiry as to his livelihood led nowhere. His clothes verged on shabby, purchased at local flea markets along Fairfax Boulevard or at Goodwill on Sunset, purposely a size too large or too small. He was not unpleasant with neighbors or strangers, yet their exchanges with the short, round-faced young man with dark heavy eyebrows and seemingly uncurious eyes, were brief and devoid of content or levity. To them he was a human cipher whose bland existence made him no more memorable than a piece of unpainted furniture. His visits via Greyhound to a purported ailing relative in Riverside explained absences often lasting weeks.

Yuri's collection of Russian and Spanish magazines and weapons manuals would likely have changed people's opinion of him. More so, had they seen the extraordinary collection of arms and electronic devices cleverly concealed in the hole he'd painstakingly dug under the decrepit closet floor.

68

Anna Popov

The following morning Izzy had a light breakfast and took a long run along the spectacular Santa Monica Palisades Park overlooking the Pacific Ocean and the fabled Santa Monica Pier. From her vantage point she could see north to Malibu and to the south the white sails of dozens of sailboats exiting the small craft harbor of Marina del Rey moving to open water. Izzy imagined a flock of doves taking wing.

An hour later, she returned to the San Simeon Hotel. She showered, wrapped the capacious hotel bathrobe around her body, and ordered a pot of coffee. It soon arrived in a silver coffee pot with china cup and saucer, cream and sugar. It was nine. She picked up the house phone and dialed.

"*Allo?*"

"*Allo,*" said Izzy. "My name is Izzy Stone. Is this the correct number for Anna Radionova Popov?"

"Izzy! It is Anna Popov! Thanks God! What a wonderful surprise!" said Anna, her Russian accent thick as ever.

"It's been a long time, Anna. I've missed you."

"*Da, da,*" said Anna, her voice bright with laughter. "I think maybe you have missed my *kasha* and *piroshki* more, my *solnyshka.*"

"My favorite was your *kolbasa* sausages, and the way you peeled them for me," said Izzy, laughing, and enjoying the moment.

"Then you must come and I will make them for you, just the way you like them. You are in Los Angeles?"

"Yes, but only for a day or two. Can I come by and see you? I'd like to get your advice on an important matter." Izzy avoided asking about Anna's aging father.

"Of course, Izzy, but you know so many important people. I'm just an old Russian professor from the past. What could I know?"

"You are too modest, Anna. You're the wisest person I know."

"Then please come. I will help any way I can."

"*Spaciba*, Anna. Are you still living on North Vista in West Hollywood?"

"*Da*, still in the small apartment. Poppa and I are happy here. Plummer Park is just five minutes away, and you remember how much Radion likes to go there."

Izzy was relieved to hear that Radion Nikolai Popov was still of this world.

"I do remember. It's your father's favorite park. How is Radion Nikolai? I would love to see him again."

"He will be so happy to know you are coming. He is not as strong as he once was, but his mind is like a twenty-year-old! He complains, of course, but I think he just likes to worry me."

Izzy laughed. "It's his Russian sense of humor."

"When can you come?" said Anna.

"This afternoon, if it is not too much trouble. I need advice from both of you."

"This afternoon? For my *solnyshka*, my sunshine, we would wait all night."

"That's sweet, Anna. Is five o'clock okay?"

"Of course, we will see you then."

Izzy ended the call and smiled. It would be good to see Anna and Radion again. The next twenty-four hours would be busy. She checked the time. I need to drop by the house once more while I can. *The more mom can see me, the better we will both feel.* She dressed and called for her car.

The next several hours passed as Izzy visited her mom who seemed revived and animated. It was so strange how an illness could give way to moments of such clarity and energy. Izzy felt rewarded by the affection her mother had shown, something that had been uncharacteristic of her.

Back at the hotel Izzy sped through a blizzard of emails and text messages from Paris and D.C. Many related to a planned global summit to be attended by the president.

Before long, it was time to see Anna and Radion.

69

Anna and Radion

West Hollywood

Izzy pulled up to the pleasant-looking brick building on tree-lined North Vista where Anna Popov and her father lived. Fond memories from years of visits to Anna's modest second floor, two-bedroom apartment flashed through her mind. Though Anna had taught Izzy Russian at Izzy's home in Santa Monica, Izzy had also visited the North Vista apartment for authentic Russian meals, music and fascinating stories about life in Russia. She climbed the stairs and knocked.

"*Izzy, dobro pozhalovat!* Come in! Come in!" said Anna, opening the door with a flourish and obvious excitement. Anna, overcome by emotion, embraced Izzy and held her close for a long moment.

"It is so wonderful to see you again, my *solnyshka*," she said, tears in her eyes.

Perhaps it was Anna's unfiltered show of affection, perhaps it was an intersecting moment of Izzy's childhood innocence and the stark reality of the tough world-wise professional she'd become, that moved Izzy.

Is it possible I love Anna more than my own mother?

Anna seemed on the verge of crying. Izzy gently placed her hands on Anna's shoulders. Her eyes met Anna's.

"Dear Anna Radionova," she said, "I did not realize how much I've missed you until this very moment."

"I can see it in your eyes, my *solnyshka*," said Anna, her smile wistful. "Come, sit. Poppa is anxious to see you."

Radion Popov soon came in.

"Isabella!" he said.

He gave Izzy a heartfelt hug and stood back. Radion, now in his late eighties, still held himself ramrod straight. Improbably, like so many soldiers who'd endured the horrors of the Soviet Union's war in Afghanistan, he seemed younger than his years.

"*Dobro pozhalovat,* Izzy! Look at you. You were once a little visitor to our small apartment, and now you travel with the president! We are honored."

"Radion Nikolai Popov," she said, "I've been gone for too many years, but I have not changed so much. As usual, I have come to ask my dear friends for advice."

"*Otlichno*! That, I like!" said Radion. "Come, sit. Tell us."

Radion and Anna sat down on a fabric-covered sofa. Izzy sat in a small wood chair facing them.

"I'm looking for a man. I hope you can help me find him," said Izzy. "I believe he is living here in West Hollywood." Her voice became serious. "But if he is here, you must be careful. He is dangerous. I won't forgive myself if any harm comes to either one of you."

"I'm sure Radion can help," said Anna. "Everybody loves him, and he has many friends."

"What has this man done?" asked Radion.

"Bad things. I cannot tell you more right now."

"I understand," said Radion. "How can we help?"

"I have a photo of a group of men." She showed them the group photo. "He is the one here on the end," Izzy said, pointing to Lalo.

Radion took the photo and looked at it. He squinted hard.

"Hmmm. He looks familiar, but I'm not sure. When was this taken?"

"About six years ago, so he'll look a bit different today. I was told he lives here in West Hollywood, and that West Hollywood is called Little Moscow. Have you heard that term?"

Anna laughed. "Little Moscow, yes, we have heard that before. But a very little Moscow!"

Radion continued to look at the photo, his expression uncertain.

"Anna, where are my glasses? I want to be sure."

"Right there in your shirt pocket, poppa."

"Ah." Radion took the wire frame glasses from his shirt pocket and adjusted them on his nose. He brought the photo closer, his gaze tightly focused on the figure. Finally, he looked up at Izzy.

"*Da*, Isabella, I have seen this man."

"Where!" said Izzy.

"Plummer Park," said Radion.

"Radion Nikolai," said Izzy, looking at him with an intensity Radion had never seen, "you seemed uncertain a moment ago."

"*Da*, but I did not have my glasses. Now I am sure. Isabella, look, here, do you see here on the side of his neck? It is a scar. The man from Plummer Park has the same scar."

Izzy took the photo and examined it carefully.

Radion was right, a scar, healed and faded. Looked like a bullet graze. She had missed it.

"Do you know his name?"

"Everybody calls him Yuri."

"Do you know his last name?"

"No, he never said. But I have not seen him in a while. Are you sure he's dangerous? When he came to

Plummer Park he was always very quiet. People said he was not very bright. He never caused any trouble. We all felt sorry for him. Always looked like he could not afford a good pair of pants."

"Yes, Radion Nikolai, he is very dangerous. Dangerous and intelligent. You must be careful."

"Perhaps my friends at Plummer Park can help."

"*Spaciba*," said Izzy. "It would be a great favor, because I must find this man soon."

"I have a friend who played chess with Yuri. My friend always let him win. Yuri was terrible, always attacked with the wrong piece. I will call him and see if he knows where Yuri is."

Izzy leaned over and kissed the old man's forehead. "*Bal'shoye spaciba*, Radion Nikolai."

Radion blushed.

"You see," said Anna, "Radion knows everyone! Now, my *solnyshka*, can you not at least stay for a cup of tea? It has been so long."

Izzy looked at Anna. There was a nostalgia, almost a need, in Anna's eyes. There was still so much to do.

How can I say no?

"Tea sounds perfect, Anna!"

A half hour later, Izzy said goodbye, got in her car and pulled away.

Her cell chirped.

<h1 style="text-align:center">70</h1>

<h2 style="text-align:center">FBI Lab</h2>

"Stone."

"Hi, this is Ed Ramen with FBI forensics in Quantico, Virginia. I was tasked to do a high value facial ID of an individual by the name of Eduardo del Valle."

"Right," said Izzy. "Long day for you. Appreciate it. What have you got?"

"Well, none of our facial recognition programs came up with a match. Our biometrics are coming up zero, and that's saying a lot. Our enhanced Next Generation database contains more than ten billion images. He's not there."

"Hmmm, not good. What about ethnicity, nationality, age? Anything?"

"Well, you've told us he is Venezuelan, and the face does appear more Central or South American. Likely in his thirties. Not that it makes a dime's worth of a difference."

"Hunh? What does that mean?"

"Well, we were pretty surprised by the lack of a facial hit, so we did a high-resolution scan of the video and the passport photo you provided."

"And?"

"We're pretty sure the face on that individual is not a genuine face."

Izzy was momentarily at a loss for words. "A mask?"

"A highly sophisticated polymer silicone mask, yes."

"Good enough to clear customs and passport control?" said Izzy.

"Affirmative. You can thank Hollywood special effects. Silicone masks have come a long way. So, long story short, we have no idea who this guy is, could be from Mars."

"Wow. Anything else to brighten my day?"

Ramen caught the dark humor and chuckled. "Sorry, yeah. We took a careful look at the body, the clothing and the physical movement."

"Awkward?" said Izzy, remembering her own misgivings about the body language.

"Spot on. We think he altered his body size, likely by wearing things that made him look considerably heavier for someone who is about five feet six inches, give or take an inch. Our guess would be some sort of padding or several layers of clothing."

"He looked a bit off, but only a little, in the video," said Izzy. "Would have been easy to miss."

"Right, so that one hundred ninety pound appearance is more like one hundred forty. Wherever he got his materials, they're good. Sorry we couldn't be more helpful."

"On the contrary, Ed, your team just gave me an early Christmas present. Can't thank you guys enough."

"Anytime."

71

It was Lalo!

So, it was Lalo in the Châtelet video! Lalo, wearing a very convincing mask, some kind of "fat suit" and outsized clothes. No wonder the Lalo that Ruben pointed out in the photo did not match the Châtelet image. Lalo was living up to his reputation as a master of disguise. According to Radion, Lalo called himself "Yuri" at Plummer Park.

Izzy was back at her hotel, the call from the FBI Lab still in her head. *Should I tell Washington what I know? Should I tell Jean-François? But other than my opinion about the sweatshirt at Châtelet and Radion's ID from the Lobos gangbanger photo, what conclusive proof do I have that Lalo and Yuri are one and the same? If Lalo's still in West Hollywood, I have a shot at finding him.* She hoped Radion Popov would come up with a lead. She opened her laptop and accessed her encrypted incoming messages.

One was from Jean-François. The body of the murdered blond woman who'd been thrown into the canal dressed in a blue outfit like Galina Federova's had been identified. The victim was an American, a tourist from Kentucky. Video footage from a neighborhood market captured two men forcibly shoving the woman into a van that sped away. The video was poor, but the two men and the van had now been identified, and detectives were searching for them.

Izzy signed off and closed the laptop. *Seven o'clock.* It had been a stressful day. Too many worries pressing down on her. She needed mental relief and comfort food and knew just where to find both. She chose a soft blue denim shirt and leather jacket, grabbed her purse, and took a cab.

72

El Coyote

A half hour later, Izzy stepped into her favorite Mexican restaurant. El Coyote was a legendary eatery where on any given night one could find Hollywood celebrities, tourists, locals and working families genially dining in close quarters.

Guillermo, the tall, lanky host, greeted Izzy with his broad signature smile.

"Isabella! *Hola!* I can't believe it. We've missed you!" He gave her a hug. She returned the gesture with genuine warmth.

"Been too long, Guillermo. Really good to see you."

"Are you alone tonight?" he said, glancing around the lobby.

"Just me."

"*Muy bien,* and I remember your favorite room. Come, Isabella," he said, sweeping his arm forward like a toreador, a large menu, rather than a cape, in hand. He escorted Izzy to a comfortable semi-circular tan leather booth in the Pink Room. And yes, it was her favorite. She'd been in the Pink Room many times with friends and relatives over the years. Always animated and cheerful, the room was decorated with large ironwork structures set in arched recesses. Multi-colored mission-styled glass windows and suspended lamps added warmth to the casual, kitschy atmosphere.

A waitress in a wide, flowing, rancho poblana dress of red and white soon appeared with a smile almost as wide as her skirt. Izzy ordered a double margarita on the rocks. It soon arrived along with bowls of guacamole, green and red salsa, and chips.

Izzy took a sip of the chilled margarita. *Perfect!* She wanted to detach her mind from all the stressful events of the day and enjoy the moment. She dipped one of the crisp chips into the red salsa, scooped guacamole onto it, popped it into her mouth, savored - and wondered why she'd ever left LA.

A few minutes later Izzy saw Guillermo heading to her table, his expression perplexed. He leaned in.

"Isabella," he whispered, "a man in the lobby asked if he could join you. I've never seen him here. I told him I would ask, but didn't think you would want to be disturbed."

"Did he give you a name?"

"No, but he said something strange."

"Yes?"

"He said he wants to know if you can recommend a hairdresser. Crazy, no?"

Izzy smiled and burst out laughing. "Guillermo, you have *nooo* idea. Of course, please bring him here, and thanks for watching my back."

"*Si, señora.*"

"And, Guillermo…"

"*Si?*"

"We're going to need a pitcher of margaritas."

"*Con plaçer!*"

A minute later, Liam Tennyson Cabot, Doctor of Philosophy, Oxford, former lover, heir to the Cabot mining fortune, and master MI6 intelligence operative, stepped into the room.

Liam Tennyson Cabot, you are something.

As Liam, dressed in jeans and open-neck white cotton shirt, strode across the crowded room with his signature unruly mop of sandy hair, long legs and fluid gait, Izzy took in the effect he always had on women when he entered a room. It was more than his intelligent green eyes, or broad shoulders and waggish mouth turned upward at one corner suggesting mischief. More than the undeniable appeal of his chiseled rugby-athlete aspect. He effortlessly radiated an easy, yet commanding presence that filled the space, telegraphed physicality and smoldering sensuality. Izzy wouldn't have been surprised if one of the women had reached out to offer him a drink. It wouldn't have been the first time.

"Just a wee dining detour, sir?" said Izzy, as Liam approached, leaned in and placed a peck on her cheek.

"*Touché*," he said, sliding into the booth.

"Well, you're a surprise," she said. "I thought you were staying in London. Still, it's good to see you, Liam. Honest."

"Honest? Honest?" said Liam.

"Cross my heart. Hungry?"

"As a California brown bear, ma'am. But you're ordering. I don't know the difference between a *chimichanga* and a *chicharron*."

"Bullshit, sir. But I *will* order for you. The menu here is a foodie's treasure trove."

"*Entonces, encantame, chamaca!*" he said.

"Show off!" said Izzy, smiling. She'd never figured out how many languages Liam spoke. He'd just asked her to charm him in colloquial Spanish with the same nonchalance he'd ordered their dinner in fluent Oromo one evening in an Ethiopian restaurant while the slender waiter looked on wide-eyed.

The waitress arrived with a pitcher of margaritas and fresh servings of guacamole, chips and salsas.

Izzy reached across the table, took Liam's left hand and guided it towards the bowl of tortilla chips.

"Now take a chip, dip it into the salsa, add a generous scoop of guacamole and enjoy," she said.

Liam did as she instructed, then feigned alarm at the size of the guacamole laden chip. "It's big. The whole thing?"

"The whole thing. Put it in, sir."

"*Si, señora.*" He placed it in his mouth. A broad grin appeared. "Ambrosia," he said.

"A good start," said Izzy. "Now," she said, pouring a margarita into his tumbler and raising hers, "here's to El Coyote margaritas!"

Liam effortlessly raised the margarita with his prosthetic right hand, and took a sip.

"Mmmm, brilliant," he said.

The food arrived and they made small talk, avoiding serious subjects while they ate. As the table was cleared and they savored the last of their margaritas, Izzy looked at Liam.

"Okay, *compadre*," she said, "you told me you were staying in London, yet here you are. Safe to say you're not in LA to drink margaritas and sample Mexican cuisine with a *chamaca*."

"Pretty simple, actually," said Liam. "We received information about a possible U.K. terrorist hiding in Denver. I've been asked to check it out. Just thought I'd do a quick side trip on my way there. That okay?"

"Honest, honest?" said Izzy.

"Cross my heart."

"How long are you in LA?"

"Outbound tomorrow morning."

Izzy was quiet for a moment. "When was the last time you were in Malibu?" she said.

"Couldn't say."

"Yeah, right. You've been to SoCal more times than Elvis. Up for a drive?"

"Always, madame."

"We'll need a car."

"Done," said Liam.

"Why am I not surprised?"

"Because you know me."

They paid the check and walked out to the parking lot.

A valet raced up to them. "*Señor?*" Liam gave him a ticket. Moments later the distinctive hum of a roadster preceded the arrival of a classic Austin Healey. The valet turned the motor off, got out and gave the keys to Liam, evidently delighted to have been behind the wheel of the impressive vehicle.

"Where in the world do you find these jewels?" said Izzy, as she opened the door and slipped onto the red leather seat. It wasn't the first time Liam had shown up in a classic. "Do you run a dealership on the side?"

Liam just smiled and stepped into the porcelain green roadster. He adjusted his position in the narrow space between the seat and the steering wheel, pushed the throttle all the way, pulled the choke out and hit the start button. The engine sprang to life. Liam depressed the clutch, moved the shift to second gear, tapped the accelerator and drove into the LA night.

Izzy directed him to La Brea Avenue then south to the Santa Monica Freeway.

"Take the westbound on-ramp," said Izzy.

"And we're going where in Malibu?" said Liam, as he shifted and raced up the westbound ramp. "Or do I need a ouija board?"

"Is that what you used to find me tonight?"

"Of course, every MI6 agent has one."

"Lovely. Drive on."

"Sooo, about Malibu?" he said.

"Paradise Cove, swami. We're going to the beach."

73

Malibu

With the roadster's top down, hair whipping wildly in the wind, Liam nudged the Austin Healey into the number one lane of the 10 freeway. The evening was warm and clear, and as they moved closer to the ocean, the air cooled, and the fragrance of the great Pacific filled the night. They entered the McClure tunnel and moments later emerged onto Pacific Coast Highway, the moonlit ocean to their left, the bluffs of Santa Monica rising to their right.

As they sped northwest, the string of lavish beachfront homes allowed intermittent views of the vast ocean. Once beyond the city limits, the ocean views became expansive and breathtaking.

"Pretty stunning," said Liam, his voice shouting above the wind.

"Always, always!" said Izzy, her voice elated.

They continued on PCH, passing wealthy Pacific Palisades and the fabulous Getty Villa high above on a promontory. Minutes later they entered the city of Malibu.

With Izzy navigating, they drove past the Malibu Pier and pulled into a small shopping center adjacent to the celebrity-laden Malibu Colony.

They stopped briefly at a Ralph's market to purchase two oversized beach towels and a large thermos, then walked to the Starbucks nearby. Liam asked the barista to wash out the thermos and fill it with coffee. The barista accommodated and added two paper cups. Moments later they were back in the roadster, continuing west and north up an incline, past sprawling Pepperdine University.

They soon arrived at a stoplight where a sign reading *Paradise Cove* marked the entrance to a narrow driveway on the left. They turned onto the tree-lined drive and followed it downhill to a parking area facing a restaurant on the sand, the ocean just beyond, a roughhewn cliff above and behind them. Liam pulled into a slot and turned off the engine.

"Welcome to Paradise Cove," said Izzy, as she opened the door and stepped out. They took off their shoes, placed them in the boot of the roadster with Izzy's purse, grabbed their towels, thermos, and cups, and made their way to the door of the Paradise Cove Beach Cafe.

"Give me a second," said Izzy, as she pulled aside the netting at the entrance of the cafe and stepped in. A minute later she came out. "All set. Offered to pay, but they said no worries. Let's get down to the water."

They walked onto the beach, the sand pleasantly giving way beneath their feet.

Izzy took Liam's left hand. "This way," she said, as they moved up the beach and away from the animated conversation and laughter of diners enjoying *al fresco* meals under garlands of colored lights. Ahead an outcropping of the cliff jutted out to the water's edge. They rounded the outcropping and walked for a few more minutes. The cafe was no longer in sight. They were alone on the dark beach, but for the waxing moon.

"Here," said Izzy, stopping where the beach became broader at the base of the bluff.

They spread their towels onto the sand, and sat down. Liam poured two steaming cups of black coffee. They sipped the delicious brew, admiring the incomparable beauty of the great Pacific at low tide.

"When the tide is out like this," Izzy said, "it's just so peaceful. People rarely come this far around the bluff." She took a sip, wrapped her arms around her knees, and pressed them to her chest.

"You love it here," said Liam.

"I do. I really do. The troubles of the world seem so far away." There was a wistful tone, a seeming sadness in her voice, and she said no more.

They sat side by side, each taking in the rhythmic sound of the lapping surf and the occasional cawing of seabirds as they dipped and soared in the moonlight. Farther out, the silhouette of an upright paddle boarder silently coursed the open water, a timeless image that added to the magic of the night.

Izzy looked out to the water and the horizon, her eyes lost in thought. Her face was luminous in the reflected light of the ocean. The fullness of her lips, her high cheekbones, firm breasts and silky red hair made her natural beauty even more striking.

They had been quiet for a while. Izzy looked at Liam. He was lying on his back, eyes closed, hands clasped behind his head, his breathing slow and even.

It's been a long time.

She leaned in and kissed him. He let his lips give way and allowed her mouth to meld with his. His breath quickened and she felt her face flush with sudden warmth.

Liam opened his eyes and looked at her. There was a gentleness in his gaze she had never seen before. It gave her a feeling of contentment she had missed. She placed a hand on his cheek.

"Hi," she whispered.

"Hi."

"Sleepy?" she said.

He stretched his arms out, and sighed. "Mmm, this *must* be Hollywood. For a moment it felt like I had slipped into an alternative version of Snow White."

"As good as the original?"

"Better," said Liam.

"Well, c'mon, Sleepy," said Izzy, "Snow White wants to go for a swim." She stood and began removing her clothes.

"Really?"

"Yes, really."

Liam got up and did the same.

They were naked, facing each other. Izzy looked at Liam's body and recalled the thrill of their lovemaking in New York and Washington. His physique evoked classic lines of a Kouros statue.

"Here," she said, her naked body brushing against his, "allow me to help." She reached for the metal snap on Liam's prosthetic hand. "You know, I do remember how to do it."

"Yes," said Liam, as he held out his arm. "And I *do now* remember how effective your hand-eye coordination was."

"Manners, manners, sir."

"Just thinking," he said. The prosthetic hand was now loose. Izzy carefully removed it and placed it on the beach towel. She took his arm and gently moved her hands to the amputation. She was always struck by the contrast between his otherwise perfect physique and the absence of a hand. She looked at Liam, a question in her eyes. *I've asked before. He's always deflected with humor or silence.*

"Liam," she said. "How? Where?"

"Chechnya," he said after a long moment. His voice was subdued, almost monotone. "An exfiltration of a Chechen rebel who had information about a stolen nuke. The guide was supposed to provide safe passage through the mountains. He decided to play both sides. It was an ambush. The exfiltration failed. The Chechen rebel was killed, as well as one of my best friends. It was a complete disaster. Lost my hand in the firefight."

"And the guide who crossed you?"

"He didn't make it."

Izzy said nothing for a moment, shaken by the mental image. She placed his wrist against her cheek.

"I'm so grateful you survived," she said, "and that you're in my life, that you crazily came to my rescue that night in Georgetown when I was about to melt into the floor at that ridiculous embassy party."

"I remember that night. You were the most beautiful woman I'd ever seen. Took my breath away. Broke me completely. I'll forever be in debt to the fool who stood you up that night."

Izzy was suddenly animated. "Let's go!" she said. She turned and raced to the breaking waves, Liam just behind. They waded quickly into the chilly waters until the ground gave way and they swam into the growing ocean swells. When they were beyond the breaking waves and into open water, Izzy pointed south as she bobbed.

"Look!" she said. "The necklace of lights."

Liam followed her line of sight. "Outstanding!" he shouted, as he bobbed next to her and took in the sparkling array of lights that extended southward like a string of diamonds along the coastline from Santa Monica to the escarpment of the Palos Verdes peninsula. It was a sublime tableau.

They swam for a few more minutes, then made their way back to the beach, wet bodies shining in the reflected light of the water. Izzy ran ahead, clearly exhilarated, and dropped onto the sand where the beach was still firm. She reclined onto her back, her breasts heaving from the exertion of the swim. Liam approached, brushing back his wet hair, salt water tracing down his body as he stood over her.

She released a slight shiver, stretched long shapely legs outward and extended her hand up to him.

"Now," she said.

74

Radion

Izzy's phone was buzzing. She looked. "Radion Popov." She checked the clock. Ten o'clock.

Damn, overslept! Liam had dropped her off at her hotel in Santa Monica at four in the morning. He had sped off to a remote airfield where a private plane awaited his departure to Denver.

"*Allo,* Radion Nikolai," said Izzy.

"I have an address for you," he said.

"Yes?"

He gave her an address on Sweetzer Avenue.

"*Spaciba,* thank you, Radion."

She quickly put on a pair of black jeans, a tan shirt, denim jacket and running shoes, and twisted her hair back into a low bun to be sure she had her best peripheral vision. Her Sig Sauer was stowed in a shoulder holster, a small derringer in her back waistband. Attached to her right ankle was an Ontario MK III knife for close combat. She did a quick make-up check in the mirror, and headed out the door.

75

Sweetzer Avenue

One hour later Izzy was sitting in her rental car, halfway down the block from the Sweetzer Avenue address Radion Popov had given her. An empty Starbucks latte cup rested in the well. A folded copy of the Los Angeles Times Classified section was on her lap. Several entries were circled in black ink.

She was worried about Radion. How much of a personal risk had he taken to get her the address? The man called Yuri was as dangerous and smart as they came. She had already screwed up by not protecting Victor and was feeling guilty about having seen so little of her mom in the last two years. If Radion or Anna were to be hurt or worse, she would never forgive herself.

She was convinced that a major attack on a nuclear power plant was coming soon. Yuri/Lalo was the point man and trigger that would set it off. Tradecraft dictated a long stakeout to have the target make the first move. But Izzy didn't have the luxury of waiting. She opened the car door and stepped out.

It was a sunny Los Angeles morning. Small surprise. Southern California wasn't called the land of the endless summer for nothing.

She ambled up the street, stopping to examine building numbers and consult the newspaper she was holding as she walked. To any observer she likely appeared a renter looking for an apartment.

As Izzy approached the address Radion had given her, she spotted a suntanned gardener, wearing a floppy canvas hat. He was noisily working a pair of pruning shears as he trimmed one of the large banana plants at the front of the building.

"*Buenos días,*" said Izzy, as she approached.

"*Buenos días, señora,*" said the man, smiling.

"*Señor,* do you know if there are any apartments for rent here?" she said.

"I think so, but you need to talk to the manager in number one," he said, pointing to the building.

"*Gracias,*" said Izzy. "I like the street. Looks like a quiet building," she added.

"*Sí, señora,* most of the time it is quiet," he said.

"Most of the time?"

"*Sí,* this morning the manager got in a fight with one of the renters."

"Oh? What happened?"

"I don't know, but I think the man in the apartment said the manager was trying to steal from him. They got into a fight, and the manager, he called the cops."

"That's not good. So, the police came?"

"*Sí,* but they weren't 'cops' cops - they were, you know, 'cheriffs.'"

"How do you know they were sheriffs?" said Izzy.

"The car, it says Cheriff on the door. They put him in the car."

"The manager or the renter?" said Izzy.

"No, the renter. Too bad, he's nice."

"Was the man in handcuffs?"

"Oh, sure."

"When did this happen?"

"'Bout nine-thirty this morning. I was watering the plants in the patio."

"Do you know the man they took away?"

"Yes. He's in number fifteen. Been here a long time."

"What's his name?" said Izzy.

"Yuri."

"Do you know his last name?"

"No, *señora*. He's just Yuri. But if you want, you can ask the manager."

Izzy headed for the manager's office. Five minutes later Izzy was back in her car. She dialed a number.

76

Secret Service

"United States Secret Service."

"This is Special Agent Izzy Stone, Presidential Protection Service. I urgently need to speak to the agent in charge."

"Who'd you say you are?" The voice sounded skeptical. Crazy folks called the Secret Service all the time. This was LA, after all, ground zero for wannabes.

"Special Agent Izzy Stone, Presidential Protection Service out of D.C. Put me through to the agent in charge, and I'll answer any questions he has."

"Hold on," the voice sounded annoyed.

Izzy had dialed the dedicated number of the United States Secret Service office on South Figueroa in downtown Los Angeles.

A few moments later she heard the phone ring through.

"This is special agent Simmons."

"Agent Simmons, good morning. It's Izzy Stone, SAIC of the Presidential Detail out of D.C. I'm in town on a special assignment. I need some help, and I need it fast."

"We've had no heads up on a visit. Can you identify yourself?"

"Right," said Izzy. She provided her government ID number and the cell number of Will Bergen in Washington.

"He's Deputy Special Agent in Charge, in my detail," she said. "You can call Will directly or just ring up the White House switchboard and they'll put you through to him."

"Hold a minute."

"No problem," said Izzy.

Five anxious minutes later Simmons came back on the line.

"Talked to Bergen. Just mentioning your name had people scrambling like you're Princess Leia. What's up?"

"A man named Yuri Kouznetsov was arrested this morning around nine-thirty by Los Angeles County Sheriff's deputies in West Hollywood. I don't have a contact at the Sheriff's station." She gave Simmons the address of the Sweetzer apartment. "The arrest was likely for assault. I have to find out where he's being held, stat. He should not be released until I can get there."

"Chasing assault suspects isn't exactly your regular brief," said Simmons.

"No kidding. But he's also a high value suspect and dangerous. I need to find him fast and have him held. I'll require backup when I arrive."

"I'll call our liaison at LA County Sheriff's Command. Get back to you in five."

"Great, thanks."

77

"They Left"

"Stone."

"Bill Simmons again. Your guy was booked at the West Hollywood Sheriff's station on Santa Monica Boulevard around ten-fifteen this morning on an assault charge."

"On my way. I'm westbound on Melrose, be there in about six minutes."

"Hold on," said Simmons. "They've already left the West Hollywood Station. He's being transported by deputies to Men's Central Jail in downtown LA. Was supposed to be put on the County jail bus, but the bus broke down on the 405."

"You mean they're transporting by patrol car?"

"Correct."

"Damn! Damn! Not good!" Heart pounding, Izzy yanked the steering wheel hard to the right in a rubber burning turn, tilted precariously off Melrose, and plunged into busy four lane La Cienega Boulevard.

"When did they leave the WeHo station?" she said, holding the phone in her left hand as she steered with her right.

"About ten minutes ago. I'll call Sheriff's Command. They'll make sure he's held at Men's Central until you arrive. What's this all about?"

"We believe Yuri Kouznetsov is involved in a terrorist operation. Can't say more right now. On my way to Men's Central. Will take twenty minutes or less. You need to tell Sheriff's Command that Kouznetsov is extremely dangerous. If the deputies transporting give him even one inch they're dead."

"Will do, stat!" said Simmons.

Izzy sped northbound and uphill on La Cienega. As usual, the broad boulevard was a bedlam of vehicles moving bumper to bumper to-and-from iconic Sunset Strip located at the top of the climb. Izzy had no time to stay locked in the motorized queue. She gritted her teeth.

No choice!

She snapped her shoulder strap once to tighten, slammed her foot on the accelerator, and swung the car into the center median, zigzagging wildly past cars left and right. As she fought her way to the summit, motorists honked horns, yelled, and made threatening gestures through open car windows.

This is hell, but the freeway would be a parking lot. Sunset's the fastest route to downtown.

Finally reaching Sunset, Izzy pulled hard right and surged eastbound towards downtown Los Angeles.

She was now pedal to the metal, the roaring Camaro clocking a gut-wrenching, sixty-eight-miles-an-hour on thirty-five-mile-an-hour Sunset. Izzy blew through red lights at Fairfax, La Brea, Highland and Vermont, utilizing every molecule of evasion and chase technique she'd ever learned. Her left hand was now buried in the car horn, the high beams on, hazard lights blinking as both vehicles and pedestrians scrambled for their lives.

Lord forbid I hit anyone.

Her phone was chirping. It was on her lap. She snagged it. Afraid to take her eyes off the road she raised it level to the windshield, and with her peripheral vision located the talk button and pressed.

"Stone!"

78

Sunset Boulevard

"Simmons, back at you. Took a few minutes to get things arranged through Sheriff's Command. There's a problem. Your guy hasn't showed at Men's Central, and Sheriff's Command Post can't reach the deputies. All hell's breaking loose."

"Not good, not good!" said Izzy. "Can you find out what their route was? I'm eastbound on Sunset right now. I can't be more than a few minutes behind them."

"I've got Sheriff's Command on the other line, hold a sec."

Izzy's mind was racing. The world's most dangerous terrorist was in LA and unaccounted for.

Simmons was talking again. His voice agitated, his words pouring out in an adrenaline-soaked clip.

"Route, Sunset Boulevard east to Cesar Chavez Avenue then north on Vignes to Bauchet and Men's Central."

"Got it! Keep me posted." Izzy pushed the accelerator to the floorboard and the beast lunged ahead, blasting through Silver Lake, approaching Echo Park as the skyline of downtown LA loomed before her.

She looked in the rearview mirror. Two Los Angeles Police cruisers were tailing, their lights flashing, sirens wailing. Entering the sharp curve at Sunset and North Glendale Boulevards, she pulled hard into it. The

Camaro's tires clawed the asphalt to maintain purchase as the car strained its stabilizers to the tipping point.

She shot a glance at the speedometer. Seventy-two. She slammed the accelerator all the way to the floor and looked ahead.

Problem!

Traffic had come to a dead stop. She wrenched the wheel left and swung into the oncoming lanes, as panicked drivers dove to the curb like windblown leaves. Downtown was approaching fast. Barreling down Sunset on the wrong side of the road, she shot over the massive concrete interchange. Below, the Hollywood and Harbor freeways intersected. Ahead was West Cesar Chavez Avenue. Still no sign of an accident or abandoned Sheriff's car. Good!

SMASH!

Izzy checked her rear view mirror just in time to see the two police cruisers airborne. *Ouch! They didn't clear that traffic jam.*

The towering Metro building came into view. Close by was Los Angeles Union Station with its rail lines spreading outward in a massive fan. She hurtled down West Cesar Chavez Avenue towards North Alameda. Just beyond were Vignes Street, Bauchet and Men's Central.

There was movement to the right in her field of vision. She looked. *Shit!* Her stomach tightened into a knot.

A crazed tangle of police cars, lights flashing, was skidding, barreling toward the main entrance of Union Station. Wailing ambulances, fishtailing wildly, were descending like whirling dervishes.

Damn! Lalo must be at Union Station!

She spun south on North Alameda towards the station. The entire driveway was clogged with vehicles.

I'm going to get blocked out - to hell with that!

She tugged the wheel left, drove across oncoming lanes, sped over the sidewalk, tore through a box hedge, careened into a parking lot scraping two cars, and braked with a howling, rubber-burning screech at the entrance. Terrified bystanders screamed and dove for safety.

She pushed her door open and sprinted in the direction of the commotion. Her long red hair, in a tight bun earlier, was now trailing wildly down her shoulders, her denim jacket flapping. Izzy pulled her Secret Service badge from her back pocket, raised it high in the air and shouted, "U.S. Secret Service! U.S. Secret Service! Make way!" In the chaotic scene, she made out a Sheriff's patrol car, its driver's side window blown out, blood splatter on the front windshield. Several people were excitedly pointing toward the main entrance doors.

He's in the station!

Shots rang out from inside.

79

Union Station

Her heartbeat clocking 170, Izzy dashed into the imposing Art Deco lobby. There was pandemonium in the immense concourse as panicked parents clutched crying children. People had fled to the former ticket hall left of the lobby searching for any kind of protection. Many were cowering behind large black walnut ticket booths, artifacts of the station's Golden Age of elegant travel.

Izzy withdrew her Sig Sauer and chambered a round, moving fast and low, eyes sweeping left and right.

"U.S. Secret Service, stay down!" she shouted to the crowd, as she advanced.

On both sides of the immense hall, rows of massive Art Deco chairs with chocolate-brown leather seats posed the danger of concealment. She moved swiftly from one to the next, checking and clearing as she went.

"He went that way!" shouted a porter, pointing towards the station tunnel.

Izzy looked. A sign over the entrance of the tunnel read: *Metro - Subway.*

Dammit!

Izzy was running fast, breathing hard, her heart thumping. She knew if Lalo made it to the subway lines before she got there, she'd lose him.

"Move! Move! Get back!" she yelled, Sig Sauer and badge raised high, as she weaved in and out of the crowd in the tunnel. Far behind, she could hear the sounds of more police rushing into the lobby.

80

In the Metro

Moments later, almost hyper-ventilating, Izzy reached the metro station and looked at the board. *Red Line, Purple Line, Gold Line.*

Which one? Which one?

The next departure, in one minute, was the Purple Line, westbound. The Red Line not for seven minutes. The Gold Line not for ten minutes.

Has to be the Purple Line!

She holstered her weapon, leaped over the ticket turnstile and made a dash for the train quai. The train's klaxon was announcing immediate departure. As the doors began to close, Izzy jumped from the platform towards one of the cars. Her body was almost in.

"Aaagh!" Her left shoulder caught in the doors. The train began to move.

She threw her full weight into the metal frame forcing the doors open just enough to get all the way in. Grimacing from the sprint and the sudden throbbing pain in her shoulder, Izzy bent forward, winded.

"No! no!" Someone was screaming in the next car. It was followed by the sharp report of a gunshot.

No time for pain, GO!

Izzy placed her hands around the Sig Sauer and assumed a tactical firing position as she advanced in the direction of the screaming. The gangway door at the end of the car burst open. Passengers tumbled in, faces flushed with panic.

"The sheriff just shot a man!" said a woman, her face bruised and bloody from her hasty retreat.

No, the shooter's not a deputy. It's Lalo! He likely killed the two deputies transporting him, is now wearing a sheriff's jacket and has at least one powerful gun on him, maybe two.

Izzy forced her way through the gangway. It was packed with terrified passengers. She stepped into the next car. More chaos. A young man lay slumped against the wall, a pool of blood spreading across the floor. She checked him. *Bad thigh wound. Clear through. Severed artery.* She turned to a man who was standing close by, his eyes wild with fear.

"Your belt. Now!" said Izzy.

Her commanding voice shocked the man to his senses. He loosened his belt and passed it to Izzy without a word. She quickly wrapped the belt tightly above the wound.

"Come here!" She pulled him down beside the wounded passenger.

"You, keep this tight until you can get him to a hospital. If you don't, he'll bleed to death."

She gave him a smart pat on the back and sprinted down the length of the car. Lalo was moving from one car to the other.

He must know someone's after him.

It hadn't been more than three minutes since the train had pulled out of Union Station. It was now arriving at Civic Center. The train came to a full stop and the doors opened. Passengers spilled out of the cars in a stampede to get as far away as possible from the mayhem. Running from car to car, she scanned for any sign of Lalo. *Nothing.*

He must have gotten off. The car doors were closing for departure. She jumped out onto the platform and

swept the noisy crowd, hoping to catch a glimpse of
Lalo.

Where the hell is he!

Passengers were scrambling onto the platform,
racing up the stairways, looking over shoulders, yelling
"Shooter! Shooter!" Fear and panic took hold of both
arriving and departing passengers. People scattered in
every direction in terror, many not knowing what they
even were running from.

Izzy holstered her Sig Sauer and surveilled the
stampeding crowd. *Nothing.*

She pushed her way to the second escalator. It rose
at a sharp angle to the street level of the station. She
took the ascending metal steps by twos and threes.
Reaching the top, she swept the crowd below, and those
on the street level. *Nothing.*

Lalo had disappeared.

As her heart rate subsided, she became aware of
intense pain in her left shoulder. She manipulated it with
her right hand. *Aaagh!*

Her cell was chirping.

81

LAPD

"Stone."

"It's Simmons. Just talked to LAPD Emergency Operations Center. They're up and running, coordinating with Sheriff's Command. They're pretty worked up. They've got two dead deputies at Union Station, and the shooter's on the run. LAPD, Sheriffs, FBI, District Attorney are all involved. Media's going crazy, but beyond the mug shot from West Hollywood and an advisory that a dangerous shooter is being sought, not much more is being released."

"Right," said Izzy. "I tracked him to the Civic Center metro station, so they'll need to set up a perimeter fast. He must have left here in the last five minutes."

"Roger that," said Simmons. "I'm going to pass you off to LA Emergency Operations Center from here. They need more information from you."

"I'll tell them as much as I can," said Izzy.

"They'll want everything. They're already pretty jazzed they weren't given a heads up on a terrorist suspect in their city."

"Got it. Put me through, but like I said, I'll tell them as much as I can and no more."

***

LA EOC had a lot of questions but got few satisfactory answers from Izzy. She told them about the chase. Kouznetsov was the subject of a sensitive terrorism investigation. The matter involved national security and she was not free to say more.

The Commander in charge was neither pleased nor understanding. In fact, he was majorly pissed.

"Who the hell are you? Swing'n all over the goddamn city waving a gun like you're Nyoka, Queen of the Jungle! We've got two deputies down, a terrorist on the loose, and you can't be bothered to say a frigg'n thing to us? I could cuff and stuff your ass in ten minutes on multiple felonies starting with reckless endangerment. Nobody screws with LAPD!"

She pushed back. "I hear you. But if you have a beef, you'll have to take it up with the White House, the National Security Council and the FBI."

She didn't like playing hide and seek with LAPD and Sheriff's Department. And she didn't fault them for wanting to know. She knew they could play hardball if they wanted.

82

Cop Killer

The cold-blooded murder of two deputy sheriffs thrust every law enforcement agency in the Southland into a full-scale tactical alert. Yuri Kouznetsov was now the subject of a major dragnet. A cop killer on the loose made it personal for every law enforcement partner, on or off duty. Bus stations, metro and railroad stations, airports, marinas and ports were placed on a high state of vigilance.

Authorities published the booking photo of Kouznetsov from the West Hollywood Sheriff's Station, and asked the public to contact law enforcement should they have any information on him.

83

SWAT

In West Hollywood, the FBI, ATF, Sheriffs and LAPD investigators descended on the Sweetzer Avenue apartment house. Residents of the building and several adjacent buildings were ordered to evacuate and a police perimeter was established. A bomb disposal team and a Special Weapons and Tactics team from LAPD's Metro Division arrived shortly after.

At two in the afternoon the SWAT team made entry to Yuri Kouznetsov's apartment, found no one, and called an all clear. The bomb detection team, accompanied by a Malinois explosives detection canine, entered the apartment. The Malinois soon alerted to the presence of explosives in a walk-in closet. A few minutes later, an ATF technician equipped with a mobile device designed to detect empty cavities behind walls and floors began scanning the closet.

"We've got something," said the technician. "A sizeable air pocket under the floor."

Several wood planks were carefully prized free. They revealed a suitcase size metal container with two heavy-duty locks, resting in a large cavity of the concrete foundation.

"Must have taken a hell of a lot of time to dig that out without having everybody in the building know about it," said one of the men.

The apartment was evacuated, and a remote-controlled Bomb Removal Vehicle was deployed. With his joysticks, a technician maneuvered the BRV into the closet, lifted the heavy container out, and slowly moved it to the manganese alloy steel Total Containment Vessel waiting on the street.

After the TCV had left Sweetzer Avenue, investigators began a meticulous examination of the apartment. Every room was photographed, inventoried, and checked for prints and DNA. The manager, residents and neighbors were interviewed in hope of discovering possible leads as to where Kouznetsov might be. Little would be gained from the effort. Yuri Kouznetsov was a neighborhood nobody who never talked.

"Are you sure," they asked with incredulity, "that you're talking about Yuri from unit fifteen?"

***

At a safe site, elite members of the LAPD Bomb Squad donned protective suits and opened the Total Containment Vessel. Using a remote vehicle they cut the two heavy locks on the suitcase-size metal box from Kouznetsov's closet, and pried the lid open. The vehicle's camera zoomed in…Empty.

84

Cedars-Sinai

It was afternoon. Izzy walked out of Los Angeles' Cedars-Sinai Emergency Room on Gracie Allen Drive. Two LAPD officers in a police cruiser had transported her to the hospital from downtown. Not a word had passed between them during the ride. She sensed the resentment. They had been instructed to take her back to her hotel in Santa Monica. They did not look happy about it.

Thanks to Anna Popov, who seemed to have an endless network of contacts within the professional Russian-speaking community, Izzy had been seen immediately by a second generation Russian-American doctor on duty.

He'd confirmed a slightly dislocated shoulder, and had quickly reset it. Fortunately, the scan revealed no broken bones. Izzy agreed to anti-inflammatory meds and painkillers, but declined a sling. She needed as much mobility as possible.

The visit had cost her valuable time, but she'd had no choice. Where was Lalo? Izzy did not believe he would remain in Southern California, nor in the United States. American law enforcement was simply too good for him to be able to evade capture for long. No, he'd find a way out.

Her phone was alerting to an encrypted message from Jean-François.

We have important new information.

She replied. *Out of country. Taking the red eye to Paris tomorrow night. Some unfinished business here.*

Izzy omitted saying her unfinished business included a stopover in Washington. Will Bergen had sent her a message telling her the meeting she'd asked the president to convene was set. She made a quick call to the car rental agency at LAX and told them where they'd find the Camaro. They would not be happy.

85

Escape

Lalo pulled out of the large storage bunker in the Valley, and revved his customized, tinted window Tesla. He kept the car there, hooked to a power source and a seven-day timer, to keep the batteries charged to ninety percent. Supplies and weapons were carefully concealed within its interior.

He'd managed to evade the person who had pursued him from Union Station to the Civic Center metro stop. By fomenting as much havoc as possible, then ditching the Sheriff's jacket he was wearing, he was able to blend into the fleeing throng of frightened souls. It gave him precious seconds to walk from the metro stop exit to a seldom-used and largely unknown elevator that took him to an underground tunnel linking the Hall of Records to the Music Center garage on Grand. There he took the escalator up to a streetside taxi stand and took a cab to Riverside Drive in the Valley. He got off, walked two blocks and hailed another cab. Ten minutes later he was dropped off a few blocks from the storage bunker.

Lalo knew he could not return to the Sweetzer apartment. He was glad he'd emptied out the metal box in the closet and disposed of the 3D printer he'd used to print several silicone masks weeks earlier.

He would need them as his plans called for a permanent departure from the United States. His mug shot would be everywhere and no place in the U.S. would be safe for him. His priority now was to leave without detection and complete his mission.

And for that too he had prepared.

86

Situation Room

White House

It was seven A.M. Izzy looked down the long mahogany table. At the head of the table and to her left, President Leyland Childs had just convened the meeting in the Situation Room, located in the basement of the West Wing.

Principals from the National Security Council, the CIA, FBI, DNI, NRC and other agencies were sitting in close quarters. Vice President Stein was out of the country.

They'd been told they would receive a briefing from Secret Service Special Agent Izzy Stone on an urgent matter of national security.

President Childs turned to Izzy.

"Agent Stone, it's all yours."

"Thank you, Mr. President," she said. "Good morning. A few days ago, I was asked by the French government to travel to Paris to assist them on a sensitive security issue. Based on what I learned there, and on subsequent events, I now believe that one or more mass-casualty attacks against the U.S. and France are imminent."

Izzy saw a mixture of alarm, surprise, and poker-face expressions around the table.

"What kind of mass casualty attacks?" said Andy Valucek, National Security Advisor.

"Cyberhacking of nuclear power plants."

She now had the full attention of the room.

"Let's hear more," said the president.

"Yes, sir," she said. She stood and surveyed the table making eye contact.

"The case I'm presenting is circumstantial. So, as you consider what I am about to say, please imagine for a moment, a crime where there is no smoking gun, yet where the evidence makes it clear that the crime was committed. Of course, this morning, I'm speaking of a crime that has yet to take place. But the circumstantial evidence strongly indicates it will."

Over the next several minutes, Izzy detailed her meetings at the Ministry and with Victor, the cataphile, who had sent the first warning of a mass casualty attack, adding:

"Victor said it was possible that North Korea was connected to the plot, but he had no proof. He also told me that the terrorist Lalo might be the mastermind. It was truly alarming news."

She paused as if having some difficulty preparing her next words.

"Soon after he passed that information to me, Victor was brutally murdered. He may have paid with his life for what he revealed to us." Izzy paused again. The room fell silent as the gravity of her words took hold.

The president broke the heavy silence. "Victor was a brave man," he said. "I knew him for only a few short hours, too short a time. He would have been a truly good friend, I believe. Victor helped save my life in Paris last year. It is a great debt I owe him." He looked at Izzy. "Izzy, please continue."

Izzy had regained her composure.

"Yes, Mr. President. When I met with French intelligence they mentioned dark internet chatter about a mass attack but they had nothing more specific. The agent from Langley who was present suggested that *if* North Korea was behind the plot, the attack might take the form of a deniable cyberattack, using proxies. When I learned of the bizarre incidents at Little River and Savoy-sur-Mer, and read the GNN interview with Brad Hollister, the prior Control Room Reactor Operator at Little River, who expressed fear that the power plant had been cyberhacked, all the pieces began to fall into place. I now know that Lalo was in Paris, and that he likely murdered Jens Alders, a man who planned to reveal details of the plot. I tracked Lalo to Los Angeles. He's a Russian-born American who grew up in Southern California. Here are his booking photos from yesterday in West Hollywood."

She passed the photos around the table. "He's the one who killed two sheriff's deputies yesterday and escaped. If a cyberattack against the U.S. is in the works, Lalo is driving it and our country is in danger." She turned to the president.

"That's all I have, Mr. President." She sat down.

"Izzy," said the president, "I know that I speak for every person in this room, when I tell you how grateful we are for your service and the personal risks you took to bring this information to us."

"Hear, hear," went around the table.

"Thank you, sir," she said, as she stood and made her way to the door.

The president looked at his watch. "I have an important call to make to the Senate Majority Leader. Let's reconvene in fifteen minutes."

***

Fifteen minutes later

The president returned, and reconvened the meeting.

"Andy," said the president to the National Security Advisor, "what's your assessment of what we heard from Agent Stone?"

"Mr. President," said Valucek, "could Pyongyang be planning the type of cyberattack Agent Stone just laid out? Possibly. The DPRK possesses cyber capabilities that are formidable, and through a well-connected terrorist like Lalo, surely has access to some of the most dangerous lone wolf cyberhackers in the world. Pyongyang is spoiling for a fight, or some payback for our recent joint military exercises with South Korea, and the economic sanctions which have truly cut to the bone. And, as you know, sir, Dear Leader believes the assassination attempt against him was an American operation."

"And if all the above is true?" said the president.

"If true, sir, it will put the United States on a deadly collision course with North Korea, triggering unknown outcomes. We're here talking about a belligerent leader with a clutch of nukes. But, at this point, sir, without more evidence, it would be a stretch to conclude that Pyongyang would risk the consequences of launching a cyberattack on one of our nuclear power plants."

"Got it," said the president, "so, without Izzy's smoking gun, we can't justify preemptive military action."

"Correct, sir. But I think we should also consider two other possible explanations."

"I'm listening."

"First, that this is a false flag operation being run by bad actors who are operating on an agenda not yet evident to us. A disinformation operation, if you will, intended to put Washington and Pyongyang on a nuclear collision course.

Second, but less likely because of the technological complexities involved, it could be lone-wolf hackers who have no political or military objective, but want only to cause mayhem, or to embed ransomware by capitalizing on a zero day vulnerability, à la Solar Winds, or by exploiting a shared zero day physical component purchased from the same manufacturer."

The president turned to Bill Reyner, head of the Nuclear Regulatory Commission.

"Bill, how vulnerable to cyberattack is Little River?"

"Mr. President, if Little River is a target, I'm deeply concerned. Cyberhackers have been probing our nuclear plants for several years looking for vulnerabilities, and getting better at it."

"Okay," said the president. "Let's say they get in. How much damage can they do?"

Reyner leaned back in his chair and extended his hands outward as if shaping his words.

"Mr. President, the potential damage runs from containable to apocalyptic."

"Go on," said the president.

"Sir, let's assume for a moment that the hackers are good enough to breach the Control Room. A big if, admittedly, but for argument's sake let's say they can, and they do. If they are good, but not good enough, Little River will be disoriented and problematic for a very short period of time, we are likely talking a few minutes, even seconds. Safety instrumented systems would automatically activate to defeat further intrusion and disruption. The reactor would be powered down.

However, if the attackers are very good and they can get control of the reactor, Little River would be at their mercy. At that point we move from containment to apocalypse, because if hackers are able to seize the reactor, it could be brought to uncontrolled overheating, supercriticality and massive explosion. Picture, sir, a thermonuclear detonation. Deadly radioactive material would be violently expelled into the atmosphere, likely resulting in countless gruesome radiation deaths, perhaps hundreds of square miles of permanently radiated dead zones, astronomical recovery costs. Water tables, land, global air currents would be infused with radionuclides. A true hellscape. Sir, Three Mile Island and Chernobyl were caused by *human* error. A cyberattack is a different animal altogether, and is all the more frightening."

"So," said the president, "if we're not talking about Three Mile Island or Chernobyl, is it more like Natanze?"

"Exactly right, sir. The 2010 malware attack on Iran's nuclear facilities at Natanze is a good analogy. In that case, the malware worm called Stuxnet penetrated the nuclear processing facility by exploiting zero-day vulnerabilities. Result? Almost one thousand centrifuges self-destroyed or were rendered inoperable, crippling the program. The astonishing backstory to that attack is that even as centrifuges were wildly spinning out of control, the operators who were monitoring the centrifuges had no inkling of the unfolding calamity, because their systems were reporting them as running nominally."

"And that could happen at Little River," said the president.

"Unlikely, sir, but conceivable, because the awesome capabilities of Stuxnet and its iterations are now in the wild. Of course, there are no centrifuges at Little River, but the exploit, the methodology, would be similar."

"I agree," said Jerry Graham, Director of National Intelligence. "The hacker group known as Dragon Fly is just one of numerous hacking groups such as Energetic

Bear and Crouching Yeti, that have probed, and successfully penetrated, our electrical and water grids - even our nuclear plants.

The troubling reality is that we have major vulnerabilities in our critical infrastructure and bad actors are exploiting them. If the attack were conducted with Stuxnet or Triton or some iteration of them, as Bill says, the malware becomes a weapon of mass destruction."

"Exactly," said Valucek. "There was a time when most of our energy providers were independent and analogue. Many of those providers had air-gapped proprietary systems that made them difficult to penetrate and sabotage. But the internet changed this profoundly. Today, even the most critical power and infrastructure systems are online. The Internet of Things means that energy providers, water plants, transportation systems, defense systems, financial centers, data providers - even your local 7-Eleven - can be, and are being, hacked. We at NSC believe, and fear, that somewhere, sometime, there will be a mass casualty cyberattack on the Homeland."

"God forbid," said the president. He scanned the table. "Anything else?" There were no further comments.

"Okay," said the president. "I believe we must assume that an attack on Little River is imminent and act upon that assumption." He turned to Valucek. "Andy, assemble a working group today. All principals need to be involved personally, no stand-ins. Starting with Little River, every nuclear power plant in this country needs to undergo a top to bottom security review. Reach out. Get as many experts as you need to do the job, and do it fast. If Agent Stone is correct, hundreds of thousands, perhaps millions, of our countrymen are in harm's way. We're not going to let that happen."

"Yes, sir."

"Bill," the president said to Reyner, "how fast can we vet our nuclear plants?"

"Mr. President, we have fifty-eight nuclear plants. It's a big lift. We should order the immediate shutdown of Little River until we can guarantee it hasn't been hacked. If it has, and we're able to identify the malware, we'll know what to look for in other plants."

"Agreed. Start working on a plan," said the president. "I need to have something on my desk tomorrow morning."

"On it, sir."

The president looked at Traficante, Secretary of State.

"Noel, partner with NSC. Draft a letter to Pyongyang for my signature ASAP. It should express our grave concern about reports we've received suggesting that North Korea plans to interfere with nuclear power facilities in the United States. We want written assurances from the highest levels that neither the government of North Korea, nor third party actors operating on its behalf, are planning, or are in the process of, carrying out an attack. We're not going to war here…yet, and Dear Leader seems to be on a hair trigger. But we need to make it clear that any such attack will present existential consequences for the DPRK and its leadership. Coordinate with the French Foreign Ministry and the Élysée Palace. No doubt President Jardin will want to send his own letter."

"Yes, Mr. President," Traficante said.

"And, Noel…"

"Sir?"

"Let's cover all our bases and make sure that the Foreign Ministries of Russia, China and Iran are all aware of our warning to Pyongyang."

"Yes, sir."

Childs looked at James Kilduff, the FBI director. "Jim, find Lalo. Stop him, do whatever it takes."

"Yes, Mr. President. Every field office and every agent in the Bureau will have photos of Lalo this morning."

"Appreciate you being here," said the president. "Let's get to work."

87

Leyland

It had been a grueling day in Washington beginning with the meeting in the Situation Room. More meetings had followed with staff from several agencies, including the CIA. Izzy made no mention of Bill Powers.

That evening she and the president had dinner in Georgetown at a small, intimate French restaurant on Thirty First Street just below M Street. It was the first chance they'd had for private time together in weeks. They shared a Caesar salad. Leyland ordered the roast chicken with *frites*, and she had the wild salmon. A chilled bottle of Sancerre arrived in a silver ice bucket.

"How's Paris?" he said.

"Wonderful, if one doesn't count the terrorists."

Childs laughed. "Izzy, you know I miss you every day," he said, "your smile and your sense of humor." He took her hand in his. "Be safe, Izzy."

She felt his strength, protective, electric. She squeezed his hand and flashed back to the raw emotion of their fights for survival in Amman and Paris. Izzy understood that although Leyland was in love with her, he was still in great mental and spiritual pain over last year's attack in Amman that had claimed the life of the First Lady. Izzy had spent weeks at Walter Reed recovering from near fatal wounds herself. Then there had been the horror of Paris only a few months later.

Leyland Childs gave the impression of a man who was indestructible. Yet it was Izzy, and Izzy alone, who knew the demons he faced when he retired to the White House residence, and the empty bedroom he once shared with his beloved wife, Meg.

He needs time to heal, to sort through his guilt and his feelings, as will I. I care deeply for Leyland, but it may be asking too much from both of us.

At the end of dinner, Will Bergen and three other Secret Service agents discreetly drove the president and Izzy in unmarked, tinted-window vehicles to her tree-lined R Street home in Georgetown. The president, in London Fog and fedora, quickly followed up the brick steps as Izzy unlocked her security system and entered her elegant home close to historic Dumbarton Oaks. Inside, they removed their coats. Leyland placed his fedora on a small table.

Will and the other agents took positions on the quiet street and the back garden with a view of the building. A light briefly appeared on the ground floor of the townhouse, then extinguished. A dim light on the upper floor illuminated. Soon it also went out.

***

They were in bed facing each other. Soft amber light filtered through the windows illuminating their nakedness. Leyland's hand rested lightly on Izzy's thigh. No word had passed between them for several minutes - prized moments, when the daily static of a thousand demands was nowhere present, and only the rise and fall of their breathing stirred the silence.

Izzy gently brushed Leyland's cheek with her fingers. "I've missed you," she said.

He leaned in and kissed her, long, hard. "I need you in my life, Izzy."

"Shhhh," she whispered, as she arched her body, pressed her mouth to his, and drew him in.

***

It was near eleven when the president walked out of the townhouse to the waiting vehicles, where Will Bergen stood with a car door open. Izzy would be driven by separate car to Dulles International for her overnight flight to Paris.

It was the last time she and the president would ever see each other.

88

The Hacker

San Fernando Valley

Eric, the San Fernando cyberhacker, knew he'd gone too far. Hacking a nuclear power plant was a game changer. He and his Belarus hackers had found a way to work around the industrial control and safety instrumented systems of Little River and Savoy-sur-Mer. They had been stunned by their success, never having really expected to pull it off. He had to admit that though he'd hacked the system, he hadn't spent a lot of time thinking about the implications.

Okay, so this Yuri guy, whoever the hell he was, had paid good, very good money for getting his Halloween jollies, the most money Eric had ever seen or likely would ever see again. At first, Eric had sized him up to be a broken-English wannabe hacker. He'd met several along the way. Guys who didn't understand hacking but wanted to play with it. Weird.

But Eric had seriously, majorly, underestimated Yuri. Been totally wrong about him. Yuri was a very bad, very dangerous dude. Now he, Eric, wanted out, but was scared shitless. Yuri had made it clear that crossing him would lead to a messy end. He was in over his head like never before, and didn't know how to climb out.

He'd considered just disappearing, but that was not only very inconvenient, it was dangerous. Yuri had shown up unannounced and told Eric he had friends who could always find him. Eric believed him. Then there was Eric's biggest mistake of all. Yuri had persuaded him to reveal "Runner," the low-rent, high-tech group of rogue Belarus hackers he'd been working with. Eric knew they were capable of real evil. It was unlikely they would reject any request Yuri made, no matter how many people might die.

"I give much, much money," Yuri had said. "How I know you really have friends in Belarus? Maybe you like to make fool of me? I want names. I don't like you make fool of me."

Yuri had spoken those words in a way that left no doubt he could dispose of Eric with no more thought than crushing an insect.

Eric began to wonder if he could strike a deal with the FBI. The more he thought on it, the more it seemed like the only way out. He'd end up doing some time for sure, but at least he wouldn't be dead. He opened his laptop.

89

Versailles

"You found Lalo," said Jean-François.

"I did. But he got away."

Izzy had returned to Paris from Washington earlier in the afternoon after an all-night flight. Jean-François had asked for a meet away from prying eyes. He said he had new information. The two were strolling down a dappled tree-lined path along the immense Grand Canal of the Château of Versailles.

"Well, we know what he looks like now. He is a suspected terrorist on the run though no one has yet publicly named him as the terrorist Lalo. His face is all over the media and the internet. Everyone from Interpol to the FBI is looking for him. He will be tracked down."

"Not so sure about that, Jean-François, he's a chameleon who's evaded capture for years."

"Let's hope his luck has changed. Why did you think you would find him in Los Angeles?"

"I played a hunch. It paid off."

"You held back information from us. We aren't happy."

"I know, and I'm sorry. But it was just a hunch, Jean-François. It could have been another dead end."

"I got a call from a reporter at *Le Monde* last night," said Jean-François.

"Is it about the LA videos?"

"Yes, they're all over the internet."

"Not surprised," she said. "During the chase I saw a lot of cell phones pointing at us."

"Well, he saw them, and he's not the only reporter who's called."

"What did the *Le Monde* guy say?"

"He wants to know what you're doing at the Ministry."

"And?"

"I told him you're visiting the Ministry to do some advance work on the Summit visit by the president."

"Won't buy that answer for too long," said Izzy.

"No doubt. I've also had calls from France 24, BFM, *Le Canard Enchaîné*, the BBC, and several American outlets."

Izzy changed the subject. "You had something else you wanted to tell me?"

"Not today. I have to get back to the city," said Jean-François, his irritation showing. "There have been developments with the Châtelet shooting. Meet me at the *Batobus* stop at Quai d'Orsay, tomorrow, eleven-thirty."

"Right. See you there," said Izzy.

***

That evening, back in her room at Hôtel de Seine, Izzy took a long soothing shower. Afterward, she made her way to the small alcove by the living room. She did a short pour of Talisker into a crystal tumbler, and turned the FM to Radio Classique. She noticed an incoming call….*Will Bergen.*

"Will, what's up?"

"Izzy, the LA videos just put a huge target on your back. How about I hang out with you there for a few days?"

"Thanks," said Izzy. "I mean it. But it might make it harder for me to take him down. If he spots protection, I'll lose him. I promise, I'll be eyes on, twenty-four seven."

"You do that. I'm not good at funerals. Besides, you still owe me a beer."

Izzy laughed. "Got it. 'Night, Will." She knew Will was right. *Lalo will find me. I'll have to be ready.*

90

Networks

Networks and digital media were airing multiple video clips non-stop, showing Izzy, gun in hand, in LA. It hadn't taken long for reporters to identify her. It was Izzy Stone, the Secret Service agent who'd famously saved the president during a Paris shootout the previous year. But the reason for her being in Los Angeles, chasing a cop killer, remained unexplained. Questions directed to local law enforcement, the White House and the Secret Service were met with a tight-lipped "No comment."

Additional digging by Washington, D.C. journalists revealed that Agent Stone had been seen arriving at the White House the day after the LA shooting. Anonymous sources suggested her presence at the White House was connected to off-the-record visits she'd been making to the French capital. Neither the French ambassador to the U.S. nor the Élysée Palace was willing to comment.

91

Chambre de Bonne

Lalo, *aka* Yuri Kouznetsov, looked out the small oval window of a tiny seventh-floor, nine-square-meter *chambre de bonne*, a former maid's quarters overlooking rue de Rivoli and the sun-bathed Tuileries garden beyond. The Tuileries were bursting with activity. Scores of fairy-tale white-tipped tents had been erected for an immense art fair. A tethered blue-striped hot air balloon rode high above the garden, providing a colorful accent to the scene.

The escape from Los Angeles after shooting the two sheriff's deputies had been a close call. The woman pursuing him had almost taken him down. Once he'd made it back to the Valley and the large storage space where the Tesla waited, fully stocked, he drove non-stop to Ferndale, Washington, dozing on and off as the autopilot maneuvered the highways.

In the small town of Ferndale, he parked the car in a remote long-stay airport lot, packed a small suitcase, and took a taxi to the bus station, where he purchased a ticket on the Bolt line bus. Two hours later, he entered Canada via Vancouver with a passport he'd obtained six months earlier by stealing the ID of a deceased Ohio man. Using several Facebook and other easily available images of the man's face, Yuri had used his 3D printer to print out a more than convincing silicone mask with a software program he'd downloaded for seventy-five dollars.

He took a taxi from the bus terminal to the Vancouver international airport, and purchased an economy-class ticket to Brussels, clearing customs at both ends without difficulty.

In Brussels he boarded the South Station Eurostar to Paris, arriving at Gare du Nord one and a half hours later. He spent the night in a forty-euro-a-night hostel in the crack-cocaine plagued neighborhood of Porte de la Chapelle. The following morning, he picked up a copy of PAP, a weekly publication carrying offers of apartments for sale and rent directly by owners. He'd seen an ad for a room located where he needed to be for his next move.

PAP provided the advantage of dealing directly with a landlord, which suited Lalo perfectly, avoiding real estate agencies with all their questions and bureaucracy. He'd offered the owner a princely sum above the asking price, no questions asked, no application forms, no middlemen, no background checks.

The owner had been in no hurry to meet, but Lalo's over-the-top offer was persuasive. He met Lalo later that day. Lalo told him he was in town to do an interview with a controversial environmental activist and needed a few days for off-the-record meetings in a place that wouldn't attract attention.

After that, the owner could rent to someone else. The owner doubted the explanation, but the money was too good to pass up.

By four in the afternoon, the maid's room was his. That gave him enough time to take a metro to a temporary luggage storage facility near the Madeleine where a package awaited in a small rental box. It was the same storage facility he'd used to deposit the Jens Alders dossier he'd taken from Galina. A Pyongyang operative had picked it up.

He entered the code he'd received in an encrypted text and opened the box. He took the package out and left. It contained a nine-millimeter Glock.

Thanks to journalists, Lalo had learned that the woman who'd chased him in Los Angeles was an American Secret Service agent named Isabella Stone. Paparazzi hot on the trail of the YouTube sensation had tracked her down to the Hôtel de Seine on Quai Anatole France. He looked at the photo of Izzy, and noticed she seemed to be favoring her left shoulder with her right hand.

The *chambre de bonne* was an easy ten-minute walk to Stone's hotel. Lalo knew she was a danger to his plans.

That had settled it. The woman knew too much and had to be eliminated. At some unfathomable level, Lalo was actually looking forward to it, in the same way he'd looked forward to shooting rival homies in LA. Violence acted on him like some palliative drug, a psychic form of payback for a childhood of abuse, fear, and abandonment.

92

Lalo Stalks

Early the next morning Lalo lingered close to Izzy's hotel, sitting in a nearby bistro nursing an espresso. A bulky backpack at his feet, he pretended to read *Le Monde* and watched the hotel entrance. He bore the face of a man, perhaps Algerian, in his late fifties. A pair of rimless, clear glasses perched at the end of his nose completed the disguise. Soon he saw Izzy emerge in running gear, jog along Quai Anatole France, and skip down the steps leading to the broad stone walkway bordering the river. He reasoned she'd return via the same path.

He paid for the espresso, picked up the backpack and walked to the quai. He took a position with a commanding view of the stone walkway below. Brushing the front of his thick peacoat with his fingers, he felt the outline of the gun and the silencer on the left side of his chest. He pulled out *Le Monde*, opened it and feigned reading again as he waited for her to return. From his vantage point he would be able to spot Izzy approaching along the riverbank with enough time to prepare. Twenty minutes later he saw her jogging toward the base of the stairs. He slid his right hand inside his coat while holding the newspaper up with his left.

SCREECH!

There was a loud noise from the street. Lalo turned and saw three blue police vans come to a fast stop at the corner. The doors slid open and police in riot gear stepped out. Two of them began unspooling a yellow police line tape across the intersection as the others formed a skirmish line. In the distance he could hear the loud chanting, drum banging, and the horn-blowing cacophony of a demonstration heading in his direction. He heard quick footfalls. *It's her.*

Lalo looked at the police. *Not here.*

He turned and began walking down the street at a rapid pace, toward the approaching demonstrators and away from the police and his target. The demonstrators came into view...***Justice Pour Les Sans-Papiers!*** read one of the large banners. One more in an endless number of Paris demonstrations, this time on behalf of undocumented persons. He quickly changed his route. He did not want to end up in the middle of a confrontation between police and demonstrators, not with a loaded gun under his jacket. He needed to burn enough time for the target to return to her hotel and re-emerge.

Lalo walked down rue de l'Université passing the back of the *Ministère des Affaires étrangères* and the *Assemblée Nationale.* Across the street Brasserie Le Bourbon and Café des Ministères were preparing for regular patrons from the corridors and chambers of the Assemblée. Over quiet wine-fueled lunches of *tartare de saumon et d'avocat* and *gigot d'agneau,* great issues of France and the world would be discussed and deals struck.

He continued down rue de l'Université as far as rue Jacob to the elite *Science Po'* university, incubator of France's ruling bureaucratic class. He returned to the bistro near Hôtel de Seine and resumed his vigil. Shortly after eleven, Izzy stepped out to the sidewalk. Lalo paid the check and followed.

93

Batobus

Izzy walked along the Left Bank from Hôtel de Seine to the stop at the foot of the Musée d'Orsay for the *Batobus,* a hop-on, hop-off river shuttle. The *Batobus* was a tourist favorite, as it plied the Seine in a large oval loop from the Eiffel Tower in the west to the Jardin des Plantes in the east, then back, paralleling historic Ile St. Louis and Ile de la Cité, home to Notre Dame, still being rebuilt following a disastrous fire.

The walk along the quai to the *Batobus* stop had only taken a few minutes. But throughout, she'd felt a baleful chill at the back of her neck. It was the same feeling she'd had earlier that morning when she'd gone for a brisk run along the river, a troubling sensation of some malevolent presence.

It's Lalo.

She bought a ticket at the *Batobus* kiosk by the river. Five minutes later the vessel arrived. Izzy boarded and saw Jean-François standing at the aft end of the boat.

"*Bonjour,* Jean-François," she said, as she approached.

"Izzy, *bonjour.*" He gave her a peck on both cheeks as the *Batobus* pulled away from the quai.

94

Lalo

Lalo saw the *Batobus* depart. He quickly located a *trottinette*, one of the thousands of electric scooters that had sprung up like overnight mushrooms throughout Paris. He took out a stolen credit card from his backpack, signed in, hopped on the *trottinette* and rolled away. Staying on the quai, he tracked the *Batobus* as it slowly moved east toward Jardin des Plantes.

95

Batobus

Izzy and Jean-François kept the conversation light until no one was close to them.

"You said you had new information," said Izzy.

"We found Galina Federova. Pretty awful."

"Dead?"

"Yes. Whoever killed her must be a psychopath. Body was burned, but the torture was still evident."

"Sounds ugly. Suspects?"

"Where does one begin? Spying is a dangerous life choice, especially when the spy has conflicting loyalties. Could be Moscow, Pyongyang, Lalo, or someone else. Who knows, Izzy, you might ask Bill Powers."

"So, why would Powers know?" said Izzy. *What is Jean-François getting at?*

"Izzy," said Jean-François, his voice sounded irritated, "our two intelligence services have been monitoring Fedorova's movements for several months. We know she met with Powers at least once here in Paris, and twice in Tangiers. The DGSE and DGSI believe she was working for your government, and if Moscow found out it's a reason why they might have wanted her eliminated."

"Well, if Powers knows, I doubt he'll tell me. We're not on the best of terms right now." Izzy was not about to share all she knew about Powers and Federova. "Anything else?"

"Yes, we have now identifed the two men seen abducting the American woman who was murdered and thrown into the Saint Martin canal after Jens Alders was killed at Châtelet. Both those men were found dead two days ago. Someone obviously wanted no witnesses who might talk to police."

"Who were they?"

"Two low-level criminals. One Albanian, the other from Mali, but not much more at the present. We're trying to find out who hired them."

The *Batobus* was nearing Pont Alexandre III.

"This is my stop," Izzy said. "I've got several D.C. matters to attend to at the American Embassy annex. I'll hop on the metro at Invalides."

"*D'accord,*" said Jean-François. "I'm staying on a bit more. Best if we don't get off together."

"I'll think about what you said." She stepped onto the quai as the *Batobus* docked and climbed the stairs to Pont Alexandre III. It was clear that French intelligence had been doing a thorough job of monitoring both Federova and Bill Powers. It was the first time that their surveillance of the two had been mentioned to her.

96

Lalo

Lalo almost lost sight of the *Batobus* when it reached Jardin des Plantes and swung westward at Ile St. Louis. He'd sped across Pont de Sully to the Right Bank and picked up the pursuit at Quai des Celestins. Several stops later, the *Batobus* arrived at the foot of Pont Alexandre III. Lalo watched Izzy get off.

97

Pont Alexandre III

Izzy looked down at the quai as the *Batobus* pulled away. Jean-François had made it clear the door was closing on cooperation with French authorities. That bothered her. The DGSI and DGSE were first-rate intelligence services that undoubtedly had more information than they were sharing. She did not want to lose those sources, or her relationship with Jean-François and Sara.

She stood at the end of the bridge and did a slow scan. She saw no unusual movement but sensed Lalo's presence. She allowed herself a moment to take in Pont Alexandre III, the most beautiful bridge in Paris, built as a tribute to Tsar Alexander for the 1900 Universal Exposition. The Art Nouveau design of its cherubs, nymphs, and winged horses was a dazzling sight. In the distance, a broad green esplanade lay at the foot of Les Invalides, resting place of Napoleon Bonaparte.

She crossed the bridge to the Left Bank and walked to the sleek entrance of the number Eight metro line at Invalides. It was one stop to the massive metro interchange at Concorde, her destination. She ran downstairs to the turnstile below, swiped her metro pass, and descended further to the train platform.

98

The Backpack

Lalo watched Izzy walk to the metro entrance at Invalides. He shouldered his heavy backpack and followed at a safe distance. He had put on a pair of dark glasses, a baseball cap and large headphones as he watched her go down into the metro station. He picked up his pace.

99

The Eight Line

Izzy had been on the Eight Line many times. During her years in Paris as military attaché to the American Embassy, she'd spent weeks with French security experts studying terrorism vulnerabilities in underground channels and the five subway routes, including the Eight Line, that transited under the Seine between the Left and Right Banks.

The Eight Line was always a roller-coaster, swinging fast and hard from side to side for twenty-three hundred feet as it roared from Invalides on the Left Bank to Concorde on the Right Bank, picking up speed as it dove deeper and deeper under the river, cars swaying, wheels and carriage screeching, screaming, drowning out all other sound until finally ascending one minute twenty seconds later at Concorde. Sometimes the run was a few seconds faster, sometimes a few seconds slower.

She was always amused by the bumpy ride and the expressions on the faces of the riders which ranged from terrified to giddy. The majority seemed indifferent to the din.

As was the case on all her metro rides, be they a short hop on the number Ten Line as it raced from La Motte Picquet to Cluny, or the twisting, rattling number Four that snaked southward for miles from

Porte de Clignancourt to Mairie de Montrouge, she'd
make a mental note of every turn, screech, minute and
second it took to go from one station to the next.

She had long ago memorized the routes and the
stops of the major lines. It was a life-long obsession with
time and measurement. It was just the way her mind
worked.

100

Dammit!

Down in the Invalides station, the five cars of the Eight Line, destination Pointe du Lac with its next stop at Concorde, pulled in. Izzy pressed the square green button to open the doors, and stepped into the front of the last car. The car was crowded. It would be standing room only. That meant six to seven hundred passengers in the five cars of the train. The signal sounded, the doors closed and the train pulled away.

Moments later, there was a commotion at the back end of the car. People were talking excitedly. Izzy could not make out the words, but the register of the voices was unnatural.

She muscled her way to the other end of the car. A woman was agitated. She looked unsettled, confused.

"A man," she said. "He forgot his bag."

"Which man?" Izzy said, scanning the car.

"A man. He got in, but then he left when the doors were closing."

"There! There!" People were pointing to the floor.

Izzy spotted a dark backpack under a seat by the door. It was partially open. She leaned down and gingerly nudged the bag open a bit more with her index fingers.

She looked in.

DAMMIT!

She leaped to her feet.

"*Allez! Allez!* Go! Go! Everyone to the front of the car. Now!" she said. Passengers froze, unsure whether to comply. She reached to the small of her back and withdrew the Beretta Nano that she used as a backup, her face crimson with fury.

"Now! Now!" she said, as she swept the gun on them.

There was a mad scramble as terrified passengers raced, pushing and shoving, climbing over chairs and benches, stepping on each other, stacking themselves like cordwood toward the front end of the car.

She was counting.

Thirty seconds since we left the station. Another fifty seconds to Concorde.

She knelt down, took slow, even breaths, and with more care than she'd ever opened anything in her life, slowly pried the bag another three inches. She now had a full view of the bomb and contents.

Twenty-eight seconds to Concorde.

If this bomb goes off while we're under the river, everybody on this train drowns.

A ragged piece from a page of the LA Times was tucked in at an angle. The page, wrinkled and torn, bore a headshot of Izzy. Next to the photo, two large silver metal cylinders wrapped in black tape were attached to a clock counting down the seconds in blood-red numbers. She took precious seconds to see if there was a way to disarm the bomb. *No, too risky.*

She looked at the clock 19...18...

We're not going to make it! Damn, damn! Izzy fought to control her breathing once more, calm her nerves....*think, think.... have to clear the river.... have to clear the damned river! Time it to the second!*

Her mind was feverishly calculating distance, time, speed. She quickly formed a plan and took a deep breath.

Lord, don't let me kill every soul on this train.

Suddenly, people were screaming hysterically. Izzy looked. A man was struggling to pull the red emergency lever to stop the train.

Christ! No choice!

The Beretta in her right hand, she raised the gun and fired.

"*Aaaagh!*" The man reeled and staggered back, his hand bleeding, as passengers rushed to him.

"Everybody on the floor, now!" Izzy said, sweeping terrified passengers with her pistol. Panic stricken, they piled on one another three-deep, frantically reaching for the safety of the floor.

Good. They're going to need a low profile .

Izzy flashed a look at the timer on the bomb….*13….12..*

The car was rocking and reeling as it sped through the tunnel, leaning into the long sweeping curve she knew was there.

We're still under the river.

She pressed her body against the side of the car to steady herself and carefully picked up the heavy bomb bag with her left hand.

Her heart was hammering wildly as the timer wound down…*wait….10…..wait…..9…..wait…..8…*

……waaaait……..Isabella McCaine Stone, don't screw this up!!.....

NOW!

She aimed, and rapid-fired into the rear window of the car. The thick glass exploded, blowing out heavy shards. A sharp blast of air from the tunnel roared in, flooding the crammed space with the smell of earth and river damp.

With a mighty throw, Izzy tossed the bag out and onto the tunnel floor as the train sped away.....5..... 4.…... 3.….. 2.…...1.…...

BOOOOM!! The powerful bomb exploded 250 feet behind them with a deafening roar as shrieks of terror from passengers mingled and reverberated off the tunnel walls.

The tunnel shuddered under the stunning force of the deadly TATP explosive as concrete, earth, metal, wires and light fixtures were blown wildly in every direction. Debris was propelled mightily toward the train as it sped toward the station. The shock wave created by the compression of the explosion in the narrow tunnel struck the train as it thundered forward. The train derailed under the impact, and cars toppled in a deafening crash as passengers screamed. Seats were ripped from their moorings, bodies flung in every direction, a hail of jagged glass from the ruptured windows shot like knives through the cabin penetrating skin and bone.

And finally, in the sudden darkness, the last of the debris came fluttering down. For a long moment, there was a deathly silence as the shock of the explosion and derailment numbed every sense.

In the distance Izzy thought she could hear the sound of dripping water. Soon, growing howls of pain became a furor in the pitch dark of the tunnel.

Izzy was on her back, something heavy pressing against her chest. Her forehead felt wet. *Blood?* She ran her fingers across her head and face. No cuts or open wounds.

Blood, but not mine. She pushed the heavy weight away from her…*Jesus! A body!* In the pitch darkness she tried to get her bearings. She located the arm of the body, then the wrist. *No pulse.* Her ears were ringing. She felt a mental fog descending.

Have to stay awake! She reached for her cell.

Still in my pocket – good!

She struggled to locate the Home button. It illuminated.

No signal.

She turned on the phone's light and panned the car. The scene was chaotic. Riders lay moaning and writhing as they called out for help. Nearby, a woman was lying against a twisted chair, her face bloodied, her body motionless. Still dazed, Izzy crawled to her and checked her vitals. *Gone.*

Izzy was blacking out. *Hold on.*

The car was on its side. A gaping hole in the car's metal frame opened out to a darkened tunnel.

Somewhere in the gloom the sound of dripping water was growing louder. Izzy was fading.

101

Oval Office

The White House – 7:30 A.M.

President Leyland Childs was seated at the Resolute, working as he watched the morning news on GNN. A chyron started streaming across the large LED screen.

.… GNN Breaking News … GNN Breaking News … Explosion in Paris Metro Tunnel … Was under Seine river … Possible Terrorist Bombing … Fatalities … Fear tunnel collapse … GNN Breaking News … GNN Breaking News … Explosion in Paris Metro Tunnel … Was under Seine river ….

Childs spun away from the monitor, muted the sound, and punched his intercom so hard it almost flew off the desk. "Hannah, get Izzy Stone on the phone, now!"

"Yes, Mr. President."

Childs picked up his phone and pressed a button.

"Yes, Mr. President," said Andy Valucek, National Security Advisor.

"Andy, watching the GNN breaking news, get me everything you have on it ASAP!"

"Yes, sir. We're monitoring the GNN feed here as well. I just got off the phone with Noel Traficante at State. She's sending a CRITIC to our Ambassador in Paris instructing him to contact the Élysée Palace stat. See what they can tell us."

"Stay on it, Andy, let me know what you get."

"Will do, sir."

Hannah opened the door to the Oval Office just a crack and peeked in.

"Find her?" said the president.

"I've called several times. She's not picking up. I get sent to voice mail. Could be a problem with the signal. Left urgent messages to call you."

"Keep trying – contact Will Bergen, her second, see if he knows what her schedule was today in Paris."

"Yes, Mr. President, right away."

Childs' insides were turning somersaults. He looked at the wall monitor and turned the sound back on.

GNN chief anchor Gerald Riddle, five-seven in his Tony Llama boots, the fabled on-site journalist who'd covered some of the world's most dramatic events, was speaking to savvy, heavy-set Gail Fowlkes, GNN's Paris correspondent.

"Gail," said Riddle, "please set the scene. Tell our viewers what you know at this time."

Fowlkes was standing near the towering Egyptian obelisk in the middle of Place de la Concorde under a crystal blue sky. Wisps of smoke and flame were emanating from somewhere along a concrete structure above the metro line.

Behind, one could see a small army of police, first responders, soldiers with automatic weapons, firetrucks, *sapeurs-pompiers*, a large bomb disposal vehicle, scores of reporters, satellite dishes, and video cameras on tripods.

Dozens of gurneys were being lined up end to end for expected victims. Beyond the long police cordon, hundreds looked on, transfixed by the scale of the drama.

"Jerry, as you can see behind me," said Fowlkes, "there has been a massive response by the French government to this horrific event, a clear indication of the severity of the blast."

"Gail, what can you tell us about the explosion?"

"Very little at this point, Gerald. Authorities have not said what caused the blast, but there are unconfirmed reports that given the deafening sound which shook buildings in the area, it must have been a large explosive device. As you can see behind me, a building across the boulevard is now fully engulfed in flames. How, where, what kind of an explosive, if there was one, we just don't know yet. One source just told me that the scene below in the tunnel is chaotic and horrifying. A press conference is scheduled within the hour."

Hannah was in the doorway again, signaling to the president. He pressed mute and turned.

"Yes, Hannah."

"Andy Valucek, line two, sir."

Childs punched the button on his console. "Andy, what have you got?"

"High confidence it was a bomb, sir. We've been monitoring French intelligence sources."

"Damned awful," said Childs.

He saw Hannah waving to him at the door again.

"Andy, hold a moment….Yes, Hannah?"

"Still no luck, sir. Will Bergen says she was spending most days at the French Foreign Ministry. It's across the street from the Invalides metro station."

"Got it, Hannah. Keep trying…Andy, get State to send an inquiry to the French Foreign Minister. See if anyone knows where she is."

"Yes, Mr. President."

A few moments later Childs' intercom light was flashing.

"Yes, Hannah."

"Sir, it's Director Kilduff."

"Andy, got to go, I've got Kilduff on the other line...Put him through, Hannah."

The phone light blinked. "Yes, Jim."

"Mr. President, we're on the Paris bombing. Just offered our French counterparts all forensic and investigative capabilities of the Bureau."

"Good move, Jim. Sounds like a bad situation."

"Must be a nightmare in that tunnel, sir. So far, looks like it hasn't flooded."

"Well, that's one blessing. Let's hope their luck holds."

"Sir, one more thing. We may have a break in the Lalo investigation. Want to brief you as soon as you have a few minutes."

"Excellent, Jim, good work. How soon can you get here? We'll need a couple of other folks in the room."

"Give me twenty, sir. On my way."

Childs hung up and buzzed Hannah.

"Hannah, Jim Kilduff will be here soon. Push the schedule. Get him in here as soon as he arrives. Tell Andy and the vice president I'll need them here."

"Yes, Mr. President, will do. And, sir, what should I tell the business executives in the Roosevelt Room who are scheduled to meet with you in a few minutes?"

"Cancel and reschedule, Hannah. Clear the rest of the day's appointments. And Hannah, hold everything for the next few minutes. I need some undisturbed time. I trust you to interrupt if it's a must-take call."

"Yes, Mr. President."

Childs sank deep into his chair. He was deeply worried about Izzy. Was she on that metro? Was she injured? Worse? She wasn't picking up her calls. That wasn't like Izzy. *Where is she? I never should have agreed to the French government's request for her help. It was a mistake.*

102

"Here, *madame*"

"Here, *madame*."

Hands were reaching down to Izzy through a gaping hole in the toppled car. Paris's *sapeurs-pompiers* were on the side of the overturned metro wagons pulling riders from the wreckage. Amidst rising pools of water, large LED floodlights mounted on tripods were now illuminating the tunnel and the area around the car. She reached up to the outstretched arms of the firefighters.

"*Merci*," she said, as they hoisted her out.

In the hour it had taken rescuers to make their way into the tunnel and assess the wreckage, Izzy had moved through the crushed debris, reassuring victims in a calm voice that the worst was over, that help would soon arrive, that they'd be alright. Other than a very sore left shoulder, and mild shock, she was uninjured.

She helped where she could. Some riders appeared okay physically, but so traumatized they could only nod in answer to her questions. Others, moaning, bleeding heavily, had major injuries.

She instructed the able on stemming the bleeding and making slings for those who could not help themselves. Several passengers were motionless. They were gone.

Ten minutes after she was pulled from the car, she was on the station platform being evaluated by SAMU medical staff. The entire area had been transformed into a gigantic triage area that extended from the platform up the stairs to the main concourse.

Teams of medical personnel moved swiftly from victim to victim, evaluating their vital signs, and transporting them to the immense convoy of ambulances queued above ground at Place de la Concorde.

Those who'd succumbed to their injuries were moved to a separate area. Gendarmes, weapons at the ready, accompanied the responders as they moved from victim to victim, watchful for any sign of a perpetrator among them.

The SAMU soon cleared Izzy, and she remained behind to speak with investigators. She identified herself, and provided a complete accounting of what she'd seen and done, but did not mention the photo in the bag, or that she'd been the target of the bomb. That would come later. Right now, her most urgent priority was finding the bomber - finding Lalo.

She checked her cell. There were multiple text messages and missed phone calls from the White House, Jean-François, Liam, Will, Powers, and others. It was clear they were alarmed by their inability to reach her in the aftermath of the bombing. She'd get back to them. She knew who she would call first.

103

Hannah

The White House – Oval Office

"Hannah Wellborn."

"Hannah, it's Izzy Stone."

"Agent Stone, thank goodness!" said Hannah. "Hold on."

"Mr. President, it's Agent Stone."

"Put her through!...Izzy?"

"Leyland, I'm okay, I'm okay."

"Thank God. Were you on that metro?"

"I was, but I'm good. Bit shaken up, nothing serious."

"Intelligence is reporting a bomb."

"It was a bomb. I managed to get it out of the train. Was powerful, likely TATP. Derailed the cars. Many injuries, some fatalities."

"Too close, Izzy, too goddam close! I need you here out of harm's way. That's it, I'm arranging immediate military transport."

"Leyland, I can feel him. I can get him. If he disappears, he'll be free to commit even worse murder. He's plotting something truly awful. You know that."

"Izzy...I...I just couldn't handle losing you too."

"That's not going to happen, Leyland. You know me, no one's taking me down."

"I know, I know, but...."

"I need to do this, Leyland. Trust me. I'll be with you soon."

There was a long moment of silence. Childs sighed.

"Understand. Be safe and God be with you, Izzy."

104

Good News

Oval Office

"Mr. President," said James Kilduff, Director of the FBI, "we've had a promising development in the hunt for Lalo."

Kilduff was sitting in the Oval Office alongside Vice President Isaac Stein, and National Security Advisor, Andy Valucek.

"We could use some good news, Jim. What have you got?"

"Yes, sir. Two days ago, our field office in Kansas City received an email from an individual who identified himself only as Eric. He said he had valuable information relating to the Little River and Savoy-sur-Mer nuclear plants. The email was forwarded to us. We were skeptical of course, but the details he provided seem to square up with what we know about both shutdowns."

"Excellent," said the president. "Have you been able to interview him?"

"No, Mr. President. Haven't even located him yet. He's very elusive, uses encryption, and multi-hop concealment. He said he would give us forty-eight hours to confirm the information he provided, and would re-contact us. If he does, we may be able to trace back to him."

“Good work, Jim. Keep digging. If this Eric is for real, we might be able to find out what is going on. Clearly, something terrible is in the works, and we have to stop it.”

“On it twenty-four seven, sir.”

105

Le Monde

Attentat Terroriste Dans le Metro!

Quatorze morts, plusieurs blessés!

The headline in *Le Monde* was only one of scores of international stories covering the bomb on the Eight Line in Paris. Commuters from the train, still in shock, were recounting events with conflicting details, so it was difficult to sort out the truth. A man had left a suspicious bag on the train. No,a woman with a gun had brought the bag, threatened to kill everybody, and had shot an innocent passenger who was just trying to help. A woman had thrown the bomb out the window and saved lives. Others said the shooter was a man not a woman. No, there were several shooters.

What was certain was that an explosive had derailed the train, causing several fatalities and many injuries. A massive police, military and medical response had descended on Place de la Concorde as investigators and anti-terrorism specialists secured the station. They coordinated treating the injured, removing the dead, interviewing witnesses, and conducted a meticulous forensic investigation of the scene. Several fissures in the tunnel under the river were leaking dangerously and were being re-sealed. Fortunately, the bomb had not detonated until a few seconds after the train had completed its transit under the river. The damage to the tunnel had been severe, but the structure under the river had held.

The government launched an unprecedented dragnet. No one would rest until the bomber had been found. Video feeds from the metro station at Invalides quickly provided images of the suspect, but a hoodie, large headphones and sunglasses made ID difficult.

Shopkeepers in the neighborhood of the Invalides station were asked to make video from their own cameras available.

City surveillance cameras immediately began downloading video of the public areas. They would not find much that was helpful. The bomber had taken every precaution to conceal his identity. He'd avoided exposing his face in the station and in public areas above. He'd managed to enter an underground parking lot on the Champs Élysées, and had disappeared.

106

Palais-Royal

"It's a miracle the bomb didn't go off while the train was still under the river," said Jean-François. "You were very, very lucky, Izzy."

They had chosen a table at a small café looking out to the flowered gardens and large fountain of Palais-Royal, just a short walk from the Louvre. Two mid-sized steaming china pots of Darjeeling tea had just been brought to their table. Honey, small chocolates and an assortment of cookies rested on a stone-white plate next to the teapots.

"Luck was part of it," she said, as she poured her tea, "but I know that tunnel and route like the back of my hand. Was pretty sure about the time and distance. Still, you're right. I did catch some major luck. The train can sometimes take a few seconds longer. If that had happened, we would have been finished for sure. Whoever made the bomb miscalculated, and assumed we'd still be under the river when it detonated. Innocent people died, and that's a tragedy."

"The bomb was for you, Izzy. You and I know it was Lalo."

"I don't know that," she said. "It could have been an Islamist terrorist, or some right-wing group, we just don't know."

107

The Hacker

THE VALLEY DAILY

Local News

- *WhopBurger chain expands to Thousand Oaks*
- *Governor blasts Washington*
- *Valley man, cyberhacker with troubled past, found dead
  Police say victim likely took own life*
- *Drug arrests up*

108

Kilduff

Oval Office

"Mr. President," said the FBI Director, "since our meeting a few days ago, we have good and bad news on the hacker who contacted us."

"Bad news first, Jim," said the president. "Hate bad news on the back end."

"Right. We found the hacker named Eric, but he's dead. Real name was Bradford Waite, twenty-six, long time hacker. Very good, but always worked the wrong side of the street. We sent him up for a year for hacking banks and the NSA. He got out and apparently picked up where he'd left off. Our Cyber Command people were able to trace his email. That led us to other information, including an address."

"Real waste of his talents," said Childs.

"We dispatched agents to the location in the San Fernando Valley, but he was gone. Local authorities say he committed suicide, though frankly, given what we know about what he was into, we have serious doubts."

"No luck, then?" said Childs.

"Not quite, Mr. President. That's where the good news comes in. We got a call from one of Eric's buddies, a guy who works at an In-N-Out burger place in the Valley. He told us Eric had asked him to hold onto a flash drive. The guy panicked when he heard about Eric.

Got scared. Didn't want to be keeping something that could get him killed. Gave it to us. The drive was mostly encrypted, but we were able to access several files. Proved to be very valuable."

"Yes?"

"We believe we've identified a cell of zero day hackers in Belarus who were working with 'Eric' Waite. They go by the name of 'Runner,' and operate out of an office complex in Minsk. They are zero day hackers, guns for hire, very good, and always on the move. Destructive as hell. We're working with partners in the region to track them down. We will use every human and technical asset available to us to locate them and interdict."

The president fixed a cold look on Kilduff. "Jim, I don't, and will not often, say these words: find them. If necessary, take them out. If we don't stop them, we will have a lot of dead Americans to answer for."

"Understood, Mr. President."

109

Showdown

Paris

This could be the day.

Izzy was up early. There was a long report to prepare, but her mind was very focused on Lalo. He had tried to kill her. He'd try again. He was stalking her, waiting for the right moment. She needed to make sure she baited him enough to bring him close. She'd provide the opportunity, then either trap him and keep him alive for questioning, or finish him off. Unless, of course, he finished her off first.

One way or the other, they were now at the end game. Lalo was a masterful evader and destructor. She'd have to utilize every hunt and kill and self-preservation skill she'd ever learned. It was almost eleven when Izzy closed her laptop. *Okay, Izzy. It's showtime!*

The immense art fair at the Tuileries was the venue she had chosen to draw out Lalo. She knew that security would be extremely tight. After the metro bombing, the city was at the highest state of alert. No weapon, big or small, gun, or explosive would likely make it through the metal detectors and physical searches that attendees entering the Tuileries would be subjected to. *At least he won't have a firearm on him.*

She dressed casually in jeans, half boots with a hardened heel, lavender blouse and camel colored tweed jacket. She picked up the Sig Sauer, checked the chamber and the magazine. It was a weapon so much a part of her life, it was almost an extension of her body. It had saved her life more than once, and when she wrapped her hand around the grip, she felt complete and confident.

She looked out to the Tuileries just beyond the river. Long lines were forming at the western gate as people streamed across Place de la Concorde on their way to the opening day of the art fair. She took one last look at the Sig Sauer, opened the carrying case, carefully put the gun in, closed the lid, spun the lock, and left it behind.

110

Jardin des Tuileries

Lalo watched Izzy walk out of the hotel. She was casually dressed, seemingly relaxed.

He followed from a safe distance, the Glock in the right hand pocket of his jacket, a cap with the name of a popular French soccer team on his head. The polymer mask he was wearing was his last. He was hoping for a quick shot as she made her way down Quai Anatole France, but the crowd of pedestrians, weaving cyclists and zipping *trottinettes* made that problematic.

Izzy walked across Pont de la Concorde then toward the *Fer à Cheval* entrance to the immense Tuileries gardens. A security checkpoint was in place at the gates to the garden. Beret-wearing soldiers with automatic weapons stood watchfully as visitors' bags and bodies were searched.

Lalo stopped. There was no way he could enter the garden with a nine-millimeter Glock in his pocket. *Not enough time to return to the chambre de bonne. I'll lose her.*

He turned and surveyed the octagon-shaped Place de la Concorde. He spotted a line of trees bordering the Champs Élysées boulevard off to the west. He walked briskly across the square to a point among the trees that provided some concealment.

Bending down as if to lace his shoes, he pushed the Glock into the soft dirt at the foot of a tree. It would require a good cleaning later.

Satisfied it was not visible, he walked across the broad square past the tall Luxor Obelisk, and entered the Tuileries. He carefully scanned the crowds as he made his way deeper into the gardens but did not see Izzy. It was near noon. Animated throngs of visitors were threading their way through the improvised sun-washed, white-tented village. Large sculptures, oil and pastel paintings, unusual jewelry, antique chests, clocks, chairs, tables, mirrors, china and silverware were on display and offered for sale.

The outdoor tree-shaded restaurants were already filled to capacity with diners enjoying their dishes, raising wine-filled glasses, celebrating the festive atmosphere. Other food vendors working from kiosks were selling burgers, pizzas, crepes, gyros, soft drinks, beer, and wine.

Lalo began walking east in the direction of the three wings of the immense Louvre, the Pei Pyramid looming ahead. Near the Grand Bassin Rond, the giant blue-striped hot-air balloon, its body secured by nylon tethers, was about to lift off. Soon the balloon would be aloft, its passengers thrilled by the view as it rose to three hundred feet then slowly returned to earth.

111

In the Tent

Izzy stepped into one of the white-tipped tents filled with still life paintings, and large oil landscapes. The art dealer approached. He introduced himself and began describing the works, their provenance, the painters, their uniqueness. Izzy listened with feigned interest as she kept an eye on the passing crowds.

The dealer was pointing out a vague reference to the Barbizon School in one of the landscapes when Izzy's attention was drawn to unusual movement in a cluster of people making their way toward the Louvre. It had only been a momentary glance, but the posture of the figure - leaning slightly back, the suggestion of a loping shuffle, shoulders moving as if arms were swinging - was enough.

It's Lalo, with his homie body language.

She said "*merci*" to the art dealer, and exited the tent. She slipped behind a tall couple as they moved in the same direction, watchful as Lalo moved ahead. Instinctively, she brushed her right hand against her jacket then quickly remembered she'd left the Sig Sauer at the hotel.

Okay. This is it. She picked up the pace.

112

Lalo Prepares

Lalo still hadn't spotted Izzy, but guessed that now he was the hunted prey. Stone was close. Los Angeles had taught him she knew how to follow and track. He quickened his step trying to keep a low profile, and headed toward one of the large outdoor brasseries located in a thick stand of trees. It was busy. Waiters moved swiftly from table to table taking orders and rushing to the open-air kitchen where chefs busied themselves preparing the dishes with well-honed efficiency.

As he passed a table that had not yet been cleared, Lalo grabbed a grease-stained knife, slipped it under his shirtsleeve, and walked to a tall, thick-trunk sycamore along the path. He stopped, slipped out of view of the path, and stood motionless, barely breathing, almost disappearing into the giant tree. He withdrew the knife.

113

Attack!

Izzy had lost sight of Lalo. She continued walking toward the Grand Bassin Rond, scanning left and right. As she passed the tree line of a sprawling outdoor brasserie, there was a sudden movement on the left of her peripheral vision. Reflexively, she stepped to the right.

"Aaagh!"

A sharp pain shot through her back as the blade of the steak knife, intended for her neck, tore into her left shoulder. She spun to her right, pivoting on her left foot, and delivered a powerful upper blow with her right leg.

WHAM!

It connected with Lalo's right temple, snapping his head to the side. She followed with two lightning rabbit kicks to his face. Lalo staggered, blood spurting from his nose. The blows were brutal, but Lalo was a force of nature. He regained his balance instantly and attacked with renewed ferocity, coming at her with slashing movements of the knife. Izzy delivered a foot strike to his groin, then a powerful hand chop to his wrist, sending the knife flying. He reeled, but came roaring back at her with demonic fury, and kicked the side of her right knee with such force she lost her balance and fell backwards. He lunged as her body slammed to the ground.

"Oooghh!"

Lalo threw his full weight onto her upper body, pinning her to the ground. His build was lean, yet his strength seemed superhuman. Izzy delivered a volley of fist blows to Lalo's right kidney. He didn't flinch. Instead, he brutally pounded her bloodied left shoulder again and again.

"Uungh, uunngh!"

With boltlike speed Lalo clasped his left hand around her neck and tightened like a closing vise. Izzy couldn't breathe. She was losing it. He increased his iron grip, formed a tight fist with his right hand, and reared his body back, preparing to deliver a killing blow.

She saw her chance.

Now!

She shot her right leg high, swinging it to the right, and then with a blow like a mighty sledge-hammer, brought her foot crashing down, heel first, onto his left ear.

"Aaarrgh!"

Stunned, blood running down the side of his neck, Lalo lost his grip. Izzy directed a powerful kick to his windpipe.

"Uunngh!" Lalo staggered.

It should have broken his neck, but incredibly, Lalo, blood spurting from his mouth, became a tenacious rottweiler oblivious to pain. He delivered a sharp palm strike to Izzy's sternum. Izzy reeled from the blow to her heart. Her breathing and vision clouded for a moment, and in that moment Lalo was running.

Gasping, Izzy stood, stumbled, grabbed her chest, and collapsed. In the deadly struggle, the voices of terrified diners and passersby had been blocked out. But now she could hear the fear of the crowd.

"Police! Police!" they screamed, as they fled in stunned disbelief at the sight of a man and woman trying to kill each other.

The bedlam brought her back. She looked. Lalo was limping, clearly in pain but moving fast. Several gendarmes were running in her direction from the gate area.

Can't stay here. If they stop to question me, I'll never catch him. Get up! Dammit get up!

Somehow, she willed herself to stand. The pain in her shoulder was intense. She could feel blood from the stab wound trickling down her back. Lalo was thirty yards away, half running, half limping. She knew she'd hurt him badly.

Shit! He's headed for the balloon!

She picked up her pace, but was still struggling for air.

Lalo was almost at the balloon, a giant teardrop sphere with gold *fleurs-de-lys* bordering its wide blue stripes. The balloon was at rest on the thick wood platform. The operator had opened the gondola and let riders out, his right hand securely wrapped around the metal activating handle of the burner. Lalo reached the gondola just as the last of the riders exited. The gate was still open. He half stumbled in.

"Take the balloon up now!" said Lalo, pointing to the handle of the burner mechanism.

"*Non, monsieur,* you must wait your turn!" the operator said in halting English, clearly terrified by Lalo's bloody appearance.

Lalo gave him a swift neck chop, and the man collapsed as bystanders screamed. Lalo shoved him out of the gondola. Izzy was close, face crimson from exertion.

Lalo gripped the thick metal handle of the burner. He'd never operated a hot air balloon, but he was about to learn. He pulled hard. The burner sprang to life.

Izzy was only a few yards away. Police not far behind.

Lalo pulled the burner handle down all the way. Flames leaped instantly. The huge sphere expanded, lurched, then awkwardly jerked upward.

The operator, still on the ground below the gondola, was shouting. "*Non, monsieur!* It is too much heat! It will catch fire and explode!"

Lalo gripped the handle even tighter as the burner raised the temperature, increasing the orb's volume at a dangerous rate as it rose. In mere seconds, the fast-rising sphere ate up the slack of the four nylon tethers securing the balloon. The tethers made a high-pitched sound as the rising globe tested the tensile strength of the five-eighths inch thick nylon cords.

Gasping for air, Izzy reached the wood platform as the gondola rose.

SNAP!

She heard a tether rupture. The massive balloon began to gyrate wildly.

SNAP! SNAP! SNAP!

The three remaining tethers broke under the mighty pull. The balloon inflated further and sped skyward, nylon tethers trailing like the long stalks of a Portuguese man o'war. Izzy lunged, grabbed one of the tethers with both hands, and was brutally yanked upward as the sphere rose.

Aaaghh! Her shoulder screamed in pain. She looked up. *It's at least thirty feet up to the gondola.*

She'd have to climb the tether to get to Lalo. The balloon was accelerating, and was now sixty feet above the Tuileries. Izzy looked downward.

It's climb up to the gondola, or take a fast one-way trip to the ground.

Tightening her grip on the tether, knuckles turning white, she used the SEAL Team method she'd learned at the Point. She pulled her knees up, let the tether fall along the outside of her right leg, then used her right foot to wrap the tether under her right and over the top of the left foot locking the rope in place. Stepping on the locked rope with her right, she reached, grabbed higher on the rope, and lifted up three feet.

"Uunngbh!"

The pain in her left shoulder took her breath away. She held on to the nylon tether, took several slow deep breaths, tried to banish the pain, and repeated the maneuver as the giant blue-striped globe shot skyward. The tethers were now swinging like immense pendulums gone mad as strong air currents took hold.

Below, the vast Tuileries garden and the gigantic Louvre museum grew smaller as the balloon rose. Izzy looked up. Lalo was holding onto the burner handle with one hand while trying to detach her tether with the other. He was looking down at her, screaming, *"Te mato, puta!* You will die, bitch!"* Part of his polymer mask had been ripped away during their combat and was hanging from his bloodied face like some grotesque disfigured gargoyle.

The wind direction, normally from west to east, had unaccountably turned sharply westward. They were moving fast. Far below she could now make out the broad Champs Élysées and the distinctive Étoile with its twelve boulevards converging and winding around the Arc de Triomphe. Cars, buses and people appeared as real life miniatures.

Pushed by the powerful winds, the balloon rose even higher.

Izzy had closed the distance to the gondola by ten feet. It was an agonizing, slow effort, and she had to stop again and again to compose her mind and body before reaching up once more.

Driven by the blustery winds, the hot air globe was now speeding west, soaring over the 16th arrondissement, transiting the immense Bois de Boulogne, the broad *Péripherique* beltway, the Seine; moving inexorably towards the towering skyscrapers of La Defense, Paris's gargantuan business center.

Just one more foot. Just one more lift.

Izzy was pulling herself upward at a snail's pace as Lalo continued to swear and work at the thick nylon tether. Bloody and damaged her left shoulder might be, still she forced herself to block out the fear, the growing fatigue, ignore the pain, the oozing blood, and reach up yet again.

There was a sharp jolt. A sudden, powerful side-draft accelerated the speed of the balloon with such force that it was now driven sideways, pulling Izzy and the other three tethers nearly horizontal in flight as they sped toward the fast-approaching high-rise buildings.

Office workers rushed to windows of the seven-hundred-fifty-eight-foot high *Tour First* in open-mouthed disbelief as the immense shape raced toward them like an incoming missile.

"This is crazy! What's that balloon doing here?" said one.

"Look, someone's hanging onto the rope!" said another.

"*Seigneur!*" shouted a third. "It's a woman!"

Now everyone was yelling.

"A woman? *Non! Non! Putain!* That's impossible!"

"Yes! Yes! Look! It's a woman."

"She's crazy to do that. It must be some stupid commercial."

They pointed and shouted "Quick! Look, Look!" as others, slack jawed at the sight, joined them, unable to take their eyes off the gigantic blue-striped globe growing larger and more menacing.

Moments later it was blocking out the sun and sky, rushing toward their building as dozens of smartphones captured the drama.

"*Putain*, it's going to hit us!" cried one.

CRASH, THUMP, THUMP, CRASH!

The balloon collided with the upper floors of this, France's tallest building, smashing its windows, shattering glass with each impact, bouncing away, then smashing again as it was propelled back in by wind gusts.

Izzy was whipped back and forth under the caroming monster. It was all she could do to avoid being crushed by each impact. The great balloon finally shot past *Tour First*, spun wildly towards *Tour CB21*, then bounced and slammed into the six-hundred-fourteen-foot tall *Tour Total*.

It continued to demolish windows, spinning, clanging, like a gigantic wrecking ball gone rogue.

As the orb and its gondola pounded the last skyscraper with strong, pirouetting blows, small fissures sprang open in the balloon's nylon sheeting.

Below on the Esplanade de la Defense, people stared upward in riveted disbelief at the sight of this strange 19th century silhouette, an improbable ghost, its immense shape hammering the buildings with so much force they could hear the impact and the sound of glass shards striking the pavement below.

The raucous, unstable trajectory of the balloon forced Lalo to ignore the nylon tether. He was being knocked about in the gondola, barely holding on to the burner handle.

With a sudden burst, the wind direction shifted eastward, the balloon spun like a top, and shot back toward Paris.

Approaching in the far distance, two prefecture police helicopters, blades thrumming, were now speeding straight for them.

Izzy continued her painful climb, but was making little progress. The loss of blood and the punishing journey had sapped her strength to the breaking point.

I can't make it to the gondola. Even if I do, I'll be no match for Lalo. Don't have the strength. He'll finish me off before I even get a chance to fight. She wouldn't be able to hold on much longer.

The immense balloon raced east, back across the Seine, then south towards the 7th arrondissement. It shot past Bois de Boulogne and headed to Passy, the Pont de Bir-Hakeim and the overhead Six Line metro railway that bridged the river from Right Bank to Left.

The balloon's fuel was gone. Its flame sputtered, died, then began descending fast, as its heated air cooled.

Izzy saw Lalo frantically pulling on the burner handle. It didn't help. The ribs of the giant form were losing shape as more air leaked from the widening tears. Soon huge folds of the nylon material were collapsing inward. The balloon dropped ever faster, now no more than two hundred feet above the ground.

As it neared the high-rail bridge spanning the Seine, one of the trailing tethers was caught in the mechanism of a metro train transiting the river.

The balloon was sharply yanked downward.

Izzy could clearly see the rails now.

If we hit the electrified rail, I'm dead.

A swift gust momentarily propelled the balloon upward. It broke free of the train, and began dropping again. Now less than one hundred feet above the river,

Izzy saw the river approaching rapidly. Above her, the massive balloon had lost most of its cubic volume, and was collapsing into an immense sheet of thick material, its blue stripes and *fleurs-de-lys* blocking her view of the sky.

The river rose fast and hard to meet her as the end of her tether struck the water. The balloon, now deflated, but still huge and heavy, hit the water with a thunderous *SPLASH!*

Izzy was in the water, desperately trying to untangle her legs from the nylon tether wound around them. The vast sheeting was taking on water. The gondola quickly swamped and was pulled deep into the fast-moving river. She could no longer see Lalo.

Izzy struggled to get free as the suction generated by the sinking giant pulled her under the surface of the agitated water. The force of the moving river made it impossible to untangle herself. She was pulling on the line, grasping, yanking, but losing the struggle. Her lungs were about to burst. She was blacking out.

Skimming mere feet above the river's surface, two huge French military Tiger helicopters, long blades spinning and thrumming with a thunderous sound, were approaching.

The two police helos had moved to a standoff position as the Tigers roared in, bay doors open, their immense rotors kicking up frothing waves on the river's surface. Two divers in wet suits stood at the open door of each helo.

"*ALLEZ! ALLEZ!*" team leaders shouted, as the divers plunged, feet first, one after the other, into the chilly, agitated water below. They swam hard, moving deeper into the fast moving river, until they reached Izzy.

They quickly placed a breathing mask on her face, cleared the water from the mask with air, and cut the entangled tethers away from her body. Wrapping powerful arms around her, they kicked upward until they broke the surface.

They pulled the mask away from her face. Disoriented, exhausted, Izzy gasped, spit out water, then took huge gulps of fresh air.

As they bobbed in the water, the divers signaled one of the Tiger crews to lower a harness.

Verging on delirium, Izzy clutched the arm of one of the divers. "Lalo…Lalo...Stop him," she said. Her eyes were wide with alarm. "Stop Lalo!"

"*Calmez-vous, madame,* you are safe," he said.

Izzy squeezed his arm. "The man, the man is Lalo."

"She's bleeding and she's in shock!" he shouted. "I don't understand what she's saying… it's about someone named Lalo."

They placed the harness around her and secured her to one of the divers. "Do not worry, *madame*," he said as they rose. "No harm can come to you now. We will tell people to find your Lalo."

The diver clasped her hand in reassurance until they reached the bay door.

"Thank you," Izzy managed to say, as her voice trailed off.

She would have kissed every one of them, but lost consciousness.

114

"It's Over, Izzy"

Paris – Hôpital Saint Joseph

"He's gone, Izzy," said Jean-François. "Lalo is dead."

"You found his body?" said Izzy.

She was lying in a sun-filled hospital room with an IV in her arm, bandages around her left shoulder. The bruises on her body were numerous, but would heal. An immense bouquet of red and white roses filled the room with pleasant fragrance. They were from President Childs, of course. A tender note had accompanied them. A fruit basket from Liam Cabot sat on a small table. A note from the Élysée Palace wished her speedy recovery. It bore the signature of President Amaury Jardin.

Will Bergen had sent a humorous message with a crazy cat video. Sara's book of poetry rested in Izzy's lap.

"Izzy," said Jean-François, "the Paris river patrol have looked for days. Nothing. With all the rain we've been having, the river was running very high, very fast. They say he must have been pulled under by the weight of the balloon. Either his body is much farther down the Seine, or he got trapped under water in tree roots and weeds here in Paris. We may never find him."

"He's a survivor," said Izzy.

"I understand how you feel, Izzy, I really do," said Jean-François. "It's a miracle you're alive. But Lalo was directly under that massive balloon. No one could've survived. He didn't have a chance."

"I hope you're right, Jean-François."

"I'm sure of it, Izzy. Lalo is finished."

"What's the status of Savoy-sur-Mer?" said Izzy.

"Savoy-sur-Mer was taken offline. It's getting intensive analysis by cyber experts. It will not be brought back online until it is safe."

"Sounds like all the boxes have been ticked then," said Izzy. Her voice became doubtful. "Perhaps it's my inner skeptic, but something is gnawing at me, troubling me. Until I see Lalo's body, I won't believe he is truly dead and the threat over."

"I understand," said Jean-François. "But it is over, Izzy. Lalo's gone. He was not invincible. He was just an evil, mortal man who is now dead. Do not worry about the plants. Savoy-sur-Mer and Little River were taken offline. They will be looked at with a microscope. Just let it go, my friend."

"Maybe you're right," said Izzy. "Once that demon gets into your brain, it's hard to banish it."

"I know what you mean by demons that don't want to leave," he said.

"You have demons?" said Izzy.

"Perhaps I'll tell you one day," said Jean-François. His voice became softer, more heartfelt. "Now get some rest. See you tomorrow. If you're up to it, Sara and I want you to spend the weekend with us at our parent's country house in Normandy. Some cross-country riding on a fine horse might do you good. Your doctors will likely forbid it," he said, breaking out a broad smile, "but they probably don't understand horses and riders."

"Life's too short, Jean-François," she said. "Doctors or no, you and Sara are on. Spirited horses, cross-country riding. What medicine could be better than that?"

"Bravo, Izzy!" He kissed her on both cheeks, said, "*À bientôt*," and left.

Izzy watched Jean-François walk out and slipped into thought. *Is he right about Lalo? He laid out a plausible, more than plausible, scenario.*

In fact, in those final moments just before they hit the water, she'd seen Lalo frantically flailing in the gondola.

Did he panic, lose his senses, hesitate jumping?? Was he still in the gondola when the balloon collapsed?

It would have been out of character for someone who was so controlled in his behavior. But Jean-François was right, the giant balloon with its enormous weight, had collapsed onto the gondola, enveloping it, folding on top of it, until it disappeared from view. Once that happened, it would not have been possible for Lalo to escape the gondola and the weight and pull of the huge swath of material as it took on water and sank.

Did Lalo even know how to swim?

115

Oval Office

Oval Office

CIA Director Roger Kiley and NSC Director Andy Valucek were seated in leather armchairs facing the president who was at his desk. Vice President Isaac Stein was seated to the side of the president.

"Mr. President," said Kiley, "French intelligence services have advised us that Lalo is dead, drowned when the hot air balloon tumbled into the Seine. They're continuing their search for the body, but say it may never be found."

"So, they say Lalo is dead, but don't have the body?" said the president.

"Correct. They say the chances he could have survived are next to zero."

"And the so-called 'Jens Alders dossier' implicating North Korea in the Little River and Savoy-sur-Mer cyberhacks?"

"Less certain. Our operative in Paris, Bill Powers, told us he was to receive the dossier from a Russian intelligence asset he'd handled for several years, a woman named Galina Federova. Federova was a highly placed agent of the Russian SVR. She passed sensitive information to us for years. She was with Jens Alders the morning he was murdered in the Paris Metro. She claimed to have the dossier and told Powers she would give him a copy."

"But Powers never got it?" said the president.

"Correct, sir. Never arrived. But he knew Federova well and considered her claim about the existence of the dossier credible."

"So, although we have reason to believe that a dossier implicating the North Korean government exists, we don't have it and have no corroboration."

"Unfortunately not, sir."

"What was her motive in offering the dossier to Powers?"

"She wanted U.S. relocation and protection."

"She wanted to defect?"

"Correct, sir. She had a good reason. According to Powers, Russian intelligence discovered she was working with us. They wanted her out of the way."

"Did you get her out of the country?"

"No sir. Afraid she ran out of time. And there's a twist to the tale of Galina Federova," said Kiley.

"This is already pretty mind-bending, Roger."

"Couldn't agree more, sir. But here's where Federova really becomes a rare spy." Kiley leaned forward placing his forearms across his legs. "Powers questioned Federova about the Jens Alders dossier. Based upon that conversation he concluded that she was likely also working with the General Reconnaissance Bureau, North Korea's intelligence service. His assessment was that Federova was witting to the alleged planned cyberattacks on Little River and Savoy-sur-Mer."

"So she crossed us, the Russians *and* the DPRK? Hard to believe," said the president. "Must have had nerves of steel."

"Exactly," said Kiley. "People wanted Federova gone. We took no active measures against her, so the question is, who killed her? Was it Moscow? Pyongyang? Someone else?"

The president said nothing. He knew espionage was a hall of mirrors and a deadly business.

"Thanks for the update, Roger. Let me know if you get any further on Lalo or the dossier."

"Yes, Mr. President."

"Isaac, any questions?" the president asked Stein.

"No, Mr. President," said Stein.

Childs turned to Andy Valucek. "Andy, what are we hearing from Pyongyang?"

"Mr. President, the DPRK is denying any responsibility. Claiming it's fake news to create a military confrontation. They're going to stick to that line come hell or high water. We expect heads to roll in Pyongyang in the coming days as Dear Leader reacts to events. Will likely be a blood bath."

"Deny, deny. Their protestations beggar belief."

"They do, sir," said Valucek, "but unless we can get first hand evidence, like the dossier - assuming the dossier even exists, we're going to have great difficulty connecting it to the DPRK. French intelligence is saying that the individuals who might have provided direct evidence of North Korea's authorship are dead."

The president looked at them, his eyes flashed with anger.

"Roger, work with Andy. By tomorrow I want a set of options laying out our response to the DPRK in the event we're able to prove that they were the instigators. And don't spare the pain."

"Andy, we need to coordinate with Traficante at State and the Élysée Palace, Palmieri at Defense and the Joint-Chiefs. When the time comes, it will be a robust response."

"Yes, Mr. President."

"I know everyone here understands," said the president, "that we'll be roundly condemned if we can't unequivocally prove Pyongyang was behind this. There will be hell to pay with China, Russia and every other damned player that thinks we're trigger-happy. Now, fellas, I've got Bill Reyner from the NRC waiting. On your way out, please ask Hannah to send him in."

"Yes, sir," they said.

***

"Good afternoon, Mr. President, Mr. Vice President," said Reyner, as he was shown in by Hannah Wellborn.

"Hi, Bill, good to see you. Have a seat," said the president, motioning to one of the leather armchairs.

"Thank you, sir."

"Bill, what's the status of Little River?"

"Scrammed, Mr. President."

"Safe, for now?"

"Safe, sir. We brought in the best from Cyber Command, Silicon Valley, and MIT to debug the entire system. First, they scrammed the reactor, shut the whole thing down tight as a drum, then did a deep dive into the Industrial Controls and Safety Instrumented Systems. They found sophisticated malware that could have taken down the reactor. Really frightening. An extraordinary feat by the hackers; deeply imbedded, designed to disable the firewalls and other defense-in-depth features. The hackers were capable of remotely taking control. They certainly knew what they were doing. But I'm glad to report our folks killed the beast."

"Good work, Bill. What's the next step?"

"We bring the plant back online in the next forty-eight hours."

"Good news. Thanks, Bill. Was a close call. Please thank the team."

"Ditto for me, Bill," said the vice president, as Reyner stood to leave.

"I will, sir," he said, "they'll appreciate the high five."

116

Chateau de Valmont

Château de Valmont, Normandy

It was late afternoon. Izzy, Sara and Jean-François had taken the TGV from Gare Montparnasse, traveling two hundred ninety kilometers an hour in a quiet, silk-smooth train with a white-tablecloth dining car, plush seats, Wi-Fi and concierge service.

They'd rented a car at the station at the small town of Valmont. Sara drove. Izzy was the front passenger, with Jean-François in the back commenting on the wooded countryside, pointing out places from their childhood and teenage days. He related anecdotes about their years there, and their wild rides at full gallop on Hanoverian stallions while the Comte and Comtesse counted prayer beads until their safe return.

As they left the main road, the eight-hundred-hectare estate of Château de Valmont came into view. Izzy was struck by the commanding black metal gates, the breath-taking beauty of the tree-lined path and the imposing sixteenth century structure that dominated the long approach ahead. Tall conical towers rose imposingly above the immaculate stone building. The sound of the wheels on gravel evoked images of horse-drawn carriages and nobility. At the end of the long path, an elegant porte-cochère framed the entrance to the circular driveway of the chateau. Floor to ceiling windows looked out from the ground level.

Ten large windows were located on the first floor. The second floor had eight mid-sized windows with handsome balconies.

The car pulled up in front of a pair of stone stairways that curved upwards to a landing with two massive caramel colored wood doors. Izzy saw an elderly man and woman dressed in casual country attire standing in the doorway. The man was of small stature, slender but poised, sporting a brown English tweed jacket, dark pants and short boots. The woman beside him was tall and imposing in her confirmation, wearing a white blouse, riding pants and boots, a blue sweater draped over her shoulders. They waved brightly.

Izzy, Sara and Jean-François got out and climbed the stairs. Sara and Jean-François rushed forward to embrace their parents and gave a kiss on each cheek.

"Maman, Papa, this is our dear friend, Isabella Stone," said Sara, as she took Izzy's hand and gently pulled her toward them, "but she prefers that we call her Izzy."

"Very well, then, Izzy it will be," said Comtesse Stewart de Valmont, her smile full and warm as Izzy approached. "Izzy, welcome."

"I second that sentiment, fully, *madame*," said the Comte, his voice strong and amiable.

"*Merci, Monsieur le Comte de Valmont et Madame la Comtesse de Valmont*," said Izzy. "Thank you for inviting me to your lovely home."

"It is so nice to have you here, Izzy," said the Comtesse, as they made their way in. "Sara and Jean-François will give you a short tour and show you to your room. The Comte and I hope you will join us for cocktails later. He has the heart of a true country chef and is preparing a tasty Normandy dinner for us."

"With help from the staff of course!" said the Comte, grinning broadly.

"*Merci, Madame la Comtesse, Monsieur le Comte,*" Izzy said, returning the smile. "I do look forward to an authentic Normandy meal."

They entered the stately chateau through a broad reception room, its walls decorated with large hunting tapestries and oil landscapes. Marble statues rested on a broad, pristine-white tile floor. Off the reception hall and to the left was an expansive, formal sitting room.

Several comfortable-looking overstuffed armchairs and sofas faced a glistening black concert grand. A massive fireplace under a tall, gilt mirror dominated one end of the spacious room. The fireplace seemed to have been prepared for a warming fire later in the day. They passed a library with floor-to-ceiling bookcases filled with books. The heavy leather bindings suggested an earlier century.

A sweeping stone staircase took them to the next level where an elegant office bureau with huge stained-glass windows overlooked the manicured, flowered gardens of the chateau. In the distance lay a large *étang* or pond, and beyond the *étang*, the thick tree line of a forest. They continued down the hall and stopped.

"This is your room," said Sara, as the three entered a sun-drenched fifty-square meter room. "It faces southwest so you will have nice light in the afternoon. It's one of our favorites. Our rooms are just down the hall."

Izzy was accustomed to lavish venues, accompanying the president all over the world. Yet this room had a unique aspect. Its portraiture and pastoral landscapes, the immense gold mirrors, thick patterned rugs and canopied four poster bed, all spoke of an alluring, storied past. She sensed a familiar presence.

"It's beautiful, Sara," she said. "It has an extraordinary aura. It's strange to say, but it's as if the room is welcoming me."

"Then it must be that you were meant to be here!" said Sara, flashing her megawatt smile.

"Sometimes a place waits for a special person to arrive," said Jean-François.

"Well, it is a perfect place," said Izzy. "I'd love to take a little time to sit and admire the room and the view. It's so peaceful, so far removed from the craziness of the last few weeks."

"Of course," said Sara. "We'll have a pot of tea sent up to you right away. Is an hour of private time okay?"

"Just right. Would you like me to come down then?"

"Yes, do," said Jean-François. "We'll be in the library with our parents. We'll all have a cocktail before dinner."

"Sounds good. See you then," said Izzy.

Sara gave her a peck on each cheek. "So glad you came, Izzy."

Izzy walked to one of the windows, sat on the broad stone sill, and looked out. Above, the sky was a delicate, pale-blue. A scattering of white clouds moved playfully across the horizon. A flock of swifts soared then swept down in perfect formation, gracefully rising then descending in majestic, timeless choreography.

Below, the grounds were arranged in regular geometric patterns of immaculately trimmed bushes and flowerbeds. The *étang* sparkled with dappled light as a light breeze moved across the water. Beyond the gardens, the stand of forest, thick, full and green, rose and spread out into the horizon without end.

The perfection, tranquility and eternal beauty of the scene swept over Izzy. She caught her breath, and a sudden sob sprang from deep within her chest. Her fingers rolled into her palms and tightened. Her head inclined forward resting lightly on the pane, tears moistening the ancient stone.

Ghosts from the past rushed at her. Her body trembled. *Dad, I miss you. Why?...Why?*

For a long moment she remained still, unmoving, a bird arrested mid-flight, wounded, vulnerable, exhausted. She knew it was all an emotional reaction to everything she had been through in the last few weeks. It had tested her mind, her physical strength, and her survival skills to the breaking point. The ever-present fear that Lalo would unleash an attack had pushed her to the edge.

She'd not slept easily for weeks as the murders mounted and Lalo relentlessly moved ahead with his vile plot. The nightmarish chases in Los Angeles and Paris had rekindled the childhood terror and helplessness she'd experienced at the age of eight as she saw her father attacked and killed. She fought to reassure, compose herself.

It's over. Thank God it's over. Lalo is dead, gone. He won't come back. Let it go, Izzy. Let it go. Jean-François is right. The monster is still too much in my head. He seemed indestructible. He wasn't. He was just a man, an evil man who is no more.

There was a slight knock on the door.

"*Oui,*" she said.

The door opened and a young woman dressed in a grey dress with a white apron appeared, carrying a silver tray with a steaming pot of tea, a cup and saucer.

"*Bonjour, madame,*" the young woman said in a voice just above a whisper.

"*Bonjour,*" said Izzy.

The young woman placed the tray on a round cherry wood table.

"*Merci beaucoup,*" said Izzy.

"*C'est moi, madame,*" she replied, and exited.

Izzy poured herself a cup, added a cube of brown sugar and cream. She took the cup and saucer back to the window and stood there, sipping and enjoying the comforting blend.

She finished her tea and unpacked the bag that had been brought up from the car. She selected one of her simple outfits, a black tube dress, black velvet flats, a thin silver necklace, then dressed and went downstairs.

"Ah, Izzy," said Jean-François, as she descended. "Your timing is just right. We were about to have a cocktail."

"I was hoping for that," said Izzy, with a brief smile. She followed Jean-François into the library.

"Izzy, please come sit beside me," said the Comtesse, gently patting a place on the sofa beside her. "Sara and Jean-François have had you all to themselves, and now it is my turn to enjoy your company."

"Thank you, *madame*," said Izzy, taking a seat next to the Comtesse.

Cocktails were served, and the evening was filled with laughter and childhood anecdotes that continued through a wine-suffused multi-course meal of scallops *à la normande*, Cornish hen with roasted pine nut asparagus, *trou-normand* sorbet with Calvados, meadow-salted lamb, garden salad, aged Pont-l'Évêque and Livarot cheeses, *tergoule* pudding, espressos, and Calvados.

The Comtesse, resplendent in a deep blue velvet vest with gold buttons, neck-high white satin blouse secured with an ivory brooch, large agate rings and jade earrings, effortlessly guided the conversation with humor and sharp wit, as she drew, with dramatic elan, on a cigarette attached to a long stem holder.

The Comte in his dark silk smoking jacket, white shirt and red bow tie, looked on admiringly, a man who could not have been more content.

They savored the Calvados and talked late into the evening. At last, the Comte and Comtesse bid Izzy good night, giving her a kiss on each cheek as they retired for the evening.

Sara, Izzy and Jean-François went for a walk outside, passing under the arched stone gate illuminated by the amber light of small gas lamps. The gravel crunched under their feet as they stepped out into the moonlit evening, the clear night sky of Normandy above, sparkling with a breathtaking profusion of stars.

"This is so beautiful," said Izzy.

"Yes!" said Sara, with equal wonder in her voice. "I never get used to it."

117

La Comtesse

Izzy sat bolt upright in her bed at the sound of someone running and a woman shouting. A disquieting energy coursed the bedroom which was illuminated only by moonlight. Izzy leaped out of bed, grabbed her robe and rushed to the door. There was a voice in the hallway, unintelligible yet full of alarm. She opened the door slightly and looked down the darkened hallway as a ghostly figure disappeared into one of the bedrooms. Barefoot, Izzy made her way down the hall, the stone floor cold under her feet.

The shouting had stopped, but a low murmuring sound came from the room ahead. She approached the door. It was slightly ajar. She peered in and was stunned at the sight. Sara, in a white linen gown, her long chestnut hair falling over her shoulders, had her arms protectively wrapped around Jean-François, cradling him, rocking him, speaking softly in comforting tones. Jean-François was leaning into her, his body limp.

Izzy moved closer and listened, transfixed.

"*C'est moi, c'est moi, Jean-François. Le Seigneur est bon, le Seigneur est juste, le Seigneur pardonne,*" Sara was softly saying, as she rocked him. "*It's me…it's me, Jean-Francois. God is good. God is just. God is forgiving.*"

Izzy stepped back into the hallway, trying to absorb the extraordinary scene she had just witnessed. *God is forgiving.* What had Jean-François done that needed forgiveness? Was this the darkness that Victor had spoken of? As she walked back to her room, Izzy heard someone call her name.

"Izzy, come."

At the top of the stairway to the next floor Izzy saw the Comtesse, a lighted candle in her hand.

"Izzy. Please come."

Izzy walked up the stairs and followed the Comtesse to a small study. The room was warm from bright embers in the fireplace, the remains of an earlier fire.

"Izzy," she said, "I'm sure you are confused by what you saw."

"Very," said Izzy. "I don't understand. How serious is it?"

"Sometimes, very," said the Comtesse. "It is about what happened to Jean-François and Sara when they were children."

"Is it about the avalanche?" said Izzy.

"Yes. When the avalanche struck, Sara and Jean-François lost not only their parents but siblings as well. It was a miracle they survived. Sara was badly injured. Jean-François's left arm was broken. There were three others, two men and a woman, who survived the avalanche, but they were terribly injured, beyond hope. Jean-François made a decision that has haunted him all his life. He knew he could not save everyone. He chose to save Sara.

The others were left to die. No child of ten should ever have to face such a heart-breaking choice."

"And Victor found them," said Izzy.

"Yes. From that day Victor and Jean-François had a sacred bond between them. To us, Victor LePrince was a saint."

"*Madame Comtesse*," said Izzy, "Victor once told me there was a darkness in Jean-François. Is this what he meant?"

"Yes. We came to call it the darkness because it took Jean-François to such a morbid place. It may always be with him."

"How did you and the Comte come to be their parents?" said Izzy. "Weren't there relatives who could have taken them?"

"There were, Izzy, distant relatives. But the people in Paris who decide such things did not believe that these children should just be sent to relatives they did not really know, who could not provide the support or education they felt they deserved."

"And so you and the Comte adopted them?"

"Yes, it was a miracle for us."

Izzy and the Comtesse talked until the early light of dawn began to filter through the stained-glass windows of the study.

118

Izzy Rides

Someone was tapping at her door.

"*Bonjour,* Izzy. It's Sara." Tap, tap, tap.

Izzy checked her smart phone. Seven A.M.

"Come in," she said.

Sara opened the door, poked her head in a bit. "*Bonjour!* Horses are ready, and the morning is just right! Brought you some riding breeches, a pair of half chaps and a sweater. Hope everything fits. I'll leave them just outside your door."

"Great, thanks, Sara," said Izzy. "I'll be right down."

Twenty minutes later, Izzy, Jean-François and Sara were downing *café crèmes* and croissants, then rushing out to the stables where stable hands were standing beside three mighty Orlov-Rostopchin thoroughbreds. Izzy, Sara and Jean-François did a full check of bridles, straps and rigging, then put on long, brown American dusters.

"Chaps, everything fit?" said Sara.

"Perfect, you're a genius," said Izzy.

"You sure you're up to it?" said Jean-François. "It will be wet, windy and bumpy."

"Jean-François, I've been looking forward to this since the Lapin Rouge!" Izzy said.

"*À cheval, alors!*" he said.

They mounted their thoroughbreds and slowly ambled away from the stables. They reached a short bridle path, and made a clicking noise with their tongues. The horses picked up a brisk trot and soon they were in open country.

The morning sky was metal grey with a cool breeze that promised rain. Ahead, a broad expanse of tall field grass extended far into the distance, disappearing into a dark green forest. They squeezed their horse's flanks with their legs and transitioned to a smooth canter.

Sara took the lead. Then with a loud *"Haaaahh!"* and a firm palm slap to her mount's hindquarters, she leaned forward low and eased her grip on the reins as the massive Orlov-Rostopchin exploded into a thundering gallop.

"Allez! Allez! Let's catch her if we can!" shouted Jean-François, as he spurred his horse into a spirited gallop.

And suddenly, the three were off on a mad, glorious, cross-country ride, the wind in their faces, dusters flapping wildly, the high grass crunching under the hooves of their powerful steeds.

Sara was still in the lead but Jean-François was gaining, his smile exuberant as they left the open field and shot into the tree line. It was an exhilarating, breath-taking gallop, and as Izzy spurred her horse on and into the enveloping forest, she felt drawn to the thrill of the ride and the newfound persona of Jean-François. There was an ebullient wildness about him she had not imagined. He was in his element - his horses, the forests, the fields, the place where he'd grown up, and loved.

Her heart quickened at the splendid sight, and she instantly understood that although Jean-François was a member of France's elite, he could walk away from the influence, the titles, the prestige and the glamour of

Paris, in a heartbeat. Chateau de Valmont was in his blood and soul.

He reined his mount in sharply, stood high in the stirrups and hailed Izzy. The wind was up and a light rain had begun to fall.

"Come, Izzy!" he said. His voice strong, full, electric. "We will miss lunch!"

She waved to him, spurred her horse harder, and in that moment knew she had never been happier in her life.

119

Change of Plans

Winded but happy from their ride, they stopped for lunch at a picturesque country restaurant. A small colombage-style family home that offered freshly cooked meals, the restaurant was one of Sara and Jean-François's favorite places. As they cooled and watered their horses in the cottage's fenced field, the elderly owners stepped out to greet them.

"Sara, Jean-François, *bonjour!*" they said, giving each a peck on each cheek. Izzy was introduced, and they all went in.

The three of them were the only diners, but it made no difference to their hosts who were accustomed to equestrians without reservations. A bottle of chilled petit chablis arrived with crab-stuffed mushrooms, cheesy onion soup, succulent white fish, tender *entrecôte,* home grown greens, raspberries and coffee. It was a delightful country meal. Their lunch finished, the three gave the old couple a hearty embrace. "*Le repas était magnifique! À la prochaine,*" they said. They paid the check, waved goodbye and left.

As they walked to their horses, Sara ahead of them, Jean-François stopped and turned to Izzy.

"Izzy," he said. "Would you have dinner with me in Paris tonight, just the two of us?"

Izzy was taken aback but said nothing.

He gently took her hands in his and looked into her eyes. "Ever since that evening at the Lapin Rouge, you've been in my thoughts. Sara says I'm quite taken by you."

He smiled. "She knows me all too well."

"Jean-François, that is so sweet, but..."

"Izzy, I understand you need time to sort through everything you've been through. It's been a *cauchemar*, a nightmare. We are all in awe of you. You're the bravest, most remarkable, loveliest woman I have ever known. It would mean a great deal to me if you would allow me to get to know you better."

"Thank you, Jean-François. I'm touched. You are exceptional, you know. It was thrilling to see the Jean-François I saw today, and I hope we will always be close friends. But it can never be more than that, because your life is here in France, and mine is in the U.S. I've seen how deeply committed you are to your country. I believe one day you may be the leader of this remarkable nation. My work in America will always be the center of my life. I could never leave it. I hope you understand."

She gave him a soft kiss on the cheek. "I will always cherish this day," she said.

***

It was mid-afternoon when Izzy, Sara and Jean-François returned to the chateau. They retired to their rooms to bathe and freshen up, then spent a while chatting with the Comte and Comtesse.

Then it was time to leave. The Comte and Comtesse reluctantly said farewell. The trio would be back in Paris by evening. Izzy planned to wrap up some matters at the Ministry and the American Embassy, then catch a return flight to Washington. She was eagerly looking forward to being with Leyland again. She missed his steady presence, his affection and companionship. There had been too little private time in the last insane weeks.

As the three arrived at the train station to return to Paris, Izzy's mobile chirped. It was an incoming message from Dr. Ebert, her mother's oncologist.

Urgent you call.

***

Izzy looked out the window of her Air France flight. The plane was on final approach to Los Angeles International.

Her mother's latest laboratory tests were dire. The cancer had spread. She was not expected to live more than a few weeks. It was a crushing blow to Izzy. She'd known that the long-term prognosis was not good, but she hadn't expected, nor had she been prepared for the suddenness of the news.

Jean-François and Sara had been wonderful, and helped with arrangements for her hasty departure. Izzy was surprised how much it meant to her that they'd been so supportive and compassionate.

Her mother was now in hospice. Izzy as an only child, had no siblings. There were relatives, of course, yet she'd had little contact with them in years. There would be feelings of guilt and recrimination. She'd chosen a career that had taken her away from Los Angeles and her mother. It now seemed selfish. In the few days that remained, she would be at her mom's side to comfort her, tell her how much she loved her, and to say how grateful she was for everything her mom had given her.

120

Little River

Little River Nuclear Generating Plant, Georgia

Jeff Adams, the Control Room Reactor Operator who'd been brought in to replace Brad Hollister, was seated at his console. Specialists from the Nuclear Regulatory Commission, techs from Cyber Command, EGI engineers and two EGI executives were standing nearby to monitor and observe the progress of the boiling water reactor as it was spooled up and brought back online.

It had been a careful shutdown with a deep dive into the system by cyber experts. After extensive investigation and reprogramming, the cyber team had successfully removed malware and certified the facility as safe to resume operations.

"Okay, let's do it," said Skip Horner, one of the EGI executives.

"You got it," said Adams. He turned the mode switch key and initiated the protocols to bring the reactor "Critical," the point at which the reactor would be fully powered.

Over the next twenty-four hours, with short naps in-between while a backup team monitored the startup, Adams sequentially pulled control rods from the reactor, taking system readings as the temperatures and pressure rose in the core, pulling more control rods until, at last, the reactor was up to one hundred percent power. Systems all registered nominal. The sequence had unfolded without incident. It had been a long, stressful twenty-four hours.

Adams finally turned to the reassembled group, and said the words they'd been hoping to hear.

"We're Critical. The spool-up was successful. We're online."

They all breathed a sigh of relief. It had been a nail-biting wait, but they felt vindicated. They'd identified the malware, and removed it. The re-start had been flawless, and the reactor was now online at full power and performing textbook.

"Beautiful, beautiful! Look'n good, look'n good!" they said, congratulating, and high-fiving each other.

"Coffee, anybody?" said one of the executives from EGI.

"Straight…Cream in mine…Sugar, no cream…"

Then…"DAMMIT! Here we go again!" said Adams.

The Control Room was being inundated by an alarm avalanche as plasma display panels began reporting problems in the reactor pressure vessel, control rods, turbines, recirculation pumps, feedwater pumps, coolant, condenser and other critical systems.

"What the….?"

Adams was looking at the master console.

Cooling System Failure-Excessive Power Surge… Critical…Critical …

He switched to his hot standby system.

Cooling System Failure-Excessive Power Surge… Critical…Critical…

Now they were all staring at the displays in disbelief. Adams was starting to sweat. His training told him to immediately SCRAM the reactor and initiate a shutdown.

"I'm SCRAMMING!" he said.

"Wait, wait! Hold on, dammit! Hold on!" said Skip Horner from EGI. "Could be just another false alarm. Those readings can't be accurate, no way, the reactor's been vetted and re-vetted. It's clean as a whistle. The re-start was textbook, the plant is online. Don't panic. No SCRAM!"

"Disagree," said one of the NRC technicians. "We can't chance it. Better SCRAM now."

"Bullshit!" said Horner. "This is going to cost EGI a fortune, and panic everyone on hell's earth! Unnecessary! The system is fine, fine. Jay Powell told me this might happen. I'm telling you, it will reset and continue safely, like Powell said. Exactly what happened the last time with no damage."

Emergency klaxons were screeching throughout the facility as the console continued to display:

Cooling System Failure-Excessive Power Surge... Critical...Critical...

Skip Horner shouted at the Operator, "Adams, do not shut down! I repeat, do not shut down!"

Adams' guts were churning like a blender. He looked at the group. Now they were yelling at each other, their faces contorted with anger, arms flailing wildly, pushing each other, menacing him, shielding him. His mind was in turmoil. He couldn't decipher their words or their intentions. It was all just unintelligible noise. He looked at the console again **...Critical...Critical...Critical...**

If I'm wrong, my career's toast. But...but..but.... "Screw it! I'm SCRAMMING!"

Adams quickly entered the password to enable the SCRAM protocol.

Control rods driven hydraulically by pressurized storage tanks underneath the reactor vessel would quickly shoot up into the reactor core. Fission reactivity in the reactor would cease within seconds, the danger would pass.

But the red SCRAM button failed to illuminate.

What the…! Get hold of yourself, Adams said to himself. *Must've entered the password incorrectly. Go again.*

His fingers trembling so much that he had to steady his right hand with his left, he re-entered the password and waited, heart pounding……..

Nothing!!

Not possible! No, No, No!

The large red button should have illuminated right away. Instead, it remained a dull red. Adams pushed the button. *Nothing.* Frantic, he pushed again, and again.

Nothing!!

He was pounding, and slamming, and cursing, and screaming.

"C'mon, dammit! C'mon! C'mon! Lord, Jesus help us!"

The Control Room was in pandemonium. The system operators were working furiously to regain control, while the experts and executives continued yelling.

Adams knew that if the readings were correct, the reactor core was headed for supercriticality. Yet not one system was responding to commands. If they couldn't SCRAM immediately, they would soon have a runaway nuclear reactor.

The Control Room began shaking. Lights and overhead display panels flickered and swayed. Hairline cracks in the ceiling appeared and spread quickly. Desks, chairs, and panels were jostled about. Jeff Adams' hands were tightly wrapped around the edge of the console. The Control Room was in full panic, stunned by the confusion and terrifying shaking.

Somewhere, someone was shouting in a terror-filled voice straight from Hell, "We have a release! We have a release!!"

BOOOOM! A massive explosion rocked the Control Room, knocking people off their feet. Dust and debris rained down and all lights extinguished.

As emergency lights activated, Adams took in the destruction. A horrifying thought crossed his mind.

The reactor just exploded!

He made the sign of the cross. *God help us all.*

He never saw the I-beam tumbling down.

121

Situation Room

The White House – Situation Room

Forty-five minutes after the first news of an incident at Little River nuclear power plant, President Leyland Childs was presiding at an emergency meeting in the Situation Room with the vice president and the heads of the NSC, Homeland Security, the Pentagon, CIA, Defense Intelligence Agency, NRC, CISA, FEMA and the FBI who had all been rushed to the White House by howling police escort.

"Bill, what do we know about Little River so far?" said the president.

"Not enough at this point, Mr. President, but it appears this is now a major Nuclear Event. Early reports from Little River are conflicting but strongly suggest there was an explosion. But if so, what part of the plant, what type of explosion, severity, damage, injuries, etc. we just don't have a lot of clarity," said Bill Reyner, the NRC Director. "The spool up was nominal and the reactor was being successfully brought online. Something went seriously wrong, and we can't reach anyone in the Control Room."

A cell phone was chirping. All eyes turned to Bobby Smith, head of FEMA. It was his cell.

Appearing chagrined by the interruption, Smith pressed TALK and brought the cell to his ear. "Yes!" he said with visible irritation. As he listened, his eyes widened in alarm. "Hold on! hold on!" he said. He looked at the president who was clearly annoyed.

"Mister President. Sir!" said Smith. "I apologize, but I have Jack Logan, one of our field directors, on the line. He has a report from just outside the facility. Sir, I think you should hear this."

"Put him on speaker," said the president.

"Jack, hold on. I'm with the president. Putting you on speaker….ok, go ahead, Jack, talk, we're listening."

"Hello, Mr. President."

"Hello, Jack," said the President. "What do you have?"

"Right. I'm about a quarter of a mile from the Little River power plant." Logan coughed loudly. "Sorry, there's a lot of dust and smoke in the air." He coughed again. "I was en route there for a safety meeting, when I heard a powerful blast and felt a quick bolt of air. It was strong enough to rock my SUV. I stopped, got out and looked north towards the facility. Can't believe my eyes. Looks like the entire side of the containment building has ruptured. Smoke is billowing out in a sort of mushroom cloud, and I can see flames shooting out of the structure."

"Are you seeing any responders?" said the President.

"Yes, sir. Looks like there are several fire engine companies on site and others approaching, but the situation looks chaotic. 'Fraid I can't give you more detail at the moment, sir."

"Got it, Jack, thanks," said the president. "I don't know if you're wearing protective gear, but it sounds like you're too close and you're coughing. Better get to a safe place and decontaminate ASAP. Keep Bobby posted."

"Yes, sir," said Logan, signing off, as he broke into a wild coughing fit.

The president scanned the table. "We need more hard information and we need it now," he said. "Get to your sources, find out what's happening. We have a national security emergency on our hands. You have thirty minutes, back here then. We have to act without delay."

"Sir," came the collective reply, as the president rose and exited.

***

A half hour later

"Mr. President," said Reyner, "we have more reports in."

"Go."

"It appears there was indeed a powerful explosion either within or in close proximity to the reactor. The containment vessel was breached, and a radioactive plume is now escaping into the atmosphere. It's severe, sir."

"What's being done to slow or stop the release?"

"We're responding with every technical and human asset available, sir."

"I need a reference point, Bill. Are we looking at a Three Mile Island Event? Something worse?" said the president.

"Mr. President, Three Mile Island was a Level Five Event. Serious, yes, but it appears that Little River will be more like Chernobyl, a Level Seven Event."

"Good lord!" Visibly shaken, the president's composure wavered for a moment. He was well aware of the scale of human and economic loss Chernobyl had wrought.

"What does Energy Global say? It's their plant. They built the damnable thing."

"They haven't been very forthcoming so far sir. Frankly, we think they're scared to death."

"I was assured the reactor was safe. How could this have happened?"

"We don't know for sure yet, sir."

"Working theory?"

"Only expert speculation at this point, sir, but leading theory is that there was another, deeply imbedded self-cloaking worm not visible to our experts, malware designed to come to life only after the reactor was brought online at full power."

"Okay, I've heard enough," said the president. "I want every nuclear plant operator in this country to report every operating anomaly or cyber event that has happened in the last three months, stat! No foot dragging or evasion's going to be allowed. Make it clear to the operators that I will declare a National Emergency and shut them down if necessary. It will create a hell of a power grid mess for millions, but if Little River was brought down by a cloaking malware that even our best people were unable to identify, we run the risk of another disaster. We've got fifty-eight nuclear power plants around the country. That's twenty percent of the nation's electrical power, and millions of lives in the footprint. Can't chance even one more Little River. Bill, I want NRC to take the lead on this. We're going to need everybody in the pool."

"On it, sir."

The president turned to Homeland Security Director Catherine Pfaff.

"Catherine. Give us an update."

"Mr. President," she said, "I've conferred directly with local and state officials, the National Oceanic and Atmosphere Administration, and, with Bill's permission, his NRC staff."

"Readout?" said the president.

"Given the projected amount of contaminant, weather conditions, wind direction and wind speed, they believe we should order an immediate evacuation of the city of Atlanta."

"The entire city?" said the president. "My god, Catherine, do they realize what they're proposing? Atlanta has about half a million residents."

"Yes, sir, they do."

"And if I order an evacuation…outcome?"

"Chaos, sir. Evacuation will result in extensive collateral damage and civilian deaths in at least the hundreds. But if we don't evacuate, the number will be in the thousands."

"Still, the evacuation of a city that large will be an almighty, unprecedented task," said the president.

"Admittedly, sir. But we have to assume that significant radiological contamination of the entire city is imminent. We don't have the full picture yet, but what we know so far is turning hair white at NRC, as Bill Reyner will attest. Like Bill says, we may be looking at a Ukrainian Chernobyl Level Seven Event…or worse."

"And if folks just shelter in place?" said the president.

"That means more souls in the city, and more dead from radiation. That was the mistake they made after the Chernobyl explosion. They did not immediately evacuate Pripyat and other towns. Consider just one logistic, sir. We'd have to have one to two million iodine pills available immediately. Few people in Atlanta have them. They're no help after exposure, and offer only limited protection in any case. Even if they were available at this very moment, distribution in the next few hours would be impossible."

The president scanned the table, his gaze moving from one to another. He raised his hands in frustration. "And even if they do shelter in place, how in the world will we provide food, water, basic services, medical supplies and emergency care to half a million people until the city is finally safe? ...assuming it will ever be safe."

122

Emergency Alert

Atlanta 12:30 P.M. EDT

This is an emergency alert for all residents in the city of Atlanta and surrounding communities ...Immediately shelter in place...Close all doors and windows...Bring pets inside...Do not attempt to leave the city...Danger to life...Tune to your local emergency broadcast stations for more information...This is an emergency alert...

The Emergency Alert warnings were broadcast via radio, television, mobile devices and internet. Police cruisers blasted the alert from their speakers as they moved through neighborhoods. Across the city of Atlanta, half a million inhabitants were stunned and confused by the sudden non-stop wailing of sirens.

People stopped whatever they were doing and looked at each other, all with the same questions reflected in their faces. *What's going on? Is this a test they didn't tell us about? Is this just a screwup like the bozos in Hawaii who scared the hell out of everybody about a missile attack for no good reason?*

Soon media were reporting that Swan Tilden, Georgia's governor, was going to deliver an important announcement within the hour. Atlanta and surrounding communities had already been ordered to activate emergency procedures. All public safety personnel, doctors, staff and hospitals were told to report for duty. Utilities were told to prepare for possible shutdown. Schools and businesses were ordered to close immediately. Police departments, government offices and public officials all declined comment, saying they had no more information than the public. The governor would soon explain the reason for the alerts.

In the absence of reliable information, panic and conspiracy rumors quickly spread on social networks. One poster reported seeing foreign soldiers wearing United Nations insignia on the streets of Atlanta. Another reported Washington, D.C. had been attacked, the president missing. Still others were saying the Yellowstone caldera had exploded, or that a meteor was about to destroy earth. No one had a clue as to what was truly going on. But one thing was undeniable. Something very, very bad was happening, and they were not being told.

123

Situation Room

Situation Room

"Mr. President," interjected Vice President Isaac Stein, "I'm afraid that I disagree with Homeland Security's assessment. Calling for an immediate evacuation of the city of Atlanta will trigger local and national panic. I feel it would be wise to wait until we have a clearer picture of the extent of the release. It may be that projections are overblown. Political damage to the government's credibility will be huge if the threat is not what is being presented."

"Not as great as the political damage that will result if thousands of Atlantans die because we waited to act," said Pfaff.

"We don't know that will happen!" said the vice president. "You're presenting us with a hypothetical scenario, not demonstrable facts."

"I'm giving you our best assessment of what is likely to happen, and time is running out," said Pfaff. "If our assessment is correct, and no evacuation is ordered, we're likely facing short-term radiation deaths in the thousands."

The president turned to Bobby Smith, Administrator, Federal Emergency Management Agency. "Bobby, if I order an evacuation, how will that play out on the ground?"

"Mr. President," said the director, "it's already starting. First responders are overwhelmed, roads and highways are becoming parking lots. Widespread panic, confusion and violence are inevitable as people try to leave the city *en masse*. Atlanta isn't prepared for this nuclear nightmare."

"True," said the president, "but what city in America *is* prepared for this? Bobby, have your folks get to work on relocation centers. We will soon have thousands of people on the run, and in need of safe shelter, food, medical care, and communications. It will be a monumental job. Cut through the red tape. Get everything you need, empty the pantry, do it directly under my authority."

"On it, sir."

"Now, what about the airspace? We've got a radioactive plume on the move."

"Sir, the FAA has declared a ground stop at Hartsfield- Jackson. Nothing's going up or down there as of half an hour ago."

"Good work, Bob. What about air traffic?"

"FAA's also issued a restricted airspace directive covering a three hundred mile radius of Atlanta. This will affect air travel around the world, of course. Hartsfield-Jackson is the world's busiest air hub. Flights will back up at every major city on the planet. Will be a colossal traffic jam."

The president directed his gaze to five-star General Paul Denser, Chairman of the Joint Chiefs, who was sitting next to Greg Palmieri, the Secretary of Defense.

"General, we're going to need serious boots on the ground. Local enforcement will be swamped. What's your plan for dealing with the civil unrest FEMA's talking about, and any evacuation orders I might issue?"

"Mr. President, said General Denser, "we have two thousand active duty National Guard personnel within an hour of Atlanta. In addition, we have active U.S. Army, Marine, and Air Force personnel at Fort Gordon, Fort Benning, Robins and Moody Air Force Bases. A large contingent of specialized medical personnel, and units equipped with radiation hazmat gear are already on the way."

"Good," said the president. "This is moving rapidly. How many additional personnel can you put into Atlanta fast?"

"Sir, we can begin to deploy five to seven thousand in three to four hours. But if you order the evacuation of the entire city, a much larger scale of deployment will be needed. As you said, it's half a million souls, to say nothing of the surrounding communities. We would need to coordinate with state and local agencies to seal off all access roads within a huge perimeter. We'd have a large number of troop transport vehicles on the move. Last thing we want is a traffic jam while we're headed into the city."

"How quickly could you deploy the main force?"

"Full throttle, sir, ten to twelve hours. Logistics take time."

"Time. Something we don't have much of," said the president. "Let's effort to shorten the timetable."

"Yes, sir," said the general. He began typing into a laptop linked to a secure Pentagon line.

"Bob," the president said, turning back to the FEMA director, "let's make sure Governor Tilden begins deploying the Georgia State Patrol to seal off major access routes to Atlanta."

"Yes, sir."

The president paused, his chin resting on folded fingers for a few moments, deep in thought. Finally, he sat back.

"Okay. Bottom line. We're looking at a lose-lose situation with two options. Option One, we don't order an evacuation. Result: we'll have casualties even if fallout is limited. If fallout is heavy, we'll have mass casualties. Option Two, we order an evacuation of the city resulting in chaos. Roads will clog, become impassable, trapping motorists in their cars as radiation rains down on them."

He looked around the table. "I need half an hour. I'll want an update on radiation levels and weather conditions. Everyone back here then." He rose and walked out.

124

The Hideaway

Oval Office – the Hideaway

President Leyland Childs walked directly from the Situation Room, up the stairs of the West Wing, and down the carpeted hallway to the small study adjacent to the Oval Office. The hideaway was his place for reflection, a sanctuary where he could withdraw from the clash of competing opinions.

No matter which path he chose, there would be fatalities. That was no longer in doubt. The question was how to best limit that number. In a mere few minutes, a gargantuan effort would be set in motion, and it was Childs who would have to make and live with the consequences of that decision. He was fortunate to be surrounded by dedicated advisors and experts. Yet in the end, it was he alone who would decide the fate of countless Americans.

The president bowed, rested his head upon steepled hands and summoned a familiar passage from a 17th century warrior's prayer. It had helped him through a bloody firefight at a remote Special Forces outpost in Afghanistan. He was grievously wounded that day but survived. He was one of the lucky ones.

"Oh Lord, thou knowest how busy I must be this day. If I forget thee, do not thou forget me."

125

Will Bergen

Santa Monica

It was morning in Los Angeles, and Izzy's cell was chirping. *Will Bergen.* She pressed CALL.

"Will, hope it's important. I'm at the hospice, and mom's sleeping in the next room. Was a very long night."

"Sorry, Izzy. But if you're near a TV, switch to GNN right now. The gates of Hell just opened."

"Got it, bye." Izzy grabbed the remote, turned the TV to GNN - and gasped.

….GNN Breaking News…Little River, Georgia, Nuclear Plant Accident…Possible Radioactive Release…

She read the chyron in alarm as it scrolled under the image of the Little River facility. It was taken from a great distance. A vapor cloud appeared to be rising from the dome.

My god! This can't be happening! The NRC said Little River was declared safe.

The picture shifted from the image of Little River to the GNN anchor booth. In the foreground, Gerald Riddle, GNN's top anchor, was speaking. He stood in front of a raised half-moon table. Behind him was a large monitor with the image of the plant in the distance.

She turned up the volume. "…so bear with us, we will shortly be moving our coverage of Little River to our New York City studios, as we'll be evacuating our Atlanta offices in the next hour. As we've been reporting, the Little River nuclear plant release came without warning."

Riddles' words tumbled out fast as adrenaline kicked in.

"Details are difficult to get, but here's what we know so far. At approximately eleven-thirty this morning, Eastern Daylight Time, an uncontrolled release of radioactive steam took place at the Little River nuclear generating plant about thirty miles northwest of Atlanta, Georgia. We don't know the severity of the release, or whether the facility has been damaged. Just minutes ago, the State Capitol issued the following statement, and I quote, 'Georgia Governor Swan Tilden will deliver a statewide speech within the next half hour to address the Little River release,' unquote. Our team of reporters is working on this breaking story, and we will bring more information to you as it becomes available."

GNN broke for a series of safety advisories.

Izzy's mind was racing. She felt everything was spinning out of control. Her mother's critical condition. Now the stupefying news from Little River. Time seemed to have warped and swept her into a new, unrecognizable, terrifying reality. She looked at her phone. She wanted to call Leyland. She was missing him desperately. But there was no room for personal indulgence. Every second counted. The president was now in the center of a maelstrom and needed to be laser focused on the crisis.

Two messages popped up on her phone. One was from Liam. The other was from Powers. She would get to them as soon as her mind cleared. She turned back to the broadcast.

126

Governor's Address

Atlanta

Phone service and internet servers, overwhelmed by panicked citizens, began to crash. The confusion and fear spread, as conspiracy trolls and wild social media posters generated confusion and fake stories. The city government was struggling to respond.

Like many large U.S. cities, Atlanta city officials had repeatedly discussed, even conducted, small-scale simulations of a radiological event. But the truth was, no one actually believed a mass casualty nuclear power plant disaster would one day happen. With the exception of Three Mile Island in 1979, only two other INES events had ever taken place at nuclear power plants in the U.S. since 1955. Both were less serious than Three Mile Island. And after all, weren't there lots of systems of protection and regulatory oversight to prevent a mishap?

It was a familiar story – state governments unprepared for devastating earthquakes in known earthquake zones; cities sitting below sea-level, unprepared for rising oceans; multi-billion-dollar corporations and key municipal agencies in denial about the growing threat of cyberattacks and ransomware; federal officials unprepared for a historic but predictable pandemic. Foot-dragging at all levels of the bureaucracy, along with budgetary concerns, powerful political and corporate interests, and pervasive, willful ignorance had stood in the way of a full-on commitment to prevent a twenty-first century cyberattack on a nuclear plant. Now it was too late.

***

"Good afternoon, fellow Georgians. This is your governor. At approximately eleven-thirty this morning, an undetermined amount of radioactive material escaped into the atmosphere from Unit Number One at the Little River nuclear generating facility thirty miles northwest of Atlanta. We currently have no indication that the health or safety of Atlantans or others is at risk. Energy Global, the operator of Little River, assures us that any radiation that may have been released is likely minimal, and presents little danger to the public.

Nonetheless, we are currently assessing the amount of contamination, if any, that may have escaped. Until we do, we urge you to follow the advice of your local officials, remain calm and listen for further announcements.

As a precaution, if you are outdoors, seek shelter and shelter in place. If you are at home or in a building, secure all windows and vents. Bring pets indoors. Do not attempt to leave the city, as traffic congestion will impede first responders, and could subject you to long delays. This is an unexpected development, but Georgians are strong and resilient. Together we will see this through. God bless you all, and God bless the State of Georgia."

***

Brad Hollister, the former Control Room Reactor Operator at Little River, got up from his chair in the living room, turned the tv off with his remote, and looked at his wife, Sue.

"Get the kids, we're leaving now!"

"But the governor seems to think things aren't that bad, Brad. Maybe we should shelter in place until we know more, like he says."

"He's lying, Sue. They're all lying. It's bad, I know it's very bad. I was there when the system went down last time. That was a false alarm. This one isn't. There's radiation this time. They're not telling us the whole truth. I told the press, I told the FBI. There's a cover-up taking place. I told them this could happen. Honey, if we don't leave now, we're gonna die of radiation poisoning in our own home."

They began packing their SUV with clothing, food, water, medicine, iodine pills, photos, documents and other important personal items. Sue saw Brad unlock the gun rack and begin to remove several weapons and ammunition.

"Brad, are you sure we should take those? I don't like guns that easily in reach."

"Babe, I know, but we have to. It's going to be a jungle out there. This is Georgia. Everybody's gonna have a damn gun. Have to be able to defend ourselves."

Neighbors noticed Brad packing the SUV. They too, had heard the governor's address.

"Brad, what's up? Do you know something we don't?"

They knew Brad had been a Control Room Reactor Operator at Little River.

"We're getting out while we can," he said.

"What do you mean, while we can? The governor said we should wait."

"He's lying, or doesn't know the truth," said Hollister. "It's a lot worse than they're saying. Stay and you…will…die. Take it from me, and head south now."

Soon neighbors were scrambling home to follow suit, telling relatives and friends to do the same.

"He knows something," they said. *"He worked there. He's got his sources. We're leaving too, heading south."*

The governor's pleas, assurances, admonitions and lack of detail convinced no one. Within minutes of his address, Tiktok, Twitter, Facebook, You Tube, Instagram and other social platforms were posting images and ghastly videos of radiation victims from the nuclear bombing of Hiroshima and the destruction of the Chernobyl nuclear reactor.

Shocking photos of red, peeling skin and grotesque burns were accompanied by horrifying accounts of cooked innards, deformed newborns, cancers and painful death.

Panic quickly began to spread throughout the city.

Georgia's citizens might not have been scientists, but they knew the word "radiation," and it was something to fear. If it was headed their way, they wanted out of the city now. They took to cars, buses, trains, motorcycles, airports. A public stampede was soon in the making.

U.S. routes twenty-three, forty-one, twenty-nine, Interstate eighty-five and other roads headed south were quickly reaching rush hour levels. Traffic collisions skyrocketed. Fights broke out. Those who chose to remain swarmed grocery stores, supply outlets, gas stations and ATMs. Shelves were soon bare, and cash quickly ran out.

Although Atlanta had initiated efforts to develop and implement a better communications system for first responders, the system was encountering major problems. Due to a lack of sufficient interagency preparation, first responders from dozens of local, state and federal agencies learned that their communication devices and broadcast frequencies were incompatible. There would be no adequately coordinated response to the unfolding crisis.

127

Southern Air

Southern Air – Flight 1287 at 35,000 feet

On the flight deck, Captain Kidder looked at his copilot, his expression grim. "Can't tell them everything. We'll have pandemonium. We've got a plane with two hundred eighty-five souls on board. Let's hope they don't find out too soon." He hit the intercom switch, and slipped into an easy drawl.

"Folks, good afternoon. This is your captain, Russ Kidder. Looks like we've got a change of flight plan today. We've been advised that due to a ground stop at Atlanta's Hartsfield-Jackson airport we're being diverted to Jacksonville International in Jacksonville, Florida. Don't have much more on the holdup right now, but we'll certainly try to keep you posted. We do apologize for the inconvenience. For those of you traveling to cities other than Atlanta, we'll be getting gate information and details on connecting flights. For Atlanta passengers, we'll do our best to get you home via other Southern Air flights or other carriers. Meanwhile, the bar is open, and we invite you to enjoy complimentary snacks and drinks. Once again, on behalf of Southern Air and your flight crew, we thank you for choosing us today, and we do again, apologize."

There were some sighs and a few grumbles among the passengers, but most understood that things happen. A storm, a control tower problem, could mess up your day. Five minutes later, the head flight attendant in First Class was jolted by the loud voice of a man in row two.

"Oh my God, oh my God!"

"What! What?" other passengers said, looking at the man with alarm. *Had he lost it? Was he having a heart attack?*

"Atlanta, it's Atlanta, I can't believe it!"

"What about Atlanta? What are you saying?" demanded a woman in the next row.

He looked at her, his eyes wild with terror. "I just got a text! There was a problem with a nuclear plant. Radiation is headed for Atlanta. The governor just now made the announcement. Oh, Lord protect us!"

"He's right!" shouted another passenger. "My husband texted. He says everybody's scared. They don't know what to do. It's radiation. Like he says, the governor said so."

Soon passengers in Business and Economy were also wailing and shouting as they read frightening texts and made phone calls to loved ones and friends. The cabin crew tried to calm people, with little success.

A passenger leapt from his seat and ran down the aisle screaming, "I've got to get to Atlanta! My family's going to die! This plane's got to turn back, they're going to die!" He reached the cockpit door and began banging, as other passengers sprang to help two female flight attendants who were trying to restrain him. They dragged him to an empty seat and bound him with belts.

In the cockpit Captain Kidder was back on the intercom.

"Folks, this is your captain again. We know some of you are receiving troubling messages about a developing situation in Atlanta. Please keep in mind that early reports are often wrong. Let's just all take a deep breath, remain calm, and wait for more clarification. At this time, for your safety, the safety of your fellow passengers and flight crew, we ask that you return to your seats, buckle up and remain seated for the remainder of the flight. Thank you for your cooperation."

The overhead seat belt sign illuminated.

128

Hartsfield-Jackson

Atlanta

The massive airline terminals at Hartsfield-Jackson International were becoming more unmanageable by the minute. With over two thousand flights per day, the airport was in danger of being overrun by people desperate to get as far away from Atlanta as possible.

Security checkpoints were swamped as rumors and panic spread. People who hadn't even purchased tickets were rushing into terminals, racing through checkpoints, leaping over barriers, ignoring barked orders from rattled TSA staff. Boarding gates were besieged by travelers forcing their way onto gangways and into planes as airport personnel attempted to close ramp doors and maintain order. On the tarmac, pilots with their aircraft loaded to capacity grew frustrated as conflicting information about a ground stop prevented them from taking off or deplaning. Adding to the chaos, people were running across runways as they crazily sought a way to board aircraft.

Ten nautical miles south of Hartsfield-Jackson, air traffic controllers at Fairfield Municipal Airport were astonished to see several single engine planes taxiing to runways without identifying themselves or requesting tower clearance.

Frantic radio calls to the pilots by the two air controllers went unacknowledged.

"Dammit! No one's responding," one of the controllers said. "They're nuts. Look at them. They're all jockeying to take off."

"Jesus! We have an inbound Cessna!" said the other.

"Wave him off or we'll have bodies on the tarmac!"

Too late. Two of the single engine planes were on the runway, gaining speed as the Cessna descended.

"Too close, too close!"

129

Little River

Little River Nuclear Generating Plant

Plant operators never had a chance. The cloaked worm had successfully disabled and bypassed critical industrial controls, closed off coolant water to the reactor, frozen control rods that would have stopped reactor fission, triggered a crippling alarm avalanche, and at every step, defeated the plant's formidable array of safety measures. Deprived of control rods, coolant and other moderating elements, the reactor had quickly moved to supercriticality and explosion. The reactor was ruptured, the pipes in ruins, the core exposed, emitting deadly alpha, beta and gamma radiation.

The force of the explosion had released massive amounts of debris and radionuclides. Billions of fine particulates infused with cesium 134 and 137, iodine 131, plutonium 241 and strontium were ejected several thousand feet into the atmosphere.

130

Situation Room

Situation Room - thirty minutes later

"Okay," said President Childs. "Where are we?" The group had reassembled. Press Secretary Mike Espinoza had been asked to join.

"Sir," said Catherine Pfaff, head of Homeland Security, "I just got off the phone with Governor Tilden of Georgia. Atlanta is approaching havoc. There have been reports of violence at gas stations and grocery stores. Two people were shot at a large box store."

"Not good," said the president. "People are frightened, getting desperate. We need to move fast here if we're going to avoid a complete breakdown of public order."

"Mr. President," said Bill Reyner of the NRC, "I asked John Patel, the director of NOAA, to join us. He may have some good news."

"We can use some. Let's hear, Mr. Patel," said the president.

"Mr. President," said the short, intense man seated next to Reyner, "we asked our computational unit at NOAA to run the atmospheric data through TELEIOS, a new artificial intelligence program using advanced algorithms and artificial neural networks that we've developed with teams at MIT and UCLA."

"And?"

"Sir, we now believe that the previous NOAA forecast of wind direction is incorrect."

"Give me the bottom line, we're out of time."

"Yes, sir. TELEIOS's analysis is that the direction of the wind will soon shift in a pronounced northeasterly direction, and away from metropolitan Atlanta. The radiation plume that was released should have only a minor impact on Atlanta. However, everything from the outskirts of Atlanta to Richmond, Virginia could be impacted to some degree."

"Minor is hardly the word to describe Atlanta's situation," said the president. "How confident are you in these projections and in this new model?"

"Ninety-five percent, sir. We can't completely rule out another change in wind direction, but the beta testing we've been doing with TELEIOS in the last few months has been close to perfect, exceeding NOAA's current weather modeling."

"Bill," said the president, turning to Reyner, "why should we trust this new prediction model when it challenges the one we've reasonably relied on for years?"

"Mr. President, the key word here is 'reasonably.' Our current system is very good. However, we need to be as close to one hundred percent as possible. Over the last six months NOAA has made dramatic progress with TELEIOS. This will be the first time we use it operationally, but we have a very high confidence level."

"Ninety-five percent is certainly better," said the president, "but we're stepping into unknown territory here with hundreds of thousands of lives in the balance. If we go with TELEIOS, and TELEIOS is wrong, we'll have mass radiation casualties in Atlanta."

"Correct, sir," said Reyner. "A direct hit on Atlanta could mean near term death for tens of thousands."

The president fell silent. A solemn quiet enveloped the room. Every person understood that the next words from the President of the United States would mark a grave and singular inflection point in the nation's history.

He sat up straight, checked his watch, looked around the table, lips pursed, nodded his head slightly, as if confirming what he was about to say. His gaze was steady as it moved from one person to the other. *I know you will remember this moment for the rest of your lives.*

His voice was clear, calm, decisive. "It's one-twenty-five. Almost two hours since the release, and we will act now. We're immediately evacuating Atlanta. The TELEIOS prediction is tempting. But if we have folks shelter in place, and that five percent error kicks in, hundreds of thousands will be trapped in their homes with dismal prospects of being safely extracted. They'll be prisoners in a city contaminated by deadly radiation for who knows how long. Providing the essentials of food, water and all the rest would be a herculean task with a high mortality rate for everyone involved." The president paused for a moment to let the gravity of the words sink in.

"I'm fully aware of the chaos we are setting in motion with this evacuation. Tragically, women, children, men will die. Atlanta may never be habitable again. We just can't know, but we can't chance having it become a mass grave. I am declaring a state of emergency and ordering the immediate evacuation of the city and surrounding communities. I'm federalizing the National Guard, and instructing our military to immediately deploy to Atlanta to maintain order and protect crucial services until the last soul is gone. Let's inform Governor Tilden ASAP. We will also notify the governors of Florida, South Carolina, North Carolina and Virginia to begin emergency preparations."

He turned to Mike Espinoza, his press secretary. "Mike, I need to address the nation in thirty minutes. It's not much lead time, but we can't spare a minute. Contact the networks and get the press corps here stat. I want a full press rollout."

"Yes, Mr. President," said Espinoza, as he grabbed his laptop and raced out of the room.

131

Atlanta

GNN Breaking News…. Two-fifteen P.M. EDT

"I'm Gerald Riddle, and we are continuing our coverage of the Little River nuclear disaster from New York as we wait to go to the Oval Office of the White House where President Leyland Childs will address the nation within the next few minutes. While we wait for the president, we have our correspondent, Dana Castro, in Atlanta with an update on the deteriorating situation in the city."

An image appeared of a youthful woman wearing a GNN jacket, holding a mike in one hand, as the other unsuccessfully tried to hold her hair in place in a brisk wind. She was standing on the Ralph David Abernathy Freeway overpass with a view of the huge serpentine intersection of U.S. routes eighty-five, twenty, seventy-five and their feeder roads, a gigantic collection of concrete spaghetti. Below, an endless stream of vehicles moved at a snail's pace, headlights on.

"Dana, bring us up to date. Looks like the wind has picked up."

"That's correct, Gerald. The wind had been minimal before this, but in the last few minutes it has definitely picked up."

"Not good news," said Riddle. "That means the plume is likely going to gain speed. Tell us where you are, and what you can see from your vantage point."

"Right," said Castro. "Well, as you can see below and all around me on the Abernathy overpass, there is now a massive river of traffic making its way southbound out of Atlanta. But, incredibly, Gerald, a stream of cars also continues to move north, in the direction of the deadly plume approaching the city. It's really getting frightening."

Castro turned away from the camera and looked to the freeway below.

"My God! Jim, quick," said Castro, pointing downward. "Pan the camera to the northbound lanes."

The cameraman panned down to the northbound lanes. Several cars were speeding the wrong way southbound, on the shoulder of the northbound lanes. A line of northbound vehicles had also moved onto the shoulder lanes. Cars were headed right into each other.

"Somebody's going to get killed," said Castro.

CRASH! WHOMP! CRASH!

The ugly sound of metal on metal, shattering glass, and the "thump, thump, thump" of cars colliding and cart-wheeling rose above the roar of the freeway. Flying debris struck other cars, causing a chain reaction. Cars burst into flames, and the freeway came to a complete standstill as riders left their vehicles, some to help the injured, others to flee in evident panic.

"Gerald, I don't even know how first responders are going to get there to help the injured. The entire freeway is a solid block of stalled and damaged vehicles."

"Looks pretty bad, Dana, and will likely get worse. Folks are getting truly frantic. Let's hope help can get to these motorists. They don't have much time. The greater danger lies in the wind you mentioned. If it continues to grow in strength, the deadly plume will arrive in Atlanta sooner than predicted. We want you and your camera crew to be safe, so use your own judgment, but you need to be ready to head south."

"Will do," said Castro. Her expression left little doubt that she would do just that.

***

A moment later the image of President Leyland Childs appeared. The camera shot moved in smoothly to frame the president. The expression on his face was solemn, his blue eyes steady.

"My fellow Americans. At approximately eleven-thirty A.M. Eastern Daylight Time today, a nuclear power generating plant located thirty miles northwest of Atlanta, Georgia, experienced a grave incident. As a result, a large plume of radioactive material was released into the atmosphere. The plume is moving slowly, but it is moving towards Atlanta and surrounding communities." He paused for a moment to let the alarming words register with viewers.

"After conferring extensively with our science and technical experts, I have concluded that an unprecedented, imminent life-threatening condition exists for all those in the path of the radioactive plume. I've just spoken with Governor Swan Tilden of Georgia. He agrees that the threat to the health, safety, and lives of Georgians in those areas is without precedent. Consequently, moments ago, I declared a national emergency and signed an executive order calling for the full, and immediate evacuation of all citizens in the city of Atlanta and surrounding communities."

The president paused for another moment. The camera zoomed in for a tight shot, the president's countenance grave.

"Now, I want to speak directly to each citizen in the path of this dangerous plume. As your president, I ask that you make no mistake about what I am about to say."

The camera shot got tighter.

"The danger to you and your loved ones could not be greater. It's likely that life-threatening radioactive material will begin to fall on Atlanta within a few hours. Do not delay. Every minute counts. Leave now. Take only a few personal items that are of special meaning and value to you and are easy to carry. If you have pets, gather them quickly. Our dedicated first responders and military personnel will direct you to the safest evacuation routes."

The camera pulled back. The president's voice became less intense.

"In a few minutes our crisis management team will brief you in more detail on what we know, and what you need to do to evacuate safely. I leave for Georgia shortly to meet with local officials and emergency services."

The camera zoomed in again. The president's face became confident, reassuring.

"To the brave citizens of the great city of Atlanta, the prayers and support of your president, your government and the American people are with you tonight. God bless the people of Georgia, and God bless the United States of America."

The camera image faded and switched to an exterior image of the White House.

***

In the ensuing hours every capital on the globe was briefed on the Little River explosion. The president ordered total transparency. This time there would be no Chernobyl-style obfuscation. A worldwide malware alert was issued. There were a total of thirty countries with nuclear power plants. They all had a right to know what had happened, and what to fear.

France, Germany, the United Kingdom, Russia, China, India and other nations had already begun to power down reactors that were located close to major population centers.

132

Jean-François

Paris

Jean-François picked up his cell as soon as he saw that Izzy was calling.

"Izzy, how are you?"

"Pretty shaken. How are you, Jean-François?"

"As of this morning, France is in a national state of emergency. I just finished another crisis meeting at the Élysée Palace. There is a sort of controlled panic there. The Little River nightmare has become France's nightmare."

"Thank god you were smart enough to keep Savoy-sur- Mer offline," said Izzy.

"Yes, but the fear continues. Like you, we're asking what if other plants are infected with the malware?"

"Does your government have a plan?"

"Yes, but it's complicated. Shutdowns will have to be strategic. Plants close to major population centers will be scrammed. Plants that are more remote will redirect power to major urban centers. Not since the war and the German Occupation has France seen the shortages of food, fuel, energy and basic essentials that are coming."

"Will be a challenge. *Bon courage.*"

"*Oui.* Let us all pray for each other."

133

Jay Powell

New York City

Jay Powell, vice president of Energy Global, was standing on the rooftop of EGI's Manhattan skyscraper next to the helipad - a cell phone in his right hand. He looked at the text message from Atlanta for the fourth time, as if hoping the message would not be there if he looked again. It had arrived two hours earlier.

Dear son, unable to evacuate. Dad still too weak from operation. Neighbors all gone. Your sister and the children left this morning. Car stolen. Called 911 but no one came. Remember us. God bless, Mom

Powell's frantic calls and texts to his parents, relatives, and police had all failed to go through. Communication systems had been swamped and had crashed. From New York, GNN was broadcasting apocalyptic drone images of a darkening city. First responders, military units and medical professionals had been among the last to leave. The plume was now raining deadly radionuclides on Atlanta. Those remaining would not survive.

There was no point revisiting his willful ignorance about the danger, telling Brad Hollister, regulators and others that there was nothing to worry about. Somewhere deep in the recesses of his mind, he'd known the truth and had chosen to ignore it. Now, his parents would have a gruesome death.

I murdered them.

He walked to the edge of the roof, crossed himself, and jumped.

134

Leaving Atlanta

Brad Hollister was at the wheel of the packed-to-capacity family SUV. Sue, his wife, was in the front passenger seat. Their two young teenage children, Larry and Margaret, were in the back with Pickle, the family terrier.

Brad was having a difficult time navigating the crowded secondary roads as they filled with other motorists who'd decided, like Brad, to avoid the main highways. They would be parking lots. But the secondary roads were narrower and had also become clogged. He checked his speed. Less than ten miles an hour. They were barely crawling. Troublemakers on foot harassed drivers, banging on the roofs of the vehicles, asking for a ride, money, food.

"Brad!" Sue shouted as a man approached her side of the car carrying a tire iron.

Brad hit the horn and held it. He lowered the passenger window two inches and yelled, "Back off, dude!"

Now the man was raining blows down on the car roof and the windshield. Brad hit the accelerator. The SUV lurched forward but soon rear-ended the car in front. They were stuck. Sue's passenger side window suddenly shattered. Sue and the children screamed in terror. Pickle began barking.

"Get the gun! The gun!" said Brad.

The man with the tire iron was smashing the front windshield.

"Sue, dammit! Open the glove compartment and give me the gun!"

Her hands trembling, Sue opened the glove compartment, pulled out the forty-five caliber semi-automatic with its nickel-plated grip, and passed it to Brad.

He pointed the weapon at the man with the tire iron. "Back off or I'll shoot your ass!"

"Brad!" Sue shouted, pointing to Brad's side of the car. Brad turned to see a man pointing a sawed-off shotgun at them.

"No, no, wait! Hold on!" said Brad, as the man fired.

135

TELEIOS

TELEIOS, for all its ability to calculate odds on near-infinite variables, had been wrong. Within hours, alpha, beta and gamma radiation, carried aloft and driven by strong currents, began falling on the city. All too quickly the deadly radiation plume enveloped most of Atlanta. By midnight, hourly milliroentgen readings had shot to hundreds of times above normal.

Streets were littered with dead and the dying. The dead, from anarchy and violence that gripped the city. The dying, from absorbing toxic doses of radiation, either because they refused, or were unable to leave. They would not survive.

Atlanta's streets were packed with thousands of vehicles abandoned by occupants who fled on foot, unable to get past the gridlock that clogged every road and highway.

People were shot, assaulted and robbed. Motorists were carjacked. Shattered glass and debris lay scattered along boulevards. Fires broke out and spread when electrical systems malfunctioned. Shopping malls, grocery and hardware stores, were emptied as looters rampaged and torched.

Emergency workers, massively overwhelmed and exhausted, focused solely on triage. Too often they had to step over the bodies of those beyond help.

Little else could be done as flames spread uncontrolled. The conflagration enveloped large swaths of the city. The elderly, sick and disabled were hit especially hard as evacuation became increasingly difficult. Some were afraid to leave, others refused to leave, insisting that officials were lying. Still others were just left behind. Astronauts, observing from the International Space Station, beamed back nightmarish images of the vast urban inferno.

With scant protection against radiation, police and military personnel valiantly struggled to contain the growing chaos. Countless Good Samaritans helped families, neighbors, and complete strangers who were stranded, confused, too terrified, or too weak to save themselves. Rich or poor, black or white, Muslim, Christian, or Jew, made little difference to those who stepped forward with open arms to provide comfort, prayer, tears, and safe passage.

As night fell and the city emptied, the only sounds remaining as the fires consumed hundreds of buildings were those of car alarms blaring into the void, glass crashing downward, vehicle gas tanks exploding, and the mournful barking of dogs running loose.

After days of heroic efforts, the fission at Little River was arrested. A gigantic concrete sarcophagus was being constructed to seal the reactor. Little River would spew death no more. But the damage was done.

In the weeks and months that would follow, repeated readings would confirm the worst. Atlanta was now, and forever would be, a forbidden exclusion zone. Once the crown jewel of the Peach State, an economic powerhouse, a cultural treasure, and an indispensable pillar of the American economy, Atlanta was now a graveyard, a ghost town, a vast, poisonous expanse of steel, concrete, glass, timber, asphalt and deserted green spaces.

In the coming decades, the concrete would crack and fail. The timber, steel and glass would succumb to the elements. Inexorably, the unique profile of the city would disappear. New trees, shrubs, bushes, flowers, vines, deer, foxes, mockingbirds, thrashers, cottonmouths, copperheads, salamanders, frogs and toads would propagate, prosper, envelop, and bury a once great American city.

136

President Childs

Memphis, Tennessee – Relocation Center Thirty Seven

President Leyland Childs, coatless, shirtsleeves rolled up, was walking through the massive camp that had been set up on the outskirts of Memphis. Special Agent Will Bergen and a small Secret Service detail walked alongside him in the mid-afternoon sun wearing casual clothes. The president wanted to avoid the formality that usually accompanied him.

As he'd done in dozens of camps in the last few weeks, sleeping little, working late into the night, he made his way, stopping to talk with people, engaging them as only he could. He was their president, their neighbor, their friend, a man who loved his country and its courageous citizens. Tragically, many in the camps had lost loved ones. Among the survivors were disfigured radiation victims and emotionally distraught children who'd been orphaned in the bedlam and death of the Great Evacuation of Atlanta.

His mind burned with rage and determination to make the perpetrators of the cybersabotage pay in blood. Both the French and U.S. intelligence services had a high level of confidence that the attacks had been orchestrated by North Korea. But Pyongyang was crying foul, insisting that the Americans and the French were employing a ruse to justify an unlawful act of war on the peace-loving Democratic People's Republic of Korea.

The inability of the intelligence services to conclusively prove that North Korea was responsible for the cyberattack was driving Childs to near distraction. All the individuals with a direct connection to the plot were now dead. He'd been given a list of names: Alders, Babin, Federova, Lalo, Chen, the hacker called Eric, and others – all dead.

Missing still was the alleged "dossier," reportedly containing incriminating evidence, and a group of hackers named "Runner," who'd disappeared into thin air. But smoking gun or not, there would be crippling payback through clandestine operations. All Childs could do for now was continue to visit the victims and hear their stories.

Camp Thirty-Seven was only one of two hundred sprawling refugee centers that had sprung up almost overnight across America. FEMA and private charities mounted a non-stop, round-the-clock effort to accommodate the mass exodus of hundreds of thousands of Atlantans and other residents from contaminated areas.

In response to the hellish calamity of Little River, the nation and the world opened their hearts to the victims of Atlanta with an unprecedented outpouring of support. Food, clothing, medicine, children's toys, phones, laptops, money, prayers, cards and letters, arrived by the planeload and the trainload from the smallest towns in the Dakotas to massive cities like New York, Houston, and Los Angeles, and from countries around the globe.

American families packed cars, campers, trucks and SUVs with food and other supplies and drove hundreds, even thousands, of miles to visit the refugee camps, share what they'd brought, and say how deeply they had been affected by the tragedy. "We Are All Atlanta" became the anthem of the nation.

Leyland Childs knew he would need to be the face of those values as he walked among the lost, listening to their powerful stories of grief, terror, flight and tearful confession. Sometimes he heard red-hot anger.

"Why didn't the government prevent this?...It's your damned fault, you're the president...All you politicians are the same, only looking out for yourselves...People died! Our families were torn apart!...Why did we have to lose everything?"

They were hard, troubling, bare-fisted questions, and he heard them out with great patience and empathy - and with hard questions of his own. *Why, indeed? Why didn't we do more to prevent this?*

He understood the symbolic importance of every comforting hug, smile, word of encouragement, or prayer he shared. His actions were captured by the multitude of ever-present media and instantaneously beamed around the world.

Leyland Childs' personal needs, his longing to have Izzy at his side, were of small import in the face of the vast and tragic cataclysm that had engulfed Atlanta. They had talked by phone, but infrequently, Izzy unable to leave her mother who was in her final days, and Childs totally absorbed by the ongoing recovery effort. His sole act of indulgence was the small black velvet box he kept close to him as he went from camp to camp.

It contained a ring.

As Childs threaded his way through the camp, providing a kind word, or a firm handshake, a young boy in his early teens approached him, tears in his eyes.

"Hello there, young man. What's your name?" said the president.

"You killed my parents!" the boy said.

"GUN!!" shouted Will Bergen, as the youngster raised the forty-five with its nickel-plated grip and put a bullet into the president's brain.

137

Izzy

"*…was pronounced dead at five-thirty-seven this afternoon, Eastern Daylight Time, at the Elvis Presley Trauma Center in Memphis, Tennessee.*"

Izzy Stone was sitting in the visitors' lounge of her mother's hospice, tears running down her cheeks, stunned, in sepulchral silence, horrified beyond horror as she watched Gerald Riddle, his voice shaking, report on the last moments of President Leyland Childs' life. People in the room were speaking to her, but she could not hear, touching her, but she could not feel.

138

Epilogue

Sylvia, the housekeeper, opened the front door. She was surprised to find a thick piece of rough material stuck in the mailbox. It was weathered and felt like canvas. She turned it over. A pattern, faded but still clear enough to make out, caught her attention. She considered throwing it into the trash, but hesitated. She took a photo of it and sent it to Izzy.

"Hello, señora, I am sorry to bother you, but I found this piece of material in the mailbox this morning. I was going to throw it away, but I thought I should show it to you first."

Izzy looked at the photo and gasped. Her heart began pounding.

It was a fleurs-de-lys pattern bordering a wide blue stripe.

THE END

ACKNOWLEDGEMENTS

Many thanks to my brother, Conrad Aragon, a gifted fellow writer, for his ever helpful comments. Conrad was always willing to read another chapter of CHÂTELET.

I could not have written this novel without the invaluable assistance of Ellen, my wise, wonderful wife, whose encouragement, support and keen advice kept me focused on the story.

ABOUT THE AUTHOR

Joseph Aragon is an American writer living in Paris who greatly enjoys his Bloody Marys at Harry's Bar, when fortune smiles and euros allow.

CHÂTELET is Aragon's second novel in the Izzy Stone political thriller series. For more information go to: **www.chatelet.us**

THE PARIS PLOT is the first in the Izzy Stone series, and is available on Amazon, Kindle and Audible, read by Ben Werling. www.theparisplot.com